TATE

STORM ENTERPRISES BOOK 2

BJ ALPHA

Copyright © 2023 by BJ Alpha

All rights reserved.

No part of this book may be reproduced in any form or by any electronic or mechanical means, including information storage and retrieval systems, without written permission from the author, except for the use of brief quotations in a book review.

This book is a work of fiction. Characters, names, places and incidents are products of the authors imagination or used fictitiously.

Any similarity to actual events, locations or persons living or dead is purely coincidental.

Published by Alpha Team Publishing

Edited by Dee Houpt

Proofread by My Notes In The Margin

Cover Design by Ever After Cover Designs

Photographer RafaGCatala

Model Albert_Iceman

AUTHORS NOTE

WARNING: This book contains triggers. It has sensitive and explicit storylines. Such as:
Violence.
Graphic sexual scenes.
Sexual assault scenes and human trafficking.
Strong language.
It is recommended for readers ages eighteen and over.

DEDICATION

To all my readers who are breeder readers just like me.
This is for you.

PROLOGUE

Tate

One night turned my world upside down, leaving me craving more.

Yet, when I discover her age, I've no choice but to let her go and spend the next four years trying to block her out of my memory.

Until an intern struts into my office and I'm catapulted back in time. Only this time, she's older, wiser, and feistier. And I'm determined never to let her go again.

We'll be the perfect family. Everything we both always wanted.

But when her past catches up with her, can we fight it and finally fly together or will it destroy us in the process.

Ava

My last summer of freedom leaves me desperate for more.

With my life about to change, I grab it with both hands and embrace it. Revel in it.

After all, I'm about to sign my life away to a monster.

When I finally break free from the chains that confined me, I'm determined to shed my broken wings and take everything that belongs to me.

ONE

AVA

FOUR YEARS EARLIER...

I've been to some parties in my short life, but holy hell, I've never been to one like this.

This place is off the fucking charts, the whole mansion is like something out of the show *Cribs*. I lean against the wall, holding my champagne flute between my fingers, acting like some debutante. Internally, I scoff at the thought because that couldn't be further from the truth.

Glancing around the foyer taking in the sea of people, I feel like I've finally hit the jackpot. Who would have thought that I, Ava Delaney, would be in some place like this?

As the waiter in the butler suit strolls by, I snag another champagne and replace it with my empty glass. Then I give the waiter an appreciative smile and raise the glass in thanks. It is my birthday, after all.

My eyes work over the crowd once again, taking in the countless socialites and obnoxious wealth of people expected to be at these events, and something causes the hairs on my arms to stand, a feeling of being watched, one I know too well. Only this feeling is different, welcomed, because the eyes scanning my body are filled with an electric heat, and what a hot specimen he is. Bingo!

Happy birthday to me.

TATE

I am late again, but I sneak in and act as though I've been here all night. My lips curl up thinking about how I'll explain to my mom what an amazing night it's been, when, in reality, all I want is to get a fuck out of it.

One of my best friends Reed, stands stoically straight as a busty blonde trails her hand up and down his chest. Reed looks uncomfortable as hell, his lip curled up at the side, and I throw my head back on a laugh. Downing my amber liquor, I survey the room. I need to get laid ASAP, but it's the regular faces I fuck at every event. I need something different.

Someone different.

One thing is for sure, whenever my parents throw a bash, I always end up fucking someone, and tonight will be no exception.

My eyes once again scan over the women here, all dressed-up, superficial socialites desperate to sink their claws into someone with status and wealth. The only thing I'm interested in is sinking my dick into some pussy for the night, not the endless tirade of questions and messages that follow after one night with these women.

Slowly, my eyes lock onto long, tanned legs and trail up to the torso of the gorgeous woman they belong to. She wears a little black dress, and her tits are pushed together in the low neckline, more than a handful but not overly huge. *Fuck.* I lick my lips. My perusal continues toward her pretty face. She's stunning in a natural way, barely a scrap of makeup. The realization that she's different from all the others has my heart race faster and my dick twitch with a need to own her. It comes alive, swelling in my pants, by the sight of her.

That's never happened before. I might be a horny fucker, but I never get hard from looking at someone—in clothes, no less. What the hell?

Her brown, wavy locks flow down her back, and the thought of wrapping her hair around my fist while I fill her cunt causes me to clench my jaw in frustration at how turned on I am, how much I crave her.

Her plump, red lips have my balls throbbing, and when she licks them seductively, my cock weeps in appreciation. My eyes flit to hers, and a knowing grin settles on her stunning face. Judging by her confident smile, the feisty little minx has been aware of my attention all along. Excitement races through my veins at the perfect scenario.

Yeah, she's mine tonight.

TWO

AVA

The blue-eyed sex god eats up my body like an addict in a drug store. He causes a tingling sensation to run down my spine and into my panties, forcing me to squirm with need.

I nibble on my lower lip and bat my eyelashes innocently as he takes strides in my direction. His daring blue eyes never falter, and my heart races in my chest at his confidence. He shakes off numerous conversations and ignores various women's attempts to snag him, trying to grab at his body as he moves toward me, but our eyes remain locked. An unmistakable connection holds us together, like a magnetic pull. It's as if we're the only two people to exist as the room continues to move around us like white noise blending into the background.

I swallow any nerves and push my shoulders back, determined to have the night of my dreams. Greeting him, I push off the wall, tilting my head, and imagine holding onto those broad shoulders as they pin me to the wall, tugging on the longer tips of his hair when he ravishes my neck with his gleaming white teeth and perfect pout. Heat blossoms from the inside out, leaving my chest heaving with need and a tremble to work through my body at his proximity.

"You look deep in thought, care to share?" He smirks as though knowing exactly what I'm thinking. His cocky, deep, gravelly voice hits me between the legs, and his scent wafts over me: clean, freshly showered, and a pinch of sandalwood—delicious.

I meet his eyes, and a confident smirk graces his handsome face as I wonder his age. Hmm, older than I expected, maybe thirty or a little over?

Honestly, who cares.

This handsome stranger is interested, and I just so happen to want a night of passion. "The thoughts in my mind, you mean? I'd much rather show you." I lick my lips for emphasis, being as transparent as possible because, let's face it, we both want the exact same thing. I allow my eyes to once again trail over his broad body, giving no room for argument about what I want.

Him.

He chokes on a grin, and I think I've shocked him with my confidence, meeting him like for like. He leans forward and tucks a wayward wave of my brunette hair behind my shoulder, then his fingers linger on my neckline. Swirling his finger just below my ear, the heat of his touch encompasses me, making my heart stutter. My eyes flick to his tongue darting out, then he licks his lips and dips his head to my ear. "You want to get out of here?" My breath hitches at the intimacy, and I can only nod in response.

THREE

TATE

I take hold of the girl's hand and tug her along; I know exactly where we're going, and the thought excites me beyond belief. Her small hand grips onto mine like a lifeline, and I almost sneer at the thought of her leaving me.

Where the hell did that come from? Since when did I become so possessive? Yet I can't help this feeling inside me that has me wanting to make her mine. All fucking mine.

Turning into the games room, I'm satisfied the lamp is on in the corner, illuminating the room enough to give it a seductive feel. I pull her in and kick the door shut, and the click echoes through the room. She startles at the sound, and I wonder if her confident bravado has now fallen. Was it all an act, after all? I turn on her, my eyes almost accusing, and the little minx smirks, as if hearing my thoughts. That naughty tongue darts out again, and my balls almost combust at the sight.

She straightens her shoulders. Nodding toward the leather armchair, her sweet, confident voice fills the silence. "Sit."

My eyebrows shoot up. If she thinks she can dominate me, she can think again. "Please," she tacks on the end, and I smile in agreement. Determined hazel eyes sparkle back at me, and my eyes dip down and check out her tits, nipples standing to attention. Fuck my life, she's hot, and I'm pretty damn sure those tits are real too. My mouth waters at the thought.

Decision made, I stride toward the armchair and throw myself down, loosening the bowtie and opening my legs wide to accommodate my steel cock.

The beauty sways her hips in my direction, allowing me to eat up her delicious curves. She has a body made for sinning, and that's just something I excel in.

She stands between my legs and her hands trail over my thighs before she slowly lowers herself to the floor, causing me to swallow past the thick lump in my throat.

Fuck, she's beautiful.

Her hands move up my legs, and my cock twitches with a need to fill her. She works my belt buckle with haste. I watch her closely, unable to take my eyes off her for a single second.

I lose myself to the moment and stroke her cheek tenderly, and she melts into my touch, her eyes now shining with a flash of vulnerability in them.

This is out of character for me, I never give tenderness. I'm all about the hard-and-fast fuck, and when we reach our orgasm, we're done, finished, and on to the next hookup. The realization that this girl is more has me dropping my hand and refusing to step over the line of a simple hookup—a fuck, nothing more.

She turns away from me but not before I see the glimmer of hurt in her eyes, and my jaw tightens in annoyance. They always want fucking more, and that's something I'm not ready for. Not yet. One day I'll want it all: house, wife, and kids. But not yet.

"Are you going to suck my cock with that pretty mouth or not?" I'm an ass, I admit it. Her head swiftly turns toward me, and fire blazes behind her eyes.

"Feed it to me." Holy fucking shit. Did she just ask me to feed her my cock?

I snatch her hands away from my belt buckle and pull down the zipper. Then I push my hand past the waistband of my boxers and tug them down slightly, my heart races with excitement as her pupils dilate when she sees the head of my thick cock. A rope of precum drips from the tip, so I graze the head with my thumb, smearing it down my cock, while using my other hand to fully expose myself to her. Taking a hold of the back of her head, I tug her forward and push my thumb into her open mouth.

My balls draw up as she sucks the precum from my thumb, then swirls her naughty tongue around my digit. A groan slips from my lips while imagining her mouth around my cock. I pull my thumb out with a pop, and without warning, I tighten my hand in her hair and yank her toward my cock. I plunge into her mouth, hitting the back of her warm throat. She doesn't gag like I expect. Her throat opens, and I almost come on the spot.

Where the hell has she been hiding?

AVA

I smile inwardly when his masculine, salty taste hits my throat. He's big but I love it. Closing my eyes, I revel in his grunts as I swirl my tongue around his velvety skin. The twitch of his cock and clenching of his thighs is a telltale sign he's struggling to control himself.

"Fuck yes." His hips rise off the chair, and when he once again hits the back of my throat, wetness pools in my panties, making me fidget from side to side.

"Fuck!" he growls on a heavy exhale.

Before I know what's happening, he pulls out of my mouth, his chest heaving up and down and his face contorted in shock. He glances down at his cock, smeared with my red lipstick, and his expression becomes feral. The cords on his neck protrude, and his forearm muscles pulsate as he attempts to rein in his need.

"Lose the dress!" he snaps. His commanding tone leaves no room for argument, so I stand on unsteady feet and unzip the side of the dress, sending it cascading down to rest on my hips. His heated glare fixes on my tits, so I give him a show. While tweaking my nipples, he chokes out a strangled laugh before lunging to his feet. "Quite the little tease, aren't you?" Smiling back at him, I raise my eyebrow in jest. He slides the dress down my hips, dropping it onto the floor, leaving me standing in only my panties and heels. Then he lifts me by my ass, and I wrap my thighs around him as he walks us over to the pool table and sits me on the edge. I open my legs in invitation, allowing him to stand between them.

"Lose the shirt," I clip back, and it's his turn to raise his eyebrow at me.

My sex god unbuttons his shirt painstakingly slow. His defined torso comes into full view. Without thinking, I trail my hands over the ripples of muscle, loving the warm solid feel of him against my fingers while I bite into my bottom lip on a whimper of need.

He watches me with affection before his mouth crashes down on mine, stealing my breath away, and I fall backward onto the table.

His hand finds my panties, and with a rough tug, he rips them from my body. His tongue devours me as we fight for possession of one another. I graze my hands across his broad shoulders and tighten them around his neck, holding on as he plunges his solid cock into me so hard my back arches off the table.

Oh Jesus.

TATE

Her warm pussy stretches to accommodate my cock—so tight it nearly chokes the poor fucker. "Fuck, you're incredible," I grunt out, the truth of the words causing me to push harder, faster into her.

Her pussy molds to my cock, as if made for me: warm, wet, and compact. The slickness between us leads to the slapping of our skin, and it's fucking incredible.

My eyes flick between her face and down toward her perfect tits. As they bounce against my chest, the friction causes her nipples to peak and, in return, I growl in delight at the contact. Fuck, I need to taste them, tug them, mark them. "Fuck."

Her pussy clenches me like a vise, and her heels dig into my ass as she squeezes my cock, painfully so.

"More, I need more." She grinds against me, her hips meeting mine on each thrust as we fuck one another.

The sound of our skin slapping fills the room. "You're a dirty little slut, aren't you?" I pant into her ear, and her pussy clenches around me. "Fuck, yes you are," I bite out.

"Yes, I am." My hips power into her harder. "Jesus, I'm so fucking dirty," she admits.

I groan on her words. "Fuck, little slut. Fuck." *Slam.*

"I need punishing." She moans.

Jesus fucking Christ she's perfect.

"Fuck yes you do." I quickly pull out of her, earning a loud moan in disapproval. Flipping her over, I spread her legs and smack her ass hard. "Little slut!" I spit. A desperate need to punish her consumes me like never before.

I raise my hand and smack her ass harder, but the little minx moans. While biting into my bottom lip, I slap her again, and a pained mewl leaves her lips. Jesus, my cock drips in approval. "That's it, little slut, cry for me. Only me." I slap her again, so hard my hand stings and my cock jumps.

How the hell can something so perfect and innocent looking let a man take her as a one-night stand? Anger boils inside me as I use the rage to surge back inside her, and the stretch of her cunt suffocates my cock. She exhales with a whoosh at the brutal force behind me. I take her hair in my hand and wrench her flush up against my chest.

My balls slap against her ass as I ram into her forcefully.

Coiling my free hand around her throat, I fuck her hard. I bite into my lip, trying to hold off my impending orgasm. Jesus, fuck, she's good.

"Oh my god. I'm close," she pants when I press hard on her pulse point. Jesus, what the fuck am I doing?

"My little slut is going to take my cum, aren't you?" I slam inside her again.

Her body freezes. "Stop, stop. Con . . . condom."

Her words barely register, but when they do, my cum shoots with vigor from my balls. "Take it, my little slut. Take all my cum in your tight cunt." I turn her head with a tilt of her chin, and her pupils dilate with arousal as I fill her. Our lips clash as her orgasm hits, milking my cock for every drop. She moans into my mouth, devouring me as much as I am her while her arms weave around the back of my neck.

Our rhythm slows, our chests heave, and our eyes remain locked as realization of the enormity of what just happened passes between us. For the first time in my life, I fucked a woman without protection, and I loved every minute of it.

Her face falls, as if realizing the same thing, and I feel the need to reassure her. "I'm clean. I've never not used one before."

Relief coats her face, and she swallows thickly before nodding. "Me too. Never. I'm on the shot."

Air rushes from my body, and I nod in approval. Not only have I had the best sex of my entire life but I'm pretty damn sure it was the best sex for her too. And we both had a first together. My lips turn up into a genuine smile, and I can't help but feel fan-fucking-tastic that I'm the first person she's ever gone bare with.

What the hell is wrong with me? I never do this shit.

My eyes remain latched on hers, and my heart hammers at the thought of her leaving. I still have so much more to give her. "There are spare rooms here, stay with me tonight?" It wasn't really much of a question, she's staying with me whether she likes it or not, but I've been brought up with manners, so I pose it as one.

My heart thuds in my chest as I watch her face for

indecision but find none as a smile forms on her plump lips. "Sure." Not giving her chance to change her mind, I pull out of her but push her against the pool table once again. With my palm pressing her spine to the table, I kick her feet apart to watch my cum slip from her pussy, and the sight has me groaning in ecstasy. When she clenches, I know she likes the idea too. Cum coats her thighs, and as I tuck my cock away, annoyance rumbles inside me at the thought of my cum leaking from her, not filling her as it should.

Grabbing my shirt from off the floor, I turn to find her standing naked, watching me. "What's your name, baby?"

"Ava."

"Ava." Her name rolls off my tongue. "I'm Tate."

Her eyes sparkle with mirth. "Your cum's dripping out of me, Tate."

I stifle a laugh and move toward her, draping my shirt over her shoulders before gently pushing her arms through the sleeves, and she smothers a giggle, presumably at my rushed attempts to dress her.

The sound fills me with warmth and has me grinning back at her. When our gazes collide, we both still, and my heart thumps against my chest like a violent drum as I come to a conclusion: we're drawn together in some way and seem to have a connection of some sort. Something beyond sex.

I clear my throat and avert my eyes, determined to stop myself from wanting more, and the words spill from my lips before I have a chance to stop them. "This is just for tonight, understood? No commitment."

Facing her, I analyze her response, and her eyes dart to mine with a serene smile playing on her lips. "Perfect."

My eyes narrow on her. "Perfect?" My shoulders tighten and I clench my jaw as anger travels through my veins like heroin.

But why the hell am I so pissed at her for being okay with what I insisted on?

Her hands weave around my neck, drawing me closer, and her soft touch relaxes me as I lift her into my arms, forcing a snicker to escape her.

Fuck me, I'm screwed.

FOUR

AVA

My brown-haired, blue-eyed sex god stalks through the corridors with purpose. He's had to have been here before because he weaves through the maze of the mansion's corridors and up the stairs without coming across a single person. He carries me bridal style with only his shirt covering me. I bury my head in his neck and grip onto his solid chest, causing his hold on me to tighten with a low growl. His enchanting blue eyes glance down at me, and I'm delighted to find them full of a protective ownership, something foreign to me but something I find myself craving. Before I can think further on it, he turns and pushes open a door with his back.

He spins us around before launching me into the air and throwing me onto the bed, causing me to giggle at how carefree and playful he is.

"I'm going to fuck you all night long, baby. You won't

remember any other man before me by the time I'm finished with you."

I smile back at him lazily. "Bring it on."

The smile encompassing his face is breathtaking, and as I roam my eyes down his deliciously hot body, I'm reminded they sure as hell don't have guys like this where I come from.

His face falls serious. "Now, get over here and clean your cum off my cock." He cocks an eyebrow high, as if testing me.

Never one to back down from a challenge, I roll onto all fours, then his lips part and his Adam's apple bobs in his throat as I crawl toward him.

"Fuckkkk," he chokes out, and I can't help but grin internally at his reaction.

Tonight, will be a night to remember. One where we soar so high, the low will be cataclysmic.

I swallow away the thought and concentrate on the sex god in front of me.

"Why do I get the feeling tonight is going to be engrained in our minds forever?" He tucks a lock of hair behind my ear with a smug smirk that has my insides clenching as he reaffirms my thoughts.

He palms my cheek in an act I don't foresee him doing often. "Just for tonight," he breathes out, as if trying to convince himself more than me.

"Just tonight," I agree on a whisper.

TATE

I roll onto my back and wince at the sun beaming through the parted curtains. Last night was incredible and just what I needed, considering what lies ahead for me, but I push those sickening thoughts aside as I throw my legs over the edge of the bed.

Glancing over my shoulder, I feel a little loss at the empty space beside me. Sure, it was a one-night stand, one we both agreed on, but the pang of hurt at being used and discarded that's become abundantly familiar over the years saddens me. I tug on the white bathrobe and ignore the purple bite marks that now litter my skin; the reminder forces my body to heat as I head toward the door. Slowly, I press the handle down and open it, then peek my head into the corridor. I run back to my room. I need a shower to wash away all thoughts of the handsome god that rocked my world.

With my future in the palm of my hands, however much I dread it, I need to concentrate on that. I've too much to lose to let my mind wander.

Besides, Tate will be long gone now.

TATE

When I made my way back to my old bedroom, I was filled with uncertainty. Why did this one woman, this one night, have to feel so prolific compared to all others?

When I closed my eyes while showering, I saw her sparkling hazel orbs shining back at me with desire and an undercurrent of vulnerability in them that made my cock twitch and beg for more.

Her touch surrounded me as my fist pumped my cock, and when I roared my release against the shower wall, her name slipped from my lips with such force I slammed my palm against the tiles.

How I fucking regretted walking away from her. So much so that before heading to breakfast, I take a little detour. For the first time in my life, I'm going to ask a woman out on a date.

I brush my sweaty palms against my shorts, acutely aware that she agreed to one night. Surely, she felt the connection and wants more too?

After all, who can resist me?

My fingers find the bite mark I discovered on my neck this morning while I brushed my teeth, and my lips tip up into a smug grin. The sign of ownership from a little wildcat. I smirk at the thought while I gently knock on the door.

When I don't hear movement beyond the wood, worry ebbs beneath my skin. "Ava?" I push open the bedroom door and step into the room.

My heart sinks. The bed is made, and the only thing left is a lingering scent of our night together. My hands curl into a ball as anger rises up my body. "Fuck!" I tug on my hair; I should have fucking stayed. Got her number. Something.

There was something about her. Something that made me want so much more than a one-night stand. I drop back against the wall, allowing my head to thud against the plaster. Such a fucking idiot letting her go.

Taking a deep breath and with my body sagging in disappointment, I head toward the kitchen for breakfast while thinking of all the ways I can get my best friend Owen to track her down.

Voices float through the corridor, and the excitement behind my mother's has me wincing. It's a reminder my parents are hosting their summer visitors and part of the reason I'm staying here for the weekend.

Steph Kavanagh is a fucking angel, her and my father adopted me and my younger brother and sister when we were all small, terrified kids.

Since then, they have set up a foundation to support foster families, helping them find placements for kids, and every school break, they take in a bunch of those kids to let them and their foster families have a reprieve during the holidays.

My parents' house is fucking impressive. They have a lagoon pool out back with water slides. A lake with boats, a basketball court they built for my thirteenth birthday, a gymnasium, a dance studio they created for my sister, a games room, and my mom even has a fucking spa in the house.

So the kids, usually teenagers, are spoiled rotten while here.

And hearing the excitement in my mom's voice means we probably have a house full of them, fan-fucking-tastic.

Approaching the kitchen, the hairs on the back of my neck stand up with the familiarity behind one of the voices. Then my best friend Owen breaks out into a loud chuckle that settles the odd nervousness creeping through me.

Stepping into the dining area, my mom throws her arms around me, greeting me in a tight hug, like I didn't see her yesterday. I grace her cheek with a quick peck and walk toward the refrigerator, ignoring the busy kitchen table like the plague. Swinging open the door, I grab the milk carton and drink from it. "Tate Kavanagh, do not drink out of my carton!" my mom chastises like she has done for the past twenty years. I reach up to the cupboard and grab a glass. "Come and take a seat, meet our guests." I roll my eyes and brush a hand over my cropped hair, plastering on a fake smile as I pull out a chair at the table. Owen grins from ear to ear, and I narrow my eyes on him. He's built like a fucking machine, taking up two places at the table, and the poor nerdy-looking kid beside him appears terrified and dwarfed next to him. I stifle a smile at the thought.

"Yeah, Tate, come take a seat with the kids." Owen smirks. I glare at the fucker. He knows how much I hate these little pow-wows my mom insists on.

Flicking my gaze across the table, my eyes lock on to hazel eyes, and hers widen with horror. Her hand pauses bringing a spoon to her mouth. My heart skips a beat, my body frozen in place while the blood in my veins fill with confusion.

"Tate, these are the children I'm housing over school break." My mom's words take a moment to register because all I see is the stunning brunette staring back at me in panic.

"This is Ava, she turned eighteen yesterday. So the party last night was as much a party for her too. Isn't that right, sweetie?" I blink. I blink again. Eighteen? My stomach drops and my glass slides through my hand and falls to the stone floor, shattering. The sound of it smashing seems to echo as a buzzing goes off in my head, and my mind blurs.

Eighteen? Birthday?

People move around me, clearing up the mess, but all I see is her.

"Tate!" Owen barks. "Sit your fucking ass down, I'll sort it."

"Owen James, do not curse in front of the children," my mom chastises, and I wince. *Children.*

Jesus.

Oh shit.

Holy fucking Christ.

As if in slow motion, my ass locates my chair while I stare dumbfounded in her direction.

Ava casts her eyes away and looks out the window toward the patio, but I can't steal my eyes away from her.

Owen clears his throat as my mom butters my toast and puts it on my plate like she has done for over twenty years.

"So, what are you two planning on doing after graduation?" she asks while I sit staring at Ava, trying to compute how this is the same woman I fucked last night. I grind my jaw in rage as anger boils beneath my skin.

Graduation? My eyes volley from the nerdy kid to Ava, as I'm still unable to grasp the woman I fucked is her. Correction, the girl. I grimace, shoving the plate away from me when sickness rises into my throat.

I fucked a child.

I'm going to hell.

"Oh, I'm going to Harvard." The nerdy kid smiles while pushing his glasses up his smug nose. My gaze darts toward Ava's, and she rolls her eyes as she picks at the muffin on her plate, refusing to make eye contact with me while I glare daggers in her direction. She seems completely unfazed, and the thought pisses me off.

Not only was I duped into sleeping with someone I thought was a fully grown woman, but she doesn't even have the decency to own her shit and acknowledge me. I pump my fists below the table in fury.

"How about you, sweetheart?" Owen asks her, and every fucking muscle in my body tightens. *Fucking sweetheart?*

"Oh, Ava has other plans. Don't you, Ava?" mocks the

spectacled little chump who I'm pretty sure is trying to have a dig at Ava.

Ava grimaces in the kid's direction, then looks down at her plate with sad eyes, and I want to ask her more. I want to protect her. What the actual fuck?

"She got an offer she couldn't refuse. Isn't that right, Ava?" The question seems loaded and full of innuendo. Her head snaps up, and she glares in his direction with the confidence she showed last night and was lacking only seconds ago.

"I'll rip your weaselly fucking head off if you breathe another goddamn word, you sad little shit," she spits, fire flaring from her eyes. The geeky kid withers under her stare, and my lip twitches at the feistiness behind her tone.

There she is, the confident little siren that gave as good as she got last night.

Again, I'm struck thinking about our night of passion, and close my eyes in an attempt to expel all memories of last night. Only, all I see is her fucking face, contorted in ecstasy as I plunge inside her, stretching her tight cunt.

I snap my eyes open, and Owen sits with a shit-eating grin on his face, as though enjoying every minute of the entertainment between them.

"Ava, honey. Why don't you take a swim? It'll be nice to relax a little, huh?" my mom suggests, clearly trying to disperse any further argument.

Ava's shoulders ease, then her eyes flick up toward my mom's as though panicked. "I don't have any swimwear," she all but whispers.

My heart hammers in my chest, so I place a hand over it to stop it from freefalling to the ground. She doesn't own a fucking swimsuit. Jesus. I exhale, then drag a hand over my hair. I want to give her every-fucking-thing she doesn't have. And so much more.

It doesn't seem like more than two minutes since I was in the same position as her. A foster kid with no home and barely any belongings.

But as I cast my eyes over her reddened cheeks, I see her for who she is. A teenager. Not the woman I thought she was. She's a scared young girl. A foster kid. And I took advantage of that. My stomach rolls at the thought, and nausea builds beneath the surface, threatening to spill at any second.

Owen doesn't miss her vulnerable reaction to my mom either; his face is laced in concern, but I give him a subtle shake of my head, and he drops it.

The geeky kid scoffs. "You won't be needing one where you're going anyway."

Like a fucking tornado, she crashes across the table, scrambling to grab the scrawny kid by the scruff of his shirt. Juice hits the table, and the dishes go flying as she tries dragging him toward her. Owen and I move, but my mom calms her down. "Let him go, sweetie. Let him go and I'll find you something to wear." She strokes Ava's arm, and I wish like hell it was me reassuring her.

Her shoulders loosen and she nods, then she releases the kid, who makes a dramatic flop on the table, heaving for air as Ava strolls away with a confident sway in her hips, and my eyes can't help but follow her.

Jesus, her denim shorts are ripped and so far up her ass I swear I can see the handprint I left there last night.

And with that thought, my cock comes to life once again.

FIVE

AVA

"Fuck!" I throw myself face-first onto the mattress with a groan. Freddie needs to learn to keep his mouth shut. I hate that someone knows the lengths I'm going to as soon as I graduate, but I don't have a choice. Whatever I need to do, then so be it. Even if it means selling myself to the devil to do it.

The door creaks open, and I glance over my shoulder. When my gaze latches onto the blue-eyed sex god, my body stills and my heart hammers to the point of pain. It was the most incredible night of my entire life, the best birthday I could ever wish for, but with the disdain oozing from him, I know he doesn't feel the same way. Once again, I'm left feeling used.

His lip curls up at the end in disgust, and his knuckles tighten on the door handle as he clings to it, as though planning a quick escape. The fact he has come no further into the room makes me feel like he doesn't want to get close, and that hurts more than anyone could imagine. Especially after I let my barriers down last night and we connected in every way possible. Maybe it wasn't the same for him as it was me. Maybe he used me like everyone else does.

"What the fuck was that?" he spits, his voice low and deadly as he points toward the door.

Exhaling loudly, I push myself up, rolling over onto my ass to face him.

He quickly peruses my body before flicking his gaze to my face.

"The little shit was causing trouble." I shrug.

His eyes widen, and he shakes his head. "Not that. I don't give a fuck about that. I'm talking about the fact you're eight-fucking-teen, Ava. You failed to mention that last night!" He's literally steaming, his face bright red and the vein in his neck pulsates in anger. Why do my eyes land on the bite mark I left there?

Licking my lips, I imagine kissing the mark, and as if hearing my thoughts of how delicious he is, his eyes bug out and he stares back at me. "Eighteen," he repeats.

I nod in agreement. "It was my birthday," I confirm with a soft smile, hoping he can see what a gift he gave me.

"Your fucking birthday?" he chokes out, his mouth falling open in shock. Mrs. Kavanagh told him this already though, so I'm not sure why he's acting so surprised.

"Yep. It was a night to remember so, thank you." I grin. See, just because I'm a foster kid doesn't mean I don't have manners.

He gawks at me, and honestly, it's adorable. My lips

twitch to tell him so, but something tells me he wouldn't be happy about it.

"Thank you? Fucking thank you?" He raises his voice, then winces when he realizes how loud he's becoming. He scrubs a hand over his head again, then starts doing some weird breathing noise while closing his eyes and dropping his head back so he faces the ceiling.

"Are you okay?"

Dropping his head forward, his eyes snap open to meet mine. "No. I slept with fucking jailbait. I'm going to hell."

Jesus, he's dramatic. I choke on a laugh. "I'm eighteen, chill out. Besides, I'm not going to tell anyone." I shrug as I push off the bed to stand. He steps back as though just being closer to me will burn him, and I smirk at his dramatics.

"You can't tell anyone about this, Ava. The shit I'll get into if anyone finds out," he breathes out in a panic.

I roll my eyes. His words sound so familiar, but at least this time it was a consensual act.

"Okay," I reply with ease.

His head rolls back as he glares at me.

In a matter of minutes, the guy has gone from shocked, to horrified, to panicked, to stunned.

"Okay?" he parrots.

"Yes, fine." I snap as I walk around my room, gathering the sunscreen and sunglasses into my rucksack.

"You don't want anything from me?" he chokes out, staring at me as though I'm the idiot.

"Nope." I pop the p to emphasize how much I don't want a damn thing from him. As much as I'd love a repeat of last night, I know damn well he will not go there again.

"So that's it, then?" he asks with his hands on his hips,

and he has a bewildered look in his eyes. The thought has my heart constricting, so I shake it off and fold the pool towel into my bag.

"Last night never happened?" he tacks on, forcing me turn to face him.

"Oh, it happened all right." His eyes bulge, and he fidgets on my words, probably thinking I'm about to go back on everything I agreed. "We both have the marks to prove it." I point at his bite mark while his gaze latches onto mine. "But I agree. We should keep this to ourselves." I gift him a swift nod.

He rubs the back of his neck and darts his eyes away before exhaling loudly. "Right. Good."

"Right," I mirror, refusing to admit how much it hurts that he wants to pretend it never happened.

"See you around, then." He stares at me but doesn't attempt to move from the doorway.

"Yeah," I reply.

Finally, he blows out a deep breath, refusing eye contact with me as he opens the door and spins on his heel, walking through it without a backward glance and taking a piece of my heart with him.

If there's one thing I'm good at, it's secrets. And Tate Kavanagh's will be a closely guarded one.

I've a feeling last night will be something I'll use to draw strength from when I need it the most.

TATE

As soon as I close her bedroom door, I drop my head against it. How fucking stupid could I have been? A fucking teenager.

This is disastrous, it could ruin my career. Everything I've worked for. Sabotage the business. I could lose it all. *We* could lose it all. My best friends would hate me.

Not to mention the hell it would rain down on my family if this got out. I swallow back the bile in my throat and head toward my room. I need to ensure there's no evidence of last night anywhere.

Although, I believe Ava when she says she'll keep it a secret. I don't even know the girl, but the weird connection between us has me feeling like I've known her a lifetime.

But I've also been the kid that was in a position where you'd do anything to get out of the hell you're in, and I can't risk her using last night as blackmail. I can't risk losing it all.

After throwing open my old bedroom door, I faceplant onto my bed, biting into my lip, unsure of who to call.

Fuck. I'm such an idiot. My best friend Reed is a lawyer for our company, maybe I should get him to draw up an NDA or something. Maybe that would ensure there are no future issues.

But why does the mere thought of approaching Ava with that fill me with a sick feeling in the pit of my stomach?

Jesus, how the hell do I manage to get into these situations?

Part of me wants to run, go back home, throw myself into work, and forget all about the feisty brunette down the hall, but then the other part of me can't bring myself to leave just yet. Besides, my best friends are coming over for a barbeque, and I can't leave them here without me.

Rummaging through my old closet, I locate my swim shorts and throw them on. If I have to stay another couple of nights, I'll be keeping a close eye on Ava.

To ensure she's as trustworthy as I hope.

Loud shrieks of laughter fill the air. My younger brother Dexter looks like he's having a fucking ball watching Ava's tits bounce up and down in the skimpy bikini my mom loaned her from my little sister. He might only be a teenager, but the kid could easily pass for eighteen, and I wouldn't put it past him to try his luck with Ava. Every muscle in my body coils to the point of pain and my teeth clamp down so hard I fear I will do permanent damage to my jaw.

"How fucking old did you say she was again?" Reed asks again.

TATE

"Eighteen." Owen grins, and I grind my teeth to refrain from the need to hit him in the balls.

We're lying on the sunbeds with a beer in our hands after my mom asked us to watch the fucking kids in the pool. I swear I almost threw up on her words. Feeling like some sick bastard for sleeping with said kid. Worse, reveling in her and showering her in so much cum she could swim in it.

"Jesus, they didn't look like that when I was a kid," Reed says, taking another pull of his beer.

I don't pay notice to either of them, my attention instead drawn toward her. With my sunglasses on, I can watch every move she makes in the pool with no one realizing. My eyes devour her: the way her bikini bottoms keep wedging into her ass, exposing the red mark on her butt cheek, the way her nipples are pebbled beneath the thin fabric, clearly too small for her. Just what the hell was my mom thinking?

My mouth waters to experience her, just one more fucking time.

A swift kick to my leg has me turning my head toward Shaw in question. "What's with you?" he asks, his gaze roaming over my stern face.

I'm normally the life and soul of the party and would have jumped in the pool by now, throwing kids over my shoulders or engaging them in dumb competitions, like who can cannon ball the best, and my best friend knows this.

But today, I lie here hating every second of the dumb prick that continues to let his hands linger for far too long on Ava's hot little body.

Maybe it's out of a sense of protection toward her that I

want to rip his hands off his arms and shove them so far up his ass they wave out his smug mouth.

"Nothing," I clip back.

He scoffs, knowing I'm lying, but doesn't press further.

"How's things with Tara, Mase?" Reed asks.

Mase's head rises from his phone. He's been married to his childhood sweetheart for years, but after she cheated on him, they started the divorce process, only for it all to come to a halt when she was in a car accident that killed her lover. Since then, he's been in a state of perpetual misery and stuck between wanting to do what's right and fight for his marriage and wanting to wipe the slate clean and divorce the manipulating bitch once and for all.

"Same shit different day." He takes a drink of his beer, then lies back on the sunbed.

"You need to get laid," Shaw suggests.

"Don't I fucking know it. I'll be like a fucking virgin in a whorehouse by the time I get to use my dick again." He sighs heavily.

"Looks like Tate got lucky last night. Right, Tate?" Shaw asks with a knowing grin, then sips from his beer.

My head snaps toward his as panic builds inside me. Does he know? Does he realize how bad I fucked up? Sweat gathers on my forehead, and heat travels over my chest.

"The hickey." He points toward my neck, and my fingers dart toward it, covering it.

I try and relax against the lounger but feeling conscious of the fact my best friends are aware I had sex last night has me wanting to throw them off scent.

"Yeah. Someone from the country club," I respond, keeping my voice monotone.

TATE

I can sense Owen's eyes on me, analyzing me. The guy is like a fucking cadaver dog, so I keep my eyes focused on the pool, pleased I have my sunglasses on to disguise the lust I feel dripping from my gaze as Ava pulls the bikini from between her ass cheeks again.

A groan escapes my lips when they lock on to the fingerprints I left on her cheek, and my cock thickens at the memory of her moans in pleasure while begging me to fuck her harder.

Jesus.

I march inside, ignoring the questions thrown my way from my best friends, opting to locate a bottle of my dad's best Scotch.

Because if I can't swim in the pool with the epitome of temptation, I might as well drown in my sins.

She spent all fucking day tormenting me, and I'm not even sure she realized she was doing it. She barely gave me a second glance. Like last night meant fuck all to her.

The cherry lotion she uses permeated the air when she reached for another burger. My body stayed stoically still and as stiff as my cock as her nipples grazed the table, and my fingers itched to touch her—just one more fucking time.

Of course, I kept my hands beneath the table, balled into fists. Telling myself to stay away.

My best friends spent the entire barbeque throwing concerned glances my way, and when the blonde wannabe surfer tucked a lock of her hair behind her ear and whispered something that made her giggle, I saw red.

But instead of kicking the shit out of a kid, I stormed inside the house and went straight to the gym, needing to take my frustration out on something.

"What the fuck is wrong with you today?" Owen asks as I throw another swing at the punching bag. Sweat drips down my body, and I swipe it from my eyes with the back of my hand, then grab the bottle of Scotch and take another swig, hissing at the burn in my throat and reveling in the tinge of relief behind it.

Owen scans my face, scrutinizing it, and my gaze darts away.

"Is it something to do with the girl?"

My body freezes, locks up tight. If I had given nothing away before, I sure as hell have now. Shit.

"Did you fuck her?"

How the hell does he do this? See straight into my soul, the depravity of my actions. My airways feel like they're closing, and I snap my eyes shut and grab my head with both hands in an attempt to block away the mistake I made. The one I long to repeat.

The pain of hearing him say the words along with the thoughts of how I've been feeling all day has me wanting to scream, and fuck, and scream, then throw the fuck up. My head is a fucking mess at the internal struggle.

"She's eighteen," he adds when my silence is confirmation. My eyes close on his words.

"It's sick," I admit on a choke, then open my eyes with trepidation, expecting to see disgust on his face.

But he's unperturbed by the fact I slept with a young girl.

And truthfully, I'm shocked he isn't repulsed by me. I know I am, and there lies the biggest problem. I hate

TATE

myself for it. She's a foster kid that's probably been through hell. Yet I crave her and her tight little body.

"You can't help how you feel. And it's legal." He tacks on the latter, as though convincing himself as much as me.

"She's too young," I snap back. "It's fucking wrong." My teeth grind as I bite the words out, the same words that have my throat burning on the venom spilling from me.

He drags his tongue over his lip, his jaw sharpening, as though angry, yet I can't figure out why. Maybe he's angry with me and trying to rein it in.

"It's not wrong. It's perfectly fucking legal," he replies with confidence behind his words I wish I felt.

I scoff. "Whatever. You and I both know you'd have to be a sick bastard to want to fuck someone so young. At least last night I didn't know her age. Now I do." I shrug. Hating every fucking word that spills from my mouth, I take another pull of the Scotch and ignore the heat coming from Owen beside me.

After all, I'm the sick bastard that wants to fuck her again. But I can't let him think that.

Owen grinds his jaw. "It isn't sick, Tate."

My eyebrows shoot up because this feels more personal, but I ignore it.

"Yeah, well maybe you're all right with fucking barely legal girls. But I'm not," I spit back, hating that our conversation is getting so heavy but needing to say the words that are tearing me up inside. "It would make us as sick as the fuckers that haunt our pasts, Owen," I snipe out.

"Maybe you need to start accepting your demons, Tate. Then you can finally embrace your future." With that, he turns and walks out of the room, leaving me stunned at his loaded response.

I pick up the Scotch, prepared to drown in my sins.

My vision blurs as I lift the glass of water to my lips. I'm not sure what the fuck I was thinking when I decided it was a good idea to finish the bottle off, but as I take another drink of water in my lame attempt to sober up, I find myself walking toward her room.

Alarm bells should be ringing in my head. Sirens should be going off with every step I take, and as my hand clamps down on the door handle, the thud of my heartbeat should shake the house.

But none of it happens, because as I open her bedroom door and her head rises from her pillow and our gazes collide, the words tumble from my lips. "One more fucking time."

She nods, a small smile playing on her lips, and then she lifts the sheet, inviting me to join her.

If I'm going to drown in my sins, I'll enjoy every damn minute of it.

SIX

TATE

FOUR YEARS LATER . . .

"Look, I don't really give a fuck how we figure the advertisement out, but we need to nail it. That presentation we just saw was shit, and with Flawless being the leading company in the market for the fragrance industry right now, we need to not look like idiots." Shaw exhales loudly in irritation.

We just sat through a presentation from our advertising department that was nothing short of shit, it has us looking like amateurs. Shaw and I are the chief executives of the advertising department, and where he deals with the negotiations and liaises with the business colleagues, I deal with the actual creation of the adverts, with Mase assisting me.

Needless to say, I've had my eye off the ball. I drag a

hand over my head. If we fail to win this contract, it's all on me.

Griffin Snider is the founder of Flawless and our leading competitor in the fragrance market. It's basically us against him in the race to sign on the Gold Fragrance deal, and I refuse to fucking lose to a piece of shit like him. I can't, not when I want to prove myself so badly. I might be the joker of the group, the one deemed the biggest bachelor who fools around, but I want to prove myself as a serious businessman also.

Besides, Griffin is an arrogant, ruthless prick with a sadistic streak who takes great pleasure in looking down on us and shoving his success in our faces at every opportunity. The man is a thorn in our sides. One I want to obliterate, damn the consequences.

I glance over my shoulder toward the window. At least Shaw has his blinds tilted so we can't see that obnoxious advertisement of his adjacent to our building.

The prick loves nothing more than to remind us he's the sole advertiser for Grandè, the creator of the Gold Fragrance.

Mase sits forward on the couch. "What about the new interns? We need a fresh approach, and the shit these kids know about social media and trends, they're the ones we should be asking. We need to utilize them."

Anger bubbles inside me; we don't have time for this shit. "They don't have the fucking experience. All they have is the papers they walk in here with. That's why they're interning with us. To get the damn experience," I snap.

Mase glares at me. "You need to give them a shot.

Some of those kids worked on some pretty impressive projects."

"We don't have time to wheedle out possible ideas. We need fucking results," I grit with disappointment at how bad the presentation went.

Mase sighs. "Look, let's just have a select few sit in on the next brainstorm. It's not going to hurt." He shrugs. "If we come away with nothing, then so be it. But Tate, anything is worth a shot right now. The only thing we can agree on is that presentation was shit!" He points toward the door.

I drag a hand over the scruff of my jaw. He's right, but Jesus, we need something quick, we need results. "Fine," I snap back.

Reed strolls into the office with his briefcase and a smug smile on his face, and it takes everything in me not to headbutt him. His smile is odd, given he rarely does. The man normally resembles Lurch from the Addams family. I smirk to myself.

"You good?" Shaw tilts his head in Reed's direction, as if assessing his odd behavior.

"I am very good." He sits down in the swivel chair Owen normally occupies, and we all watch him like he's losing the plot.

I ball up the bundles of paper from the meeting that went to shit and launch them at his head. "Fucking share, then, dick!" Because clearly, he's smug about something.

"I just had a meeting with George Fanzio." We all sit forward in our seats. Jesus, this is great news. George Fanzio is a billionaire property mogul, just being in the man's presence is a business honor. "He wants me to complete a sale on a plot of land and then he's selling us the land at a reduced fee." His face brightens even further, if that is humanly possible. "It's perfect for an entertainment venue." He smiles.

Fucking smiles.

"Wait. Back the fuck up, why would he sell it to us cheaper?" Shaw asks, raising an eyebrow.

I sit back and widen my legs, watching the exchange take place.

Reed grins. "Because he knows how ruthless I am."

"Fuck." Mase sighs while slumping back in his chair, and we all laugh. He rolls his head toward Reed. "What the hell have you got to do?"

Reed smirks. "He needs me to shut down a community project and clear a few houses." He waves his hand as though it's nothing. My eyes bug out at the thought.

"Clear a few fucking houses?" Mase mumbles.

"This could be bad publicity, Reed," Shaw snaps.

"I have a plan. Don't worry. We'll be the heroes, the good Samaritans." Reed grins back.

"What the fuck ever. I have a wife to get home to. Just don't rock the boat, we've created an empire here. People get angsty when you want to touch their properties." Shaw pushes back in his chair.

Reed's eyebrows furrow. "It isn't their property to begin with, they pay rent."

Mase snorts. "And that is the exact reason why we should be worried." He points toward Reed, whose face is contorted in confusion.

"How's the wife going, anyway?" I wiggle my eyebrows in Shaw's direction. "Is it true what they say, happy wife, happy life?"

"She's great," he replies like a lovestruck idiot.

When Shaw discovered he'd knocked up a Mafia princess, he was forced to marry her by her ruthless brother. It was that or be killed.

Luckily for him, Emi, his new wife, seems like a decent catch. Apart from the whole Mafia thing and the fact he had to break up with his on-again-off-again psycho girlfriend in order to marry her. Yeah, apart from that, everything is going great for him.

I'm pleased for him, but each time I hear about them creating a family together, a pang of longing hits me square in the chest. An insatiable need for my own family overwhelms me. I scrub at the pain.

"Great?" Reed responds with a wrinkle of his nose.

Shaw's eyes roam over us all. "What?"

Mase shrugs. "You seem . . . happy."

I throw in a grenade to alter the mood. "I heard that pregnant women are horny all the time. Is that true?" I wiggle my eyebrows.

Shaw's eyes turn murderous. "I'm not discussing our sex life with you!"

"Never stopped you from discussing Lizzie," I counter, referring to his psycho ex.

"She wasn't my fucking wife." His eyes drill lasers into me.

I hold my hands up playfully, knowing I overstepped, while throwing a wink in Mase's direction, who struggles to stifle a laugh against his fist.

Luckily, Shaw just shakes his head and leaves.

As soon as the door closes behind him, Mase turns to face me. "So, shall I arrange a meeting with the interns?"

My head drops back against the couch with a groan. "Ugh, yeah." I throw up my hand. "Fuck it. I've already wasted hours of my life today. Why not waste a couple more."

"Great!" He claps eagerly like an idiot and jumps to his feet.

"Fucking great," I mimic in a childish voice, like the immature prick I'm known to be.

SEVEN

AVA

TWO MONTHS LATER...

I glance around the office again, an unusual buzz of excitement in the air makes me want to roll my eyes.

The room is full of interns desperate to impress the management with their skills and ideas, and in doing so, willing to sell their souls.

My stomach rolls at the memory, but I refuse to look back. After all, I've been there myself and know only too well how far people are willing to go to get on in life.

"Ava, everyone is heading up there already. Come on." Steve, my supervisor, lingers by my desk, tilting his head toward the elevator. My lip curls, and I cast my eyes up toward him. His gaze bores down on me with those green eyes I know so well. Refusing to acknowledge his words, I glance away and continue typing. He sighs and leans against the side of my workstation. "You know, it could be a good opportunity for you too."

This time, I give him my full attention, and his face softens as his eyes lock with mine. I'm not stupid, I know Steve is falling for me, that's why I stopped our regular fuck sessions. I don't need nor want a relationship. Not now, not ever.

"I don't need it." I raise my chin.

He smiles down at me. "It's not up for discussion, Ava. The boss requested all interns be in the meeting."

I roll my eyes and push back in my chair with a huff, and he chuckles at my dramatics. I gather a notepad and pen and follow Steve and his tight ass toward the elevator. He presses the button for the top floor, where the owners of STORM Enterprises work from, then presses his fingerprint to the screen. "Can you believe this shit?" He raises an eyebrow. "My fingerprint is only valid for access to their floor today."

Feeling his eyes on me, I stare ahead toward the doors, refusing to continue the conversation. I'm being an ass but also well aware if I give Steve an inch, he'll take a mile. The mile being me.

"You know, we could always just . . ." The doors open and I march ahead, not acknowledging whatever the hell he was about to say. Instead, I pull open the door and try to ignore the excitable hustle and bustle of the room.

Jesus, anyone would think some sort of god was descending on us. They might own the building, but they don't own me. Nobody will ever have that hold on me again.

I take the last seat. It faces a kid who has what looks like hives all over his face, his fingers tremble and sweat

TATE

beads his forehead. How the hell do they get this far when they can barely hold a pen?

Glancing around the table, I notice some have dressed up for the occasion, one girl has heat traveling up her face as she slinks back in her chair while another guy stares ahead at the blank whiteboard, as if waiting for a test to begin.

My gaze roams over the room, it's a blank canvas, apart from the odd photo on the wall that shows who I imagine are the owners of the company.

Floor-to-ceiling windows fill one side of the office, but the view is obstructed by the blinds being closed. That doesn't draw away the brightness of the room though.

The doors open, and feet thud against the floor as a soft hush fills the room. I almost want to scoff at how dramatic this all is.

"Hello, everyone, and thank you for joining us. I'm Mason Campbell, Chief Executive here at STORM Enterprises. I've gathered you all here today because we need your help." I stare at the spotty kid, wondering whether he's on some medication for his trembling condition, while blocking out the god executive's voice.

"We refuse anything other than success. And with success comes gold. Literal Gold. We want to become the leading advertisement company in the Gold Fragrance franchise, and in order to do that, in order to succeed, we need you. A new set of eyes, a fresh approach." The confidence oozes from him while his words register.

They want the Gold contract, the contract I know has opposition.

Whispers and mumbles of enthusiasm buzz around

me, but I barely take any of it in while I consider the fact Steve could be right, this could be an opportunity for me.

I doodle on my notepad, the way I always do when my mind is full of ideas.

Feeling eyes on me, I glance up to find Steve leaning against the wall with his clipboard in hand. He nods toward the Chief God, as though prompting me to listen. I give him an uninterested head shake and continue doodling while, unbeknownst to him, I take in every little detail.

"Without further ado. I'll hand you over to my co-owner, Tate, who will tell you what we would like to see."

My heart hammers faster, but I don't know why.

"Hi everyone, I'm Tate Kavanagh. You've already had the meet and greet from Mase here, so I'll get straight to the point. Every idea placed in front of us so far has been shit. So, here's the latest idea . . ."

My heart thuds harder and harder. Surely not? It can't be. My stomach flutters with a feeling of panic.

"Holy fuckkk," I gasp.

Everyone's eyes turn toward mine, and I duck my head down at the epic screw up. I most definitely thought it, I just hadn't realized I'd said it. Steve's eyes are practically burning through me with anger.

"Exactly, holy fuck. It's a mess, right? So, give me what you've got." The room falls silent, everyone stunned at his words, or mine? I'm not sure.

"Miss Potty Mouth Intern at the end of the table, trying to skulk down in her chair, can you give us an alternative, or are you just one of those people without anything constructive to say who just enjoys tearing down other people's hard work? Maybe keep your mouth shut and you might learn something, or better yet, you might get to keep the position you should be grateful for having instead of creating this little outburst of yours in an attempt to garner attention."

My jaw falls open, my temper skyrockets, and pain at the back of my eyes forces my pupils to dilate while the blood in my veins pumps wildly around my body like an inferno threatening to combust.

How fucking dare he? He cannot be serious. Because of one slip up, he thinks he can speak down to me like this? All because he was born with a silver spoon in his impressively talented mouth, he thinks it's okay to belittle other people? I've spent my entire life being submissive, and when I finally broke from my cage, I told myself I'd allow no one to take advantage of me again. I'm fucking free!

I did what I had to do, when I had to do it. But now, now I have a choice and a voice, and I'm not afraid to use it. I'm not about to let Tate Kavanagh, the arrogant prick, get away with this.

In a move that stuns the room further, I straighten my shoulders, push back in my chair, and stand tall.

Steve's eyeballs almost fall to the floor as I raise my chin and stride toward the presentation desk and projector screen.

They all think I'm about to walk out of the room. *Idiots.*

But what I'm about to do is give them all a lesson in never judge a book by its cover. Or an intern who they think lacks experience. If they read my résumé, they'd know otherwise.

I lift my head as I walk with a confident swagger toward the desk, ignoring the whispers and wide eyes from my colleagues.

Not giving Tate a glance, because quite frankly I'm not sure I can even go there, I turn my back to him and give them the critical feedback they were not expecting from the intern—the potty mouth.

I stare up at the screen, taking in the numerous reels laid out on a vision board. "Well for starters, the shading is all off. You're trying to sell a fragrance that represents the highest of quality, yet your advert currently shows lack of exclusivity and indulgence. You chose black as your main color scheme. When you said yourself, the contract is for Gold." I smirk at their lack of intuition and the irony behind the name. For a company doing so well in the advertising industry, they're really off the mark with this one.

"Even the models are all wrong. You've gone with an older-looking model with your typical billionaire approach. It's been done. It's being done. It's irrelevant. Much like the Lamborghini Aventador in reel number four. Last season." I cluck my tongue as I point at each reel.

I can't help myself, I'm on a roll. "You say you want a fresh approach, a young mindset, yet your reels and advertisement are none of these things. In fact, the ideas are completely outdated and have been used before." My body swells with pride.

"And what the fuck would you know? You're just an intern," he spits from behind me with so much venom I wonder if he realizes it's me.

"I have experience," I reply while scanning over the reels, analyzing each and every one of them in much more detail.

He scoffs. "In what? A school project?"

I take a deep breath, ignoring the snickers filling the

room at my expense. Oh, how I can't wait to set the smug prick straight. Walking over to the blinds, I press the button on the side of the wall, allowing the blinds to draw open, revealing the Flawless advertisement I'm sure had been blocked out on purpose.

I can practically feel the triumph radiating from Tate, but I ignore him and his ego trip. "In that!" I point toward the advertisement glaring back at us all. Heads turn, and the whispers become louder as everyone in the room discusses the incredible advert I created. "I created it. That's my experience." I turn and shrug with a sly smirk as mouths fall open.

When my eyes finally lock with Tate's, the color drains from his face and he stumbles back as though he's seen a ghost. I'd almost feel sorry for the poor guy if he wasn't being such a prick.

"You created that?" Mase stands with a huge smile encompassing his handsome face.

"I did." I give him a tilt of my head, grinning with pride, and ignore Tate and his flaring nostrils as fury emanates from him.

Mase holds out his hand for me to shake. "I think we just found our hidden gem, huh, Tate?" Mase glances toward Tate, whose focus is fixed so firmly on me I struggle to swallow.

Not acknowledging Mr. Grumpy Pants, I step forward and slip my hand into Mase's, ignoring the sound of a petulant growl from Tate.

"Welcome to the team . . ." He tilts his head and smiles at me but doesn't finish his sentence, realizing he doesn't even know my name.

"Ava." I smile back sweetly.

"Ava," he replies with a hint of uncertainty flashing behind his eyes, then I wonder if he was one of the guys at Tate's parents' home that summer.

"Let's organize a meeting." He grins from ear to ear.

Tate looks like he wants to tear me apart, and not in a good way.

TATE

I toss back another Scotch while glaring down at the desk. How the hell did this happen? It's been four fucking years since I last saw her. She still has that snarky attitude I dream of spanking out of her. That summer, I spanked the attitude out of her so many times her ass was raw. Followed by spending years jerking my cock over the memory, and now it feels like an eternity ever since.

For four years I've filled as many holes in New Jersey as humanly possible trying to eradicate as many thoughts of Ava as I could.

Like a poison in my veins, she invaded my cells, and I haven't been able to find a cure no matter how hard I tried. And boy have I fucking tried.

I refused to allow myself to dig any deeper into where she came from or what became of her, knowing if I did, there would be no turning back for either of us.

The feisty little brunette that rocked my world and tilted it on its axis has been forever embedded in my mind.

I struggled in the days, weeks, and months to follow

since that summer, wondering what sort of home she had come from and if she had made it like the geeky kid bragged.

But if I'd have dug into her life, the ramifications could have been catastrophic. Not just affecting me but my family and my best friends too. So instead, I buried my cock in as many women as possible, hoping to wash away my sins in a never-ending wave of women. All while craving the one out of reach.

My friends queried my behavior, and even picked up on my attraction to her at some point. While I was shit-faced, I spoke about her, but none of them pressed me. Owen stayed silent and it irked me. He never pushed me for answers, when, if I'm being honest, I could have done with someone to speak to about her. I realized it was because of her age and how fucked up he considered the whole situation I was in. But still, I needed someone.

Sighing, I scrub a hand over my head, feeling myself coming undone. I tug open the top button of my shirt and attempt to do the deep-breathing technique I've witnessed Reed doing countless times. How can this be happening?

My office door reopens, and Mase reemerges. After everyone left the room with praises of congratulations in Ava's direction, I followed behind, ensuring my office door was closed before slamming my forehead against it. Multiple times—hard.

Then I hit the bar in the corner of my office and threw myself into my chair while every memory of her came flooding back while drowning my sorrows in Scotch.

"Are you okay?" Mase asks, staring down at me in confusion with his hands on his hips. "Are you pissed about me asking the intern to join the team?" I don't answer him, unable to construct a single word, let alone an entire sentence, a testament as to how in shock I am right now. "I know I should have given the other kids a chance, but fuck, man, her résumé is impressive, and her experience is the kind we need. She's incredible." I wince at him calling her a kid.

He pulls out the chair and parks his ass in it, ignoring my obvious meltdown. I can literally feel the sweat trickling off my forehead. I take another drink, gasping at the burn in my throat.

Jesus, she's changed so much. I swallow back the thought. She's nothing like the girl I met four years ago. Yet the moment she opened her mouth, it was like she hadn't changed a single thing.

She was wearing ripped jeans and chunky boots along with a black hoodie. I mean, who the hell goes to an office job dressed like that? One where you're trying to make an impression, no less. Surely, we have a dress code for this shit.

And the piercings, her ears are lined with them. For some odd reason, I want to know how many she has.

She still has the fire behind her eyes. Eyes that refused to acknowledge just who the hell I am. Does she not remember me at all?

Did I not leave the same impact on her as she did me?

"Tate. Fucking answer me, otherwise, I'm going to stage an intervention." Lifting my gaze to Mase, I shake my head, trying to settle the thoughts rushing through my jumbled mind.

Did he ask me a question? "What?"

"I said, explain what the fuck is going on with you."

His eyes ping pong over my face, his brows pinched together.

Rubbing the back of my neck, I shift in my seat and swallow back the lump of anxiety building in my throat while trying to ignore the bouncing of my leg. Do I tell him, do I open the door to my fucked-up memories of something that should never have happened. Yet happened repeatedly.

"Tate!" he snaps again, and my head jerks back at his bitter tone.

"Jesus." I drag a hand down my face and stare down at my desk, as I'm about to admit my truths that weigh me down.

"You can trust me, man. You're as good as my brother." My eyes snap up to meet Mase's green ones. The sincerity seeps from them, forcing me to take a deep breath while my throat remains dry. Out of all my best friends, he's the most compassionate, the most understanding.

"You remember the summer I attended my last foster event?" My Adam's apple slides slowly down my throat as Mase nods, fully aware of the last foster event I went to and have since avoided. "There was a girl." Our eyes remain locked, and he gifts me with a reassuring nod. I lick my dry lips. "The night before, at the party. I slept with her." He closes his eyes and pinches the bridge of his nose. Panic builds inside me. "I didn't know she was a foster kid. I swear it," I blurt. He exhales, and I watch in apprehension as I wait for him to open his eyes and stare at me in revulsion, but when his eyes finally open, they're filled with sympathy.

"Okay." He sighs and gives me a nod, as though knowing there's more to come.

"After I found out her age—" I swallow again, knowing the enormity of what I'm about to admit. "I slept with her again." The disappointment in my voice reflects how I feel about myself.

"Jesus, Tate. Are you fucking stupid?" he admonishes.

I blow out a deep breath to try and convince my friend to understand I'm not some weirdo that goes after barely legal girls. "I know, Mase. Fuck, I know. But after, I never saw her again. I swear it. It was just that summer."

"But you wanted to?" he queries, raising his eyebrow, his eyes drilling straight into me, as though seeing every sick, twisted, and obsessive thought.

Sweat slides down my spine as I struggle with the decision to be honest with my best friend. But him sitting there when he could be out the door, and knowing how supportive Mase is, leaves me with no choice.

"I wanted to."

Mase's shoulders relax, as though pleased with my reply, which is odd. He gives me a reassuring nod. "You never looked her up?"

I scoff. "Fuck no." I drag a hand over my face again. "I couldn't, man." I shake my head. "It was for the best."

"It was," he agrees in a monotone voice. But I ignore it, instead tackling the issue head-on.

"What am I going to do?"

Mase rubs the back of his neck, then fidgets in his chair. "Do you have feelings for her?" His vulnerable eyes meet mine.

It's not often we talk about fucking feelings like a bunch of girls.

"Fuck." I slump back in my chair. "Yes. It's not like I really know her, though, Mase. But we had a connection. I thought about her every damn day since seeing her. She fucking consumes me, and I can't even hate her for it." I shake my head in wonder. "And now she's here. She's finally fucking here."

He studies me for what feels like hours before he speaks. "I mean, she's an adult. And as long as she doesn't say anything about the past." He shrugs while talking so low I almost don't hear him. He snaps his head up. "Maybe we should have Reed make her sign an NDA?"

I shake my head. "Fuck no. I don't want the guys knowing, Mase. Please," I practically beg, my heart racing at the thought of disappointing my best friends. "Reed will be a fucking nightmare; you know it as well as I do. Shaw has too much on his plate." Mase's lip curls into a knowing smirk.

"Okay. We stay quiet about the past, but judging by the look on your face, she's your future, Tate. Just don't fuck it up."

My shoulders relax. He's right, she is my fucking future. She might have gotten away from me once, because it was the right thing to do, but never again.

Mase clears his throat and taps on the desk with his fist. "We have her in the office first thing in the morning and let her know she's here to work. Anything that happens between you guys stays out of the office." He glares at me in warning. He doesn't want me to fuck this up, because if I do, I screw up the project too.

"Agreed."

Mase stands, giving me a weird smile that has me wanting to hit him in the balls for how smug he looks.

I sigh into my chair, throwing my head back against the headrest.

"Oh, and Tate?"

I lift my head, and his hand lands on the door handle. "All those jibes about my blue balls over the years? Seeing her today just made me realize you're about to have them now too."

My eyes narrow at him as he swings open the door and laughs, leaving me more confused than ever.

Because if there's anything I've never suffered from, it's blue balls.

And I'm not about to start now.

No, Ava is mine. I just need to get her on board with it.

EIGHT

AVA

As soon as I strode out of his office, I went to the restroom to gather my thoughts, splashing my face to wash away the look on his face when he realized who I was. There is no doubt about it, he knows who I am.

I stare up into the mirror, hating the reflection staring back at me. I'm not the same girl I was back then, and I wish for nothing more than being the carefree, confident girl full of dreams and aspirations. But things change, and although, ultimately, I got what I wanted in the end, I had to live in hell until I got there.

The things I've done, I had to push myself to go above and beyond every boundary I never knew existed to get where I am now. So, I push away from the sink and out the door to go back to my desk, reminding myself of the same two things I've told myself countless times in the past four years.

You did what you had to do.

The man with the blue eyes isn't your savior.
Nobody is.

I can feel Steve's eyes on me as he walks toward my desk, but I feign being busy, instead concentrating on the design ideas in front of me.

As much as I don't want to cause waves working on a task that pits me against my ex-employer, Flawless, I can't help but be excited about the prospect of creating something to rival them. A big fuck you to how I've been treated. It drives me forward, spurs me on, motivating me to create the best damn advertisement ever.

Steve clears his throat, giving me no choice but to glance up toward him. A soft smile plays on his lips, and his tongue drags out over the bottom one. I can't deny the guy is hot and decent in bed when I have the itch, and right now, I have the itch; it's been a while. Squeezing my thighs together, he chuckles, as though knowing my thoughts.

He lowers his head. "I wish I was coming here to take you home. But you're wanted upstairs." He flicks his eyes toward the ceiling, and I swallow back the ball of nervousness I feel at his words.

Gathering the tablet provided to us by STORM, I pick up my phone and folder. "Are you coming with me?"

He pushes off the desk and glances over his shoulder. "No. I have a project to finish. You have access to their floor though. But maybe you could come over later?" He brushes the strands of loose hair from my messy bun off my shoulder. His insinuation cannot be missed, and frankly, I revel in it. I need to blow off steam and get this never-ending vision of Tate out of my head. His phone buzzes, severing the connection, and with a roll of his eyes, he sighs. "They're waiting for you."

Giving him a nod, I step back and swing my hips as I walk toward the elevator. I take a deep breath, scan my finger, and press for access to the top floor, then close my eyes and give myself a pep talk. *Stay focused. Remember your endgame. Do what you need to do.*

When the elevator pings, I snap my eyes open, pull my shoulders back, step out, and stride toward the reception desk.

The woman behind the desk is filing her nails, oblivious to my presence.

"Excuse me, I have an appointment with Tate and Mason. I'm already running a little late, so if you could hurry and finish that nail." I point toward her talons.

Her eyes lazily meet with mine, and she gives me a languorous once-over, a sneer on her heavily painted lips, with disdain oozing from her thick mascaraed eyes. Locking eyes with me, she blows on her nails, as if giving me a big fuck you. Before finally getting to her feet, she snaps her fingers, forcing my eyebrows to shoot up in shock.

"Come."

Is she for real?

Utterly gobsmacked, I follow after her. She teeters on ridiculously high heels; her skirt is so short if she bends over, her ass will be on full display, but something tells me that's part of her plan. Her shirt is almost an inch too short for her, exposing her waist as she walks. And with that exaggerated swing of her hips, it's a wonder she isn't disjointed. I roll my eyes.

With a knock on the door and a blink of her eyes, she transforms from brutal bitch to flirtatious and flighty. "Yeah," a gruff voice that sends a shiver down my spine penetrates through the door.

She swings the door open, and I try not to meet Tate's face, acknowledging Mase first, but I can feel the glare radiating from him. "Hi, good to see you again."

Mase is hot. Broad shoulders, cropped hair, and bright eyes would have any woman wanting to melt into a puddle. "You too, Ava." He winks, and I shudder behind the hidden meaning of his words. Shit, does he know? Does he remember me? "Take a seat." He points toward the two empty chairs opposite Tate's desk.

I slump down, somehow finding the seat, and I cling to the items in my grasp, as though anchoring me.

"You're fucking late!"

Lifting my head, our eyes clash. His face a mask of fury, his temple pulsates and his nostrils flare. His shirt strains across his shoulders, his muscles pulled so tightly it threatens to tear. Jesus, he's even more built than I remember. My fingers twitch to explore his flesh, and my mouth waters to lick him. Every-fucking-where.

"I'm sorry, I was waiting—"

He holds his hand up. "Shut the fuck up."

I jolt at his venom.

"Tate!" Mase chastises, his voice deep and seething.

Tate exhales, and his fists clench and unclench on the desk before he shoves them beneath the desk, out of sight, as though annoyed I can see the strain he's under.

"Would you both like a drink?" the receptionist asks,

darting her eyes from Tate to Mase and back again, ignoring my presence.

Tate lifts his head, his shoulders relax, and a sweet smile plays on his handsome face. "Sure. Thank you, Tiffany." She smiles like the cat that got the cream before strutting over toward the bar, and his eyes follow her movements.

"Oh, please," I mumble at how pathetic this guy is.

His head whips around to face me. "Problem?"

Jeez, what an ass. He might be gorgeous, but clearly, Tate is a player, and worse, he doesn't care to hide it.

Tiffany brings two drinks over to the desk and lowers Tate's right in front of his face, therefore pushing her cleavage into him. Then she creates a show of sashaying around to Mase and doing the same. He fidgets in his chair, as though uncomfortable with her antics, while Tate beams up at her like she's the answer to all his desperate cock prayers.

"Did you want a drink, Ava?" Mase asks.

"No. I'm good, thanks." I smile back at him.

"Okay, Tiffany, if you can shut the door on the way out that would be great. Thanks," he adds, earning a bitter huff from her before she slowly leaves the room.

Mase clears his throat. "Okay. I'm going to be honest with you, Ava." I nod, keeping focus on Mase and not the burning glare opposite me. "I know you and Tate have a bit of history." I suck in a sharp breath as heat travels over me. He told him?

"But I'd like this to remain professional. Whatever happens between you two stays out of the office." I frown on his words, happens between us? I open my mouth to reassure him that nothing will happen, but he holds his hand up to stop me, then carries on. "We really need your support in getting the best advertisement out there, and with your experience, I'm sure that's something we can achieve. How does that sound to you?"

That's it? My body relaxes. "Of course. Whatever me and Tate shared was over a long time ago." I notice Tate flinch from the corner of my eye, but otherwise, pay him no attention.

Mase claps. "That's great. Right, Tate?" He smiles at Tate with mirth in his eyes.

Turning my head to finally look at Tate, I'm shocked at the seething anger focused on me. He bites into his cheek, as though struggling to hold back saying something.

"Right." He fake-smiles, dropping it in an instant, letting us both know he's anything but happy.

TATE

"Of course. Whatever me and Tate shared was over a long time ago." I flinch at her words. How the fuck can she dismiss me so quickly? After what we shared. Is that what she's done for the past four years? While I've sunk myself in as much pussy as possible to drown out her scent, she's not so much as given me another thought? I refuse to accept it. There's no fucking way she didn't think of me. We had a connection; we were drawn to one another.

I wonder if she thought of me when she fucked other people like I did? Every time I sank inside someone, I would imagine it was her all along. Jesus. I crack my neck from side to side, trying to ease the tension building behind it.

"So, I studied your résumé, Ava. And I have to say it's rather impressive." Mase praises her as I watch on like a fucking voyeur.

"Thank you," she whispers with a smile toward Mase that has my body vibrating with a need to brutalize my friend's good looks.

My gaze bounces back to her, as if magnetic, and travels over her body, taking her in. She sticks out like a sore thumb in this place, and I can't find it in me to hate it, as much as I want to.

Her black T-shirt is pulled tight across her tits, her ripped jeans fit her like a second skin, and her unlaced combat boots are something I've only ever seen on TV. Her fingers have multiple rings on them, and when she brushes her hair from her face, I note a small scar on her neck I'm certain wasn't there before. How the fuck did that happen?

I lick my lips while her and Mase's conversation drones on as background noise. But when Mase mentions the owner of Flawless, Griffin Snider, her spine bolts straight and her body shudders. Did he do something that made her leave?

"I mean, the guy is well-known for throwing money at things he wants, instead of working for it." Her face pales, and my eyes narrow.

"Right." She exhales before clearing her throat. "Do you have a vision for me to work with?"

Mase scrubs his hand over his cropped hair and exhales loudly. "Honestly, we're all out of ideas. That's where we were hoping you would come in."

Ava chuckles and moves her notebook to the desk. I sit back and watch the exchange with jealousy coursing through my veins at how easily they're getting along.

"So, I started producing some notes, and honestly, I think you've been trying too hard." She giggles. Fucking giggles!

Mase leans over her to get a closer look at the tablet. I pump my fists beneath my desk, itching to tear him away.

He's close, so close he could smell her. Does she still smell like cherries? My nostrils flare at the thought of him inhaling her.

She's fucking mine!

"Jesus, Ava. This is incredible." He gasps, and annoyance grumbles inside me. Her glossy lips tip up into a smile she's trying to fight. Does she still taste like cherries too?

"Can you send us these? We can look them over and put another meeting in our diaries for next week?"

"Sure." She nods eagerly with a bright smile, and I grind my teeth at how she refuses to acknowledge my presence yet smiles at Mase like he hung the moon and the fucking stars, screw it, the sun too.

"Okay, so I'll get the dates added to your diary and we'll reconvene later."

"Thank you, Mase." She rises from her chair, gathering her notebook and tablet. "Tate." She nods in my direction, but I glare straight through her, refusing to look at her and the five cute freckles I memorized on her nose.

She leaves the office, taking my breath with her. Finally able to relax, I drop my head back against the chair with a heavy sigh.

"You are so fucked." Mase chuckles, and I can't help but groan in agreement.

NINE

TATE

It's been six days since I saw her last, and I can't take it anymore. We have a meeting tomorrow and I need to start paying attention to the task at hand, that's my excuse for venturing down on the floor I have no reason to be on. I spin from left to right like an idiot.

To be fair, the last time I was down here was ten years ago when we started the company and they were moving the furniture in.

"Mr. Kavanagh, how can I help you?" A blonde flicks her hair over her shoulder, beaming at me with her pearly whites. Maybe I fucked her one time? I'm not sure. They all look the same. Apart from *her*.

I clear my throat. "I'm looking for Ava?" Her face drops, and she wrinkles her nose.

"Sure." She smiles but it doesn't reach her eyes. "This way."

She guides me down the corridor and into the open

office space where dozens of desks are littered haphazardly around the room, blocking views from others with their workstation screens. Jesus, this looks like hell. And she works here? I grit my teeth, not liking the thought one bit. Not when there's plenty of space for her on my floor.

Near my office. Inside my office.

We turn a corner, and the blonde points to indicate which desk. I give her a nod and push past, ignoring her feigned smile and whispered thanks I did nothing to earn.

As I approach, her loud giggle cuts through the air and into my soul, grabbing it with both hands and squeezing painfully, stealing my breath. *Fuck.* Why the hell do I feel nervous all of a sudden?

My palms become clammy, and my heart rate picks up.

What the hell is wrong with me?

I step around the workstation, and my veins pump with fury as I take her in. Her legs are stretched out in front of her, and her feet are crossed at the ankle, resting on her desk, her ripped jeans tight around her legs, and her camisole is pulled across her chest, showcasing her ample tits, but thankfully, her arms are covered in a black hooded cardigan. She leans back on her chair with her tablet in her hand, laughing at something some smarmy little fucker says to her. Anger boils inside me, and I want nothing more than to tear the prick apart.

She barely spared me a second glance in the meeting, yet her eyes are focused on this dipshit.

Without thinking, I stride forward, ignoring her shellshocked face at seeing me. I swipe her boots off her desk, sending them thudding to the floor and startling her in the process. The douche jumps up from his chair. "Oh, erm,

TATE

Mr. Kavanagh. N-nice to see you again," he stutters like an idiot.

I scan him from head to toe to ensure he sees the glare of contempt on my face. He fidgets from foot to foot. I recognize him. He helped on a project last fall, but I'm not about to take things easy on him by letting him know I remember him, not when it's clear he has a thing for Ava.

I act unfazed. "Sorry, do I know you?"

The douche blinks, stunned by my response. Then he clears his throat while I look down at him. I must be a good foot taller than him; I broaden my shoulders for emphasis, not missing Ava's eye roll at my show of dominance.

"I'm Steve. I assisted on the Harley Project." He holds his hand out for me to shake, but I turn away, directing my attention toward Ava, whose beautiful hazel eyes are seething with fire.

"What the hell are you wearing?" I snipe out.

Her eyebrows shoot up.

"We have a fucking dress code," I bite out. Not actually giving a fuck about her work attire, more of the fact she's flirting with other men.

She raises her chin in the air. "Not down here you don't. Up there"—she points toward the ceiling—"of course you do," she mocks and glares back at me.

"Well, you're going to be working up there from now on. So I suggest you embrace office chic."

She scoffs, and my eyes bulge. What the hell is wrong with her? "You want me to dress like one of your minions?"

Douche's wide eyes ping pong from me to her, his mouth gaping like a moron.

"I want you to dress appropriately." I smile back, condescension oozing from me.

Ava exhales in a huff. "Let me guess, like the receptionist?" She raises an eyebrow in my direction, and I can't help but wonder if she's jealous. I like the feeling of her being possessive of me, so I roll with it.

"Exactly like that." I smirk, crossing my arms over my chest. I feel like I won this round.

"I personally think your look gives you character. It says far more than how most people dress here," the douche spouts off while practically drooling over Ava.

I seethe in his direction; the fact this punk thinks he can steal my girl. Not a fucking prayer. "Of course you do. Get your shit together, Ava. We're going for lunch."

Her mouth falls open, and I internally smile at the shock on her face, plus the jolt from the prick. And when the dipshit tightens his palms and stuffs his fists into his pockets, I almost preen with delight. I roll back on my heels, grinning and raising my eyebrows in his direction while Ava stuffs her phone in her purse.

"Ready?" I question as she lingers around her desk.

She nods but refuses to look at me, and I want nothing more than to grab her chin and force her eyes on me.

"I'll text you later," the jerk mumbles.

I don't give her a chance to reply as I push her along the corridor with my palm at the base of her spine. The heat from our touch seems to seep through her clothes and into my skin, scarring my flesh, like she's scarred my mind and heart.

Walking into the elevator, nerves dance in my stomach. I fucking hate how she causes me to come undone, how I unravel in her presence and crave her approval. Leaning past her, I press the button for the ground floor. Her familiar scent catches in my nostrils, and nostalgia sweeps in, taking my breath away.

She lies on my chest as I stroke my fingers lovingly through her hair. Holding up a lock, I note the hint of red in it that stands out against the whites of my fingertips.

I've never taken much notice of these details on a woman before now. But I suddenly want to consume her, discover every freckle, every single piece of her. Why is she so different? I want to know every part of her, learn every inch of her, before our time together ends. I want a lifetime of memories.

I was determined not to poke and prod into her life. Determined not to exceed the invisible boundaries I had in place when I stepped over the threshold of her room. But I can't help myself. I have an odd feeling in my stomach that won't shift. Like something is going on with her. Like she's screaming out for help behind those confident, feisty eyes. As though they're begging for someone to rescue her. My throat is dry as I mumble the words, scared of her response. "Are you going to be okay?"

Her breath stutters, and I wonder if anyone has ever asked her that before. She takes a minute to answer, but when she does, I don't believe a word of it. "I'm going to be just fine, Tate."

But I refuse to dig deeper. Because if I do, will I find myself in a scandal I can't get out of? Will it force me to regret stepping into her room? That's not something I'm prepared to do.

So instead, I bury my head in her hair, breathing in her cherry scent, and tell her, "Butterflies are meant to fly, Ava. And you're going to do just that," before rolling her onto her back and sliding my cock into her tightness, embracing every fucking second of it while I still can.

"Where are we going to lunch?"

Her sweet voice makes me jump, and I clear my throat

to respond, dragging a hand over my hair. "Erm," I breathe out, because honestly, I've no fucking clue.

Glancing at Ava, her hazel eyes sparkle as she bites into her lip. "Have you ever been out for lunch, Tate?" Her words are playful, so I grin back at her.

"No." I choke on a laugh, and my cheeks grow hot, because how fucking ridiculous.

"I know just the place." She smiles back, unperturbed at how much of an idiot I am for not even knowing where to eat. The way her smile affects me is hard to fathom. How can a simple smile have me feeling so fucking happy, so alive?

I follow beside her as we head through the doors and out of the building. My palm twitches to feel her hand in mine. I've never held a woman's hand before, yet I want to hold hers and never fucking let it go.

We walk in a comfortable silence as my mind tries understanding all the feelings so foreign to me. Turning down a side street I never knew existed, she pushes open the door of a small coffee shop. My nose turns up at the cramped, outdated space, but when I glance down and see her soft smile, I find myself mirroring it.

"Looks good." I beam.

She stifles a laugh, digging her teeth into her bottom lip. "Liar."

This time, I chuckle.

"Come on, you'll love it. I promise." She pulls me along by my shirt, and I allow her to.

"Doubtful," I mumble, and she giggles.

AVA

I went from being angry with Tate to finding myself relaxing in his presence and enjoying our conversation. He let me order for him, and I made fun at the fact he was probably only used to prime steak or caviar.

Denny, one of the servers, places our burgers down and lingers beside me, so I turn to face him. "Hey, Ava, just wondered if you were going to the game next Saturday night?" Denny asks, his tone as sweet as ever. Denny is nice, but he can't be any older than nineteen. He's a cutie but too young for me, more like a younger brother. Besides, I seem to be attracted to older guys with brooding eyes and a territorial streak in them.

I can feel Tate's eyes on me, and my cheeks pinken under his scrutiny.

"She's busy next Saturday," Tate grits out.

Denny rubs his hands down his pants. "You normally come on a Saturday with—"

"She's with me on Saturday, kid." Tate takes my hand

in his and entwines our fingers, and my eyes bug out from mortification.

"Okay, right." Denny steps back before scurrying away, and I wince.

I pull my hand away; the action causes his jaw to sharpen as I spin and face him. "What the hell was that?" I spit out.

He clenches his teeth as he stares back at me with his bright-blue eyes. For the first time today, I allow myself to look him over. Jesus, he's gorgeous, even if he knows it.

His white shirt is pulled tightly across his broad shoulders, his short light-brown hair is longer on top and styled perfectly, the sharpness of his jaw and high cheek bones, along with a bronzed complexion, have him looking like a model, and I swoon over the fact that at one point, we were intimate.

And every day since, when I closed my eyes and wished for tenderness combined with passion, I saw his face. And above all else, the need in his eyes, the longing that was then so quickly washed away with guilt, turned my stomach at the very thought of his regret.

"You're thinking too hard, baby."

I jolt, realizing I was staring and getting lost in my head. The term of endearment that slips from his lips like velvet has me wanting to purr while widening my legs for him in invitation.

"I'm not your baby," I breathe out low, and even I can hear the need in my voice, and my heart aches at the pain of my words.

His lips tip up into that smug smirk of his. "Sure you are." He leans closer, so close I can smell his minty breath and his sandalwood cologne, and all I want to do now is lick him, all fucking over. "Now that you're older, there's no stopping us." My pulse races on his admission.

"Here's the bill." Denny slams the bill onto the table, breaking the moment between us.

Tate's jaw tics in annoyance, then he stares down at his untouched burger. He glances around the room, roaming over the tables before he turns back in confusion. "Do they always bring the bill before you start eating?"

I pop a fry into my mouth. "Nope. They just want to get rid of you." I smile back at him, and his eyes narrow back at me.

"Eat up. My boss won't be pleased if I'm late back from lunch." I nudge his plate toward him.

He breaks out into the smile that sends a pool of wetness into my panties. "I am the boss. And I'd be happy to assist in eating. Preferably your pussy, do you still taste like cherries?"

I choke on a fry. So much so I gasp, and Tate jumps up from his seat in panic.

"Get her a water. Holy shit. We need a medical team. Some fucker help me."

If I could roll my eyes right now, I would. I've choked on dicks worse than this coughing episode.

My face feels like it's on fire from embarrassment when a group of customers take notice.

Denny thrusts a glass of water in my hand as I start to compose myself, and he glares daggers in Tate's direction. He's oblivious to my discomfort, he's too busy growling like a raging bear at Denny.

After swallowing the water, I clear my throat. "I'm fine. Thank you, Denny." I smile up at him, and he returns it.

"Are you fucking him?" I turn my head to face Tate.

His eyes are shooting venom in Denny's direction. "Are you?" They flick back down to mine. His sharp jaw works from side to side, and his chest heaves. Clearly, he's struggling to rein in his temper.

Any other time, I'd be amused, but right now, I'm pissed.

I push back in my chair and ignore him as I march toward the door.

No way after four years am I allowing him to step foot back in my life thinking he can take over. Besides, if he knew the truth, he wouldn't want to be anywhere near me. I know it.

Tate Kavanagh can go screw himself, because the only person I can ever rely on is me.

TEN

TATE

I cast my eyes up toward the clock on the office wall; she's due here in two minutes.

After I spent yesterday pissed once she marched out of the diner as though she had a right to be angry at me, I'm determined to force her to understand the situation today.

What I don't understand is, I saved her fucking life, yet she was pissed at me. For the rest of the day, I considered all the ways I could punish her for her behavior. The sooner she realizes we're a thing, the better, and the sooner I get my cock inside her, the sooner I can finally relieve four years of pent-up need.

"Are you listening to me? What's with you?" Mase clips from the opposite side of the table, where he's spread out an array of ideas presented by Ava.

Glancing up at the clock again, I note the time—one minute. A small knock on the office door fills me with excitement, and my cock stirs to life at the prospect of her presence.

I stand taller, trying my best to hide from Mase the excited vibes bursting to get out. "Come in."

The clinking of heels has my eyebrows furrowing, and when I glance over my shoulder to look for Ava, my mouth practically drops to the floor, because holy fucking shit.

My eyes travel from her come-fuck-me heels, over her bronzed legs, and up to her skintight pencil skirt, then over her white, fucking see-through blouse. I can see her goddamn tits through her shirt. Her tits!

Holy shit. Is one pierced? My mouth goes dry, and when my tongue becomes lodged in my throat, I choke. Jesus, I'm fucked.

My cock becomes hard as steel, my balls ache for her, and precum drips from the tip, crying out for release.

Her red lips are beaming with a bright smile, and her brown locks flow down her back in big waves, reminding me of when we first met.

Mase clears his throat, and it's only then I remember we're not alone. Darting my eyes toward his, I can tell he's trying not to look at Ava's tits, darting his eyes around the room. The thought sends a red haze over my vision, and anger boils through my bloodstream.

My temple pulsates with fury, and I ball my hands into fists.

"What the fuck are you wearing?" I snap, ignoring Mase's presence. I feel like ripping the shirt off my back to cover her.

"Office chic." She smiles back broadly. Office fucking chic?

She approaches the table, ignoring the tension radiating off me. "Office chic?" I spit the words out in disgust.

"Mmhm." She doesn't even look at me as she stares down at the papers on the table while I literally stand beside her vibrating with rage that has me shifting from foot to foot, unable to expel it.

Before I know what I'm doing, I snap, spinning her to face me. "Office fucking chic, Ava?" My eyes go wide and roam over her body, but she rolls her eyes, infuriating me all the more.

"Do you guys need a minute?" Mase asks, and his gaze bounces from mine to Ava's, then back to mine again.

"Yes," I snipe out, not taking my eyes off Ava.

"No," she replies, and my jaw locks tight.

Out of the corner of my eye, I watch Mase scrub a hand through his hair before exhaling loudly, then he walks out the room.

As soon as the door closes, I take her in further. The way her chest rises rapidly and the way her cheeks flush under my perusal has my cock throbbing with desperation. She's a maelstrom of innocence and filth all rolled into one. The blend creating the ultimate perfection.

"You're gorgeous," I breathe out on a deep exhale.

Her breath hitches as my hands find her hips, giving them a gentle squeeze. Her nipples harden and then I remember her piercing.

"You pierced your fucking nipple?"

She attempts to pull away from me, but I hold her in place with a firm grip, biting into her flesh.

"Answer me." My eyes search hers, needing her attention on me.

Hers flare with desire, the same desire I witnessed four years ago. The same desire I've craved every day since.

"Yes," she breathes out.

"Show me."

Her eyebrows shoot up, and her eyes dart toward the door. I shake my head and squeeze her hips again, growing aggravated she's taking so long to do as I command. "Show me," I repeat.

She swallows thickly, and her fingers tremble as she unbuttons her blouse, starting from the bottom.

I watch in awe as she releases each button. The submissiveness behind her has my cock twitching and thickening so much it's painful. My mouth becomes dry as she reaches her tits and exposes her bare chest to me.

"No fucking bra, Ava?" I growl.

I take her in, her tits have grown, I'm certain of it, and my cock jumps with appreciation. "Fuck, my cock is so hard for you right now, baby," I breathe out, closing my eyes for a moment as I try and control myself. The last thing I want to do is come in my pants before I even touch her.

Opening my eyes, I don't miss the way she squeezes her thighs together, and it only heightens my arousal.

Our eyes remain locked as I work my hand from her hip up toward her tit while her hands clutch the table behind her, as though supporting her. I gently palm her tit, brushing my fingers over her pierced nipple, and she whimpers beneath my touch. My cock pulsates, and I hiss with vigor as I push my hard, straining cock against her waist, needing some relief while I explore her soft skin begging to be marked.

Groaning in pleasure, I squeeze her tit harder, lifting

the weight into my palm. I tweak her nipple between the tips of my fingers, and she pushes her body against me in response, allowing me to grind into her. "Tate?" she whispers. We both know it's not a question at all. She needs me. And fuck, do I need her.

Towering above her, I lean down, brushing my lips against hers. "I need to fuck you so bad, Ava."

She sucks in a sharp breath. "Please."

My wavering restraint snaps, and I lift her onto the table, shoving her skirt up to her hips to find her in fucking garters. Gritting my teeth, I growl in anger and arousal when I see her thin black lacy panties.

Our mouths clash together, and I bite into her lip, determined to make her feel me as I frantically unbuckle my pants.

Her arms band around my neck, holding my head in place while I tug my aching cock from my boxers. I waste no time in placing my cock at her pussy, and her slickness coating it causes my eyes to roll to the back of my head at the sensation. Fucking beautiful.

I've waited years for this moment.

Pulling my hips back, I drive inside her, and the force behind my thrusts causes the table to shift below us. "Fuck," I hiss when her pussy molds around me, holding me in. I pull back and repeat the motion harder this time. So fucking hard I want it to hurt her like her absence hurt me, and when she winces into our kiss, I know I've achieved it. I smirk at the thought, and she punishes me by biting my lip and tugging so much copper floods our mouths.

Using one hand to hold her hip in place, I use the other

to roll her piercing between my fingers, and her tight cunt squeezes me on each flick of the barbell.

"Mmm." She moans against me.

"You like that? My dirty little office slut."

"Fuck, Tate. Harder."

"Shit." I bite into my cheek, trying to fight off my desperate need to orgasm so soon. My cock works like a jackhammer, pounding her against the desk with such force it shakes beneath us. Her nails dig into my neck, and her tongue pushes against mine with equal aggression.

I move my lips, licking a path down her neck. Determined to feel that piercing in my mouth and around my tongue, I travel down. Then her pussy clenches around me, and I know she's close. "Tate?" She taps my shoulder. "Tate."

I ignore her, focused on waning my orgasm until she reaches hers. "I'm not on birth control." *Fuck me. I want that. I want that more than I want anything in the entire world right now. Me, Ava, and a baby. Our own fucking family. Finally a family. Finally together.*

Her words send me wild, like a man possessed, and I slam into her frantically, determined to fill her cunt with my cum. Fill her. Giving her no choice but to carry my baby. The pleasure hits me like a freight train as my balls draw up, the slit of my cock widens, and my mouth falls open at the power behind my cum flooding her bare cunt.

My body shakes, and my hips work uncontrollably, it's like an out-of-body experience, the pleasure so intense I feel like I'm floating. I'm aware her pussy has locked securely around me, and it's damn near impossible to continue my onslaught. She's thrown her head back against the table as her orgasm hits her and the last of my cum coats her womb. I fall on top of her, my head landing in the crook of her neck.

Her fingers work through the fine hairs on my head, and I practically purr beneath her touch. Our chests rise in unison, and our bodies coated in a sheen of sweat.

"Fuck, I missed you so damn much, Ava."

I raise my head to stare down at her. Those hazel eyes of hers soften at my words before she seems to realize something, and her face falls. I pull up onto my elbows. "What's wrong?" I swipe the blood from her bottom lip, then realize it's mine, and my lip tips up into a grin at the thought of her marking me.

Glancing away from me, she severs the moment between us, and I hate it. I want her eyes on me, her thoughts on me, and ultimately, every fucking thing of hers on me.

She closes her eyes with her head tilted to the side, effectively locking me out, and I hate it. Gently, I turn her chin to face me. "Open your eyes, baby. Talk to me," I implore.

Her throat works on emotion. "I'm not on birth control."

Fuck, is that all she's bothered with? My lips curve into a smile, and I gift her with a half assed shrug. "Good."

She pushes me to stand while she sits up. I allow her this, because, in all honesty, I was expecting a fight about this shit at some point. May as well get it over with now.

"Good?"

My cock twitches inside her, and her eyes bug out in horror. "Good?" she repeats, dumbfounded.

As much as I want to flip my shit at the look of disgust on her face, I remain calm, hoping to soothe her. "I'm all in, Ava. I waited four fucking years to feel you again." I bring my lips down to hers. "You own my fucking heart." I place a kiss on her parted lips. "You own all of me," I breathe out against her while her eyes remain wide in shock. "I'll give you every-fucking-thing. Just agree. Tell me you want this too."

The office door begins to open, she scrambles in a panic, pushing me away, my cock slips from her slick pussy, and my cum splashes against her thighs. My jaw grinds, I wanted my cock inside her for as long as possible, not discarded and used.

"Tate?"

My spine bolts straight at the secretary's shrill voice.

Oh shit.

I fumble to tuck my spent cock away and buckle up my pants while internally kicking myself as to how unfortunate my situation is about to become.

The heels come to a stop. "Oh, Tate. I have the files you wanted for the Gold project," she drawls. And I fucking know she's taking in Ava. I step in front of her to shield her while she continues to button her blouse.

"Oh, another one." The secretary sighs.

Ava's hand freezes, and my jaw locks tight.

"Oh, honey. Don't look so worried. It was me last month, it'll be another next. The ones he keeps around the office long enough learn quickly. Right, Tate?"

I close my eyes at her words and try to regulate my breathing. Not only is every word she's saying true but the fact she's saying it in front of Ava has my heart hammering against my chest and a lightning bolt of pain surging through it at the way Ava's face pales.

"Av—" She shakes her head and brushes my hand

from her shoulder.

Raising her chin, she stares back at me, the softness in her eyes evaporated, the look that tells me I fucked up.

Big fucking time.

"Wait, what's your name, honey?"

"None of your fucking business," I snap back, determined to get her out of the office. "Leave the file and go."

Her heels draw closer, and I squeeze my eyes shut. "I was talking to your latest office conquest." Yeah, she needs firing, but I can't think straight to compute the words right now.

Ava's lips part, and I will myself to slap my hand over her mouth, but I'm frozen with rage and fear rolled into one. I'm already losing her before I even got her.

Again.

"Ava," my girl breathes out.

The heels stop moving, and my nostrils flare, knowing she realizes the enormity. "Ava?"

Ava stands taller and straightens her shoulders, but I drop my head, unable to think straight.

"As in *the* Ava?"

I lick my dry lips. "Can you just fucking leave?" I snap

The bitch throws her head back on a condescending laugh that has me wanting to rip her vocal cords out, because if she even so much as thinks about screwing with Ava, I'll rip her a-fucking-part.

A cunning smirk plays on her face as she turns and walks toward the door, allowing me time to come to my senses.

I need to make this right. I need her to understand my playboy ways are in the past. That she's my future.

My only future.

AVA

I shrug off his touch, ignoring the flash of regret and hurt on his face as I push past him.

Knowing I'm one of many women he screwed in his office is really no surprise. However, I just didn't expect it to hurt so much.

So damn much.

Instead, I straighten my shoulders and respond to her question. "Ava."

She comes to a standstill and stares at me in shock. "As in *the* Ava?"

I glance back at Tate in confusion, but he's ducked his head, as though trying to compose himself. His hands are balled into fists, he breathes through his nose, and his chest rises as though he's struggling to rein in his reactions.

"Can you just fucking leave?" he snaps.

"What is she talking about?" I try to catch his eyes, but he refuses to look at me. I'm not even sure he heard the words.

The secretary doesn't budge, but I refuse to participate in this pissing contest any longer. If she wants Tate, she can have him.

I'm sure he expects me to leave the office, judging by the way his eyes bounce between mine and the door. But I refuse to be a damsel in distress and run from the situation. So instead, I own it, hitting it head-on, and do what I'm here to do. I take one of the folders, open it, and lay out the remaining designs I created, ignoring his searing gaze as I line them up.

"Put the rest of the files on the desk and get the fuck out," he screams at the secretary, gesturing toward the door.

"Av—" I hold up my hand to stop him, but I refuse to meet his eyes and give him another minute of my attention.

"Ava, I—"

"I'm trying to work, Tate. Just let me work," I snap.

"But"—he shifts from foot to foot—"I just want to explain."

I snap my eyes up to meet his, mine alight with fire. "You don't have to explain anything. It was sex." I shrug, ignoring the tic in his forehead and the way his chest heaves.

"Hey, guys. How are we getting on in here?" Mase appears at the table during our stare off.

"Fine," I reply to Mase with a smile I struggle to muster. He pulls out a chair and moves the images to face him. "I think we need to go back to the root of the product. They want gold. We give them gold." I point to my idea and feel a sense of pride wash over me when Mase beams back at me.

I can feel the searing heat from Tate glaring into me. But I ignore him and push another image toward Mase.

"You're fucking incredible, Ava." Mase grins.

Tate turns on his heels and storms from the room, slamming the door behind him. The sound echoes around us, forcing me to wince.

"I'm sorry about him." Mase grimaces toward the door. "I'll speak to him."

My heart sinks at his departure, but I refuse to acknowledge it. "It's fine." I feign a smile.

Mase rubs his forehead and shifts in his seat. "He's my best friend, Ava. He's like a brother to me, and I know whatever is going on between you guys, it's been happening for years. In here at least." He taps his heart, and I swallow hard with emotion at the recognition. "He'll never let you down on purpose. He's too good a guy for that."

I flip the file shut with a slam, unable to hear anymore.

"He already did that," I tell him as I push back in my chair and stand to gather the remaining files. As I walk toward the door, I try to block out the memory of the way he let me down, the way he knew I lied to him but refused to push me further to, no doubt, save himself.

"Are you going to be okay?"

My heart hammers against his, beating in time with one another. My body screams to tell him, "No. I need help." *But I remain frozen.*

Why now? Why does this person come into my life and allow me to feel free for the first time when I'm about to become so caged? When I'm about to sign my life away to a monster.

His heart quickens, his grip on my body tightens, and I know he knows. He knows something isn't right. I squeeze my eyes closed, fighting the internal battle of letting it all out, changing everything.

But then what? Will my knight in shining armor become another monster, letting me down like everyone else? Will my plan crumble? I can't risk it. There's too much at stake, and worse, I might hate him for not helping me.

So instead, I swallow past the lump in my throat and utter the words he wants to hear.

"I'm going to be just fine, Tate."

His body barely relaxes, and I know he knows I'm lying. But he doesn't press me further.

He let me down.

And worst of all, I expected it.

"Butterflies are meant to fly, Ava. And you're going to do just that." *His voice soothes as he kisses my head tenderly.*

A tear slides down my cheek.

How do I tell him I can't fly because my wings are about to be broken?

ELEVEN

TATE

My mind has been working a mile a minute, and every second of those minutes have been consumed by her.

I need to fix it, I'm just not sure how.

I've barely slept and look like shit. Does she regret me fucking her? Who else is she fucking? Has she taken the morning-after pill? She better not have. I want her pregnant with my baby; I want to secure a future with her. Fate brought her back, and I'm determined to ensure this works between us.

My mind wanders to what the diner kid said, and I wonder if she's seeing him. Or the guy in her office. They both salivated over her, and the thought enrages me and consumes me with jealousy and a possessiveness I've only ever felt toward her.

Casting my eyes up toward the expensive apartment building, uncertainty gnaws at me. Surely, she doesn't live here? I can't help but check my phone for her personal details once again. Because how the fuck can an intern afford this place?

Luckily, we have the technology that gives me access to security systems, so when I enter the building and follow the instructions on my screen, I type in the code allowing me access to the elevator. Stepping inside, I grin from ear to ear at how easy this all is. With my leg bouncing in anticipation, the elevator ascends to her floor, and when the doors finally open, I swallow the nervousness away, give myself a quick once-over in the mirrored walls, and stride out with determination.

Pressing the doorbell, I try and listen beyond the thick wooden door, noting the numerous locks sliding out of place. Odd to have so many when this building is one of the most sought after and secure in the area.

The door opens and I'm rendered speechless.

Standing in front of me is a guy with a towel wrapped around his broad waist. "Who the fuck are you?" He scans me up and down.

My head pounds, the cords of my neck tighten, and a growl escapes my chest. I seethe at seeing another man in her apartment after I fucking came inside her, giving part of me only she has received.

My hands clench and unclench beside me.

And when I hear her sweet voice call to him, "Todd?" I fly into a fit of rage. Throwing myself at the dude, I tackle him to the floor. He's so shocked at my outburst he doesn't see my fist coming. I slam it into his jaw before delivering a swift blow to his stomach.

"Oh my God, Tate!" she screams, but I ignore her as I

raise my fist again, preparing to pummel the fucker who touched my girl. "What the hell are you doing?"

"Jesus!" the guy spits as he thrashes below me, trying to throw me off.

Ava's arms wrap around my neck, as if trying to pull me from lover boy. "Tate, stop. Please," she begs, her words laced in a sob. She's protecting him? I slam my fist into his face again, and she cries out in response. Her fists hit me, but I ignore her while he bucks against me, trying and failing to move my body off his. The rage behind her need to protect him sends me wild, landing another punch to his stomach. "Tate. He's my brother!" she screams, and I jolt with my fist in midair.

Slowly, I lean back on my heels, releasing him while my chest heaves and my mind whirls over her words. "Brother?" I question in shock.

Her tear-streaked face makes my heart skip a beat as I jump to my feet to reassure her. She bats my hands away when I try to pull her against me. "He's my little brother, you idiot."

The guy stands with a wince, and blood drips from his face. He's anything but little, that's for sure, the dude is taller than me. "Little?" I jerk my head back.

"I'm almost eighteen, Ava! Not a fucking child," he spits in her direction. With his words on repeat in my mind, I find myself agreeing with him. Eighteen isn't a child. Every path carved has led them to that very age, and sometimes their experiences have left them wiser beyond their years. I wince, knowing I let her go at eighteen. I let her go when I could have fought for her, for us.

"You're still my little brother. Here, let me clean you up." She steps around me, and I almost want to pull her hand away as she tugs the towel from his waist, exposing his boxers.

"Oh my fucking God." He groans and his cheeks redden, forcing me to grin at her motherly antics. She's completely oblivious as to how embarrassed Todd is right now.

He winces when she touches his lip. "Sorry about the . . ." I wave a hand toward his busted lip.

Ava spins her hazel eyes in my direction, fire burning behind them. "Just what the hell did you think you were doing?"

"He was jealous." Her brother grins like a Cheshire cat. "He's into you. Is this the guy you've been hung up on?"

My heart hammers waiting for a response. It better be me.

She ignores his question. "He shouldn't even be here."

I scoff. How dare she tell me I shouldn't be here. Brushing off her snide remark, I remain on target. "I came to apologize."

Her mouth falls open as she tends to his forehead. "Apologize? I should call the cops."

I glare back at her, holding her eyes hostage. "Do it. They'd have to shoot me to get me out of here until I speak with you."

She exhales and rolls her eyes. Dabbing his face once more, she taps his shoulder. "You're all good to go. The jerk didn't do too much damage." I raise my eyebrow at her.

"Thank fuck. I don't want to be late for my date," Todd throws over his shoulder as he rushes down a corridor, which I imagine takes him to his room.

Scanning over the apartment, I take in the open-plan

concept; light-gray furnishings and soft blues complement the room. Decorative artwork hangs from the walls, and I can't help but be impressed with the way she's put everything together. She's already proved herself to have an amazing eye for design, and her apartment is just an extension of that.

Ava finally turns to face me, and when our gazes clash, it's like nothing else exists. Time freezes, my blood pumps fast, and her pupils dilate under my scrutiny.

"Jerk, huh?" I question.

"If you guys are going to fuck really loud again, can you please put some music on?" Todd reappears fully dressed, and I wonder how the hell he dressed so quickly.

"Be home by midnight. And use protection." He gifts her with a peck on her cheek, gives me a swift nod, then heads toward the door while I replay his words.

My temple pulsates and my heart rate picks up while glaring at Ava, and she swallows. "Who the hell have you been fucking loud?"

TWELVE

AVA

When Tate crashed through the door, it took me a moment to realize what the hell was happening. For him to become a crazed beast was not only jaw dropping but also a turn on. His possessiveness has me feeling wanted, needed, treasured even. It's a shame my little brother got caught in the crossfire.

Thankfully, Todd is a tough guy. He's forever coming home with cuts, bruises, and sore muscles from his football training, so he took it on the chin, caring more about his date than the guy standing before me with steam coming out of his ears.

"Who the hell have you been fucking loud?" I jump at his words. He steps forward, and I step back, and this continues until I'm pressed up against the wall with his arms above me, caging me in. "I asked you a fucking question, Ava." His voice oozes possession, smooth with a guttural edge to it that sends a flood of need to my panties. "Who the hell have you been fucking loud?"

I roll my eyes. How he calls me out on my past transgressions when he has so many, is beyond me. "That's nothing to do with you. Besides, you've fucked nearly the whole of STORM Enterprises." I jut my chin out.

"Wrong, it's everything to do with me," he snaps, grinding his hard cock against me.

"Who the hell do you think you are?" I try to ignore the dull throb between my legs and concentrate on the fact Tate has burst into my apartment like a jealous long-term boyfriend, when, in reality, we're nothing more than a hookup.

"I'm yours," he breathes in my ear while traveling his hand down my arm and to the hem of my oversized T-shirt where he slips his hand beneath the fabric, then his fingers graze over my panties.

Struggling to swallow back the moan gathered in my throat, I bite back, "My past fucks have nothing to do with you, *Tate*."

When I expect him to glower with anger, his lip curls into a serene smile. "I'm pleased we can agree on them being in the past." He withdraws his hand, and I sag against the wall in disappointment, then he tucks a strand of hair behind my ear before dipping his head into my neck and placing a gentle kiss against it. "We both have a past, Ava. But you're my future." He raises his head for our eyes to meet before resting his forehead against mine. "You want that too, don't you?"

I breathe him in, every part of him: the way his muscles flex as he waits for a response, the way his veins protrude on his strong arms that lock me in, and the way his eyes seep with truth yet swim in lust.

"Yes," I breathe out, so quietly I didn't think he'd hear.

A growl tears from his throat, and he lifts me without warning. I wrap my legs around his thick waist when his mouth crashes down against mine. "Where's your room?" He nips at my lip, causing my head to swim. "Your room?" he questions, giving my ass a tight squeeze when I don't respond.

"Down the hall, first door on the right," I pant out.

"Good girl." I whimper on his words as his tongue clashes with mine. Desperate to please him, desperate to be his good girl.

We crash through my bedroom, and as he lowers me to the bed, I cling to him like a koala, then his lips tip up into a smile as he kisses me with passion. Slowly, he pulls back to look at me, and the desire pooling in his eyes has me willing to drown in his consumption. Flutters fill me when he tugs on my shirt, and a wave of arousal flows through me when he lifts his shirt over his head in a move only someone so godlike could achieve.

My gaze roams over his bronzed chiseled body, down to the distinct V where his jeans sit, until he flicks open the top button like one of the Magic Mike guys I watched last winter.

Moving quickly, I pull the T-shirt over my head. When our gazes clash, my heart jumps in my chest. He swallows thickly, and his fingers tremble as they wrap around my throat. "You're mine, Ava," he pants as his soft lips coax mine open. "Every part of you is mine." I moan into his touch, helping him undress, as he does me.

TATE

She opens her legs for me, and I take in her fully exposed body. Her arms are littered in tattoos, something I've not noticed before now but desperately want to explore, preferably with my tongue. Her tits are perfect, with big round nipples for my mouth to toy with, and that piercing has my cock jumping at imagining flicking it with my tongue.

Her bare, glistening pussy is like an aphrodisiac to my already aroused state. It begs to be sucked, licked, and eaten; it weeps for me to drink in her pleasure. "Scoot up the bed, baby. I need to taste you." She gasps but quickly scoots her ass up the bed, laying her head on the pillow and watching me as I lower myself toward her pussy.

Breathing her in, I delight in the fact that even her pussy smells of cherries, fucking delicious. Her slit is slick, waiting for my tongue to savor her, so I lash it out over her pussy lips. My cock jumps, reveling in her thighs attempting to clench around me. I slam them against the bed with a firm grip, holding her open for me to eat. Then

I go to town on her, licking up and down her slit with fervor, shoving my face against her pubic bone, hitting her perfect spot when I suck on her clit. She bucks up against me, and my cock spurts at the sensation of her fucking my face. "Oh fuck, Tate."

"Yes. Fuck, yes. Scream my name, baby." Moving my hand, I slide a finger inside her wet cunt, pumping it in and out while my other hand digs into her soft skin.

The bed rocks under my movements and the way she bucks her hips to meet my face. "Such a slut for me, Ava."

"Tate, oh god."

"More?" I question with a smirk as I pull my finger from her pussy and my mouth from her clit.

"Please, more." Her begging has me grinding my dripping cock into her mattress.

"Fuck yes," I pant in approval while plunging two fingers into her sweet pussy. Pumping them in and out, in and out, her pussy juice coats my fingers and runs down my hand.

"Oh fuck, baby. You're dripping." Her pussy clenches on my words, spurring me further. "Filthy girl. You like dripping down my fingers, you little slut, don't you?"

"Yes. Oh god, nearly there, Tate." She tugs on my hair and lifts her ass, pushing her pussy into my mouth.

"Fuck, yes, little slut. Fuck my face." She grinds against my mouth while the sloshing of my fingers pumping in and out of her mingles with her heavy pants. I twist my fingers and find her G-spot, rubbing over it with each controlled pump. "Holy fuckkk!" she cries as her pussy clamps around my digits, causing me to wish my cock was feeling her orgasm ripping from her.

I slow my tongue, lapping up her cum while she comes

down from her high. Her body softens, and the grip in my hair lessens, so I reluctantly withdraw my fingers from her pussy with an audible slurping sound.

When I lift my face from her pussy, I'm overwhelmed at her beauty once again. Her hair is splayed over the pillows, her cheeks are red, and a flush travels over her chest toward her peaked nipples. She looks thoroughly fucked, and I'm only just starting.

I pump my cock, letting her see the precum dripping onto my fist. Then, moving forward, I coat her pierced nipple with her essence, using the fingers that were inside her only moments ago. Dipping my head, I latch onto her tit, sucking the flesh into my mouth to leave a mark before trailing my tongue around her nipple, finally licking her piercing coated with her pussy juice. She watches my every move, and I fucking love it.

Her fingers find my hair again as she grips me against her, encouraging me, while I use my free hand to stroke my cock up and down her dripping slit. Sliding inside her, I bite on her nipple and tug on her barbell. "Fuck. Tate." She exhales heavily, and I smile with pride at the pleasure oozing from her. My cock stretches her pussy, and her muscles contract around me, and I groan in response.

My body moves faster above hers. The bounce of her tits in my face encourages me to drive into her harder. "Fuck yes, little slut." Our hips work to counter one another, hers bucking against me, as mine surge my cock inside her with vigor. "Fucking take it." *Slam.* "Take all my cock, Ava."

"Jesus. Yes, Tate. Yes."

I push my hand beneath her ass and grip it while fucking her ruthlessly, and our bodies slap against one another. I growl in pleasure as my balls draw up, and I suck in her peaked nipple while embracing the clench of her pussy. "Fuck. Fuck," I chant, forcing the bed to smack the wall.

"Yes, yes. Oh godddd," she screams, throwing her head back. I slam deep inside her, roaring when my cum shoots out of me, forcing my eyes closed and my lips to clamp down on her tit.

"Mine."

THIRTEEN

AVA

Wave after wave of pleasure consumes me, and my body falls lax against the mattress while Tate's weight drops on top of me.

"Fuck," he breathes out before rolling off me, taking me with him and giving me no choice but to comply. Our legs tangle as we lie facing one another.

I open my eyes to find his bright-blue eyes sparkling back at me and a smile playing on his lips. "That was incredible, baby."

"Mmm, it was." I practically purr in admittance, and his smile widens further.

His cock is still stuffed inside me, but the feeling of his cum leaking down the inside of my thighs has my body freezing and his eyebrows furrowing at the sudden change in my demeanor.

"You didn't use protection," I blurt out.

I watch his face for the same horror marring mine but

find none. Instead, he offers me a shrug. "I've only not used protection with you."

Anger fills my veins. "I could get pregnant, Tate. I'm not on birth control." His cock twitches inside me, and my eyes widen in shock.

He shrugs again. "Good. I'm in this for the long haul." He leans forward, pressing a soft kiss to my forehead before pulling back and scanning my face.

My mouth falls open. "Close your mouth unless you want it stuffed with my cock, baby." He wiggles his eyebrows in jest, and I continue to stare at him like he's lost his damn mind.

Eventually he sighs. "Ava. I want a future with you. What happened in the past is just that. In the past. You want me too; I can feel it." He taps his hand over his heart, and mine falters at how sincere his words are. My lips go dry at the sincerity in his voice. "Tell me you want me too." The flash of vulnerability in his eyes makes my heart ache.

"I do," I admit weakly. His shoulders relax, and he grins playfully once again. "Fucking knew it."

I swallow past the bundle of nerves gathering inside me. "But, Tate, we both have pasts and barely know one another. What you're considering is crazy."

The smile falls from his face in an instant, and his body tenses. "I don't give a shit about your past. Nor should you give a shit about mine. I fucked a shit ton of women trying to erase your memory, Ava." I wince on his words, but he continues regardless. "No woman has ever made me feel how you do. Not a single one. You were too young before, Ava. But you know what?" Tears fill my eyes as he speaks. "If I could go back, baby, and change the past, I'd have never let you go back then. I'd have conquered every fucking demon to step in our way." His lips find my forehead. "Four years without you has felt like a lifetime of punishment for my stupid decision."

He has no idea what punishment it's been like for me. How could he? I wish with all my heart he could go back and recreate that decision, chase away the monster in my nightmares. His thumb grazes over my cheek, catching the lone tear I hadn't realized was descending down my face. He sucks it into his mouth.

"These tears are mine, baby. The only time you cry is for me. You understand?"

I nod. "Yes."

"Good girl. Now anything else you wanna get off your chest?" He crooks an eyebrow at me.

"No. But . . ."

He sighs with a groan. "But?"

I chew on my lip, unsure of how honest I can be with him about my concerns. "A baby?"

Before I know what's happening, he has me flipped onto my back and grips my wrists between one hand, then pulls his hips back and drives his cock into me full force. "Yes, a fucking baby, Ava. Our fucking baby."

"Oh god, Tate." He clamps down on my neck, biting me while his cock hits that perfect spot only he can reach. "Fuck, Tate. More," I beg.

He rears back, and his muscles stretch across his chest as the feral gleam in his eyes takes over his entire face. "My slut wants to be fucked hard, huh? She wants reminding who this dripping cunt belongs to?" *Slam.* "If I wanna put a baby in here, I fucking can. You hear me?" *Slam.*

My pussy pulsates as he powers into me. "Shoving my cum so deep inside your cunt." He grunts. "You'll give me a fucking baby." *Thrust.* "I wanna watch this hot little body stretch for me." *Thrust.* "I've fucking dreamed of putting a baby in you, Ava. Making you mine forever."

My head rolls back on a moan at his words. "Filling you with my baby. Watching your tits fill." He groans, and his cock thickens while my spine arches in pleasure at the sensation. "Jesus. Fuck, yes." Feeling his hot cum splash inside me has my orgasm flowing through my body, has me floating in a wave of pleasure. "I'm putting a baby in you, Ava."

He finally collapses beside me, and this time rolls me onto his chest. Our hearts beat rapidly against one another as we lie in silence, and the enormity of our actions doesn't sit heavily in my stomach like when he came in me in his office. No, they fill me with promise.

A promise of a future I've only ever dreamed about.

A future with Tate beside me.

TATE

Her breathing evens out, and a gentle snore escapes her, allowing me to finally take in her room. It's just how I imagined it to be, nothing girly or fancy. Instead, it's colored in various grays with the furnishings white. But it doesn't feel cold or clinical. How the hell could it when she possesses such warmth.

She whimpers in her sleep, so I clutch her tighter. "Stop. Please, sir." I freeze and my pulse races.

I have demons of my own that can visit me in the night, and the thought of Ava struggling with hers has me wanting to slay every fucker that dared to ever look in her direction. Breathing in the cherry scent from her hair, I relax when she softens against me, allowing my fingers to slip through her locks as I stroke her hair with the palm of my hand. Lifting it into the light, I smile at the familiar tinge of red in her hair, something I've longed to see. Something I thought I'd never see again, yet a reminder of how badly I missed her and how determined I am to keep her this time.

My hands play in her hair. If anyone found me here with her, all hell would break loose, but I can't bring myself to care, not when it feels so right. She relaxes her back against my chest as the sun dries out her hair.

When Ava walked away from the pool, I followed her down to the lake, ignoring my best friends' questions of where I was heading. I made the lame excuse I had a headache and was heading inside. Instead, I slipped out the garage door and quickened my pace, only for my breath to be stolen at the sight before me. Her dark locks shine with a hint of red as she slips off her bikini top and dives into the lake, barely leaving a splash behind her.

I damn near stumble kicking off my sneakers and follow behind her, making her squeal in delight when I come up behind her and nuzzle into her neck. "You said last night was the last time," she quizzes, looking over her shoulder with a smile that has my heart throbbing and my cock pulsating.

"I know."

I turn her, lift her into my arms, and encourage her to wrap her legs around my waist. "I'm leaving this evening."

Disappointment flashes on her face before she quickly masks it. Instead of analyzing the look, I line my cock up against her bare pussy. My eyes roll as I enter her, stretching her.

"I'll never forget you, baby."

"Never," she pants.

My breath hitches at the memory of our last time together while my arms band around her so securely she flinches, so I ease up. Gently, I place a kiss on her hair and maneuver myself from beneath her. With my bladder about to combust, I head toward the bathroom for a piss.

Washing my hands, I take in the reflection of the man staring back at me. He has hope in his eyes and can look at himself in the mirror without feeling self-loathing, and he can finally think toward a future. One with her by his side.

I have a chance now, one I never thought possible, and I'm not prepared to do anything that's going to risk changing that.

After drying my hands, I do a little snooping. I open the cabinet door, but my eyes lock onto a medication box that sends my blood cold, and my mouth dries as I struggle to swallow. Clutching the box, I close my eyes at the pain when I read it's the morning-after pill.

Fuck.

I can't help the feeling of disappointment lining my stomach. Then, as if an inferno rages deep inside me, fire burns through my veins and I throw open the bedroom door to confront her. Did she think I'd be okay with her trying to get rid of my baby?

My body freezes and my eyes widen. What the fuck?

She lies on her stomach with her back exposed. And covering her back is a full tattoo. My eyes roam over it: a bird's cage at the bottom followed by dozens of bright-blue butterflies floating out of it all the way up to the base of her neck.

My cock jumps when she stirs, reminding me I'm pissed at her. Glancing at the pills in my hand, I throw them onto the bed, then quickly straddle her ass. Positioning my cock at the entrance to her pussy, I surge inside her and hiss through my teeth in pleasure when she attempts to push up from beneath me.

I rear back and slam inside her harder. "Did you really think I wouldn't know?" She tries to turn her head to face me, but I use my thick palm to pin her down while slamming my cock into her again and again. "I'm going to use this cunt." Her pussy muscles grip me. "Fuck, yes. My little goddamn slut wants filled with my cum." I spread my thighs further, allowing her room to grind her ass against me while giving me the perfect position to drive into her. Her hands move to push me away, but I take ahold of them in one firm grip while digging my knees into the mattress, and I ride her. Hard.

"Fuck, little slut. That's it, try and fight me, try and stop me from filling you with my cum." Expelling all my anger through my words, I continue with my onslaught. "You'll have my fucking baby whether you like it or not. You hear me?" I grind my hips against her, and she moans at the contact, and the sounds resonate in my balls. "Fuck, my slut likes that, huh? You like me forcing a baby into you?" I lean down against her ear, my voice laced in darkness, laced in need, a tone reserved purely for her. "That's what I'm doing, fucking a baby into you. Forcing you to take my cum." I grunt in approval when she whimpers. "My beautiful little cum slut." I groan. "Filling my little slut with our baby."

"Jesus, Tate." She clenches me tight. So fucking tight I see stars. "Ohhh!" Her mouth falls open into an O, and she screams against the sheets, the sound penetrating through my skin, searing into my blood, and forcing my balls to draw up, then rope upon rope of thick, warm cum shoots from my cock in a magnitude of pleasure.

"Fuckkkkk!" I roar into the room, imagining her filled with my child.

Filled with our future.

AVA

He collapses on me, pinning me to the mattress. The look of hurt marring his face when he threw down the pills will be forever engrained in my mind as something I hope to never witness again.

"I didn't take them. I didn't take them, Tate," I pant out from beneath him. "I swear it. You can check."

His solid body lifts off me, and he rolls me over to face him. "You didn't take them?" His features soften while he scans over my face. "Why?" He licks his lips.

Swallowing back the ball of nervousness gathered inside me, I decide to be truthful. "Because I wanted to be close to you. I wanted a part of you that I could keep forever." Tears glisten my vision. "I know it's selfish to want a baby under those circumstances." He opens his mouth to speak, no doubt to rebuke my claims, but I shake my head. "I was prepared to be selfish, Tate. I've spent my entire life doing things for other people. Being something for someone else." Sickness sits heavily at my admission.

"But having a part of you inside me. That's something I want for me, Tate. A future for me."

His eyes soften. "For us, Ava. A future for us."

Our focus remains on one another as his lips find mine in a tender, intimate kiss that sets my skin on fire. Then he slides his cock deep inside me. "I'm going to make love to you now."

When his words should shock me, they don't. They bring with them warmth, possession, and a knowledge of the future.

And if truth be told, I love him too.

I'm just not ready to admit it yet.

Not when my past could destroy our future.

FOURTEEN

TATE

"So, tell me about the tattoo on your back, baby." She places a plate of pancakes down in front of me, then leans against the counter.

"I wanted them, so I got them." She shrugs, unwilling to give me more explanation.

"Butterflies, huh?" I crook my eyebrow. We both know what I'm implying, but I'd rather hear her admit it than me ask her if I had anything to do with her choice of tattoo.

"What can I say, I like butterflies." She stares back at me nonchalantly.

"So, I had nothing to do with that decision, then?" I smile at her and revel in her pinkened cheeks, so unlike her usual confident self. Pushing back in my chair, I strut toward her, tugging her by the waist until she's flush against my chest. "I'll spank your ass if you don't tell me the truth, baby."

Her fingers grip my T-shirt, and her breath hitches, then she swallows. "M . . . maybe you had something to do with it."

I take my hand from her waist and use my fingers to tilt her chin up to meet my gaze. "Maybe?"

She rolls her eyes and pushes back against my chest. "Okay. I remember what you said to me, and it stuck, okay?"

"And what did I say?" I grin back at her.

She gives me the stink eye. "Don't be clever, Tate."

A door opens down the corridor, breaking our conversation, then Todd comes into view. "You're going to be late, Todd," Ava snaps in his direction.

He leans over the kitchen table and grabs my plate before rushing to stuff the pancakes in his mouth. Jesus, the kid can eat. I notice the similarities in him and Ava that I never saw before now. His brown hair has a wave to it, he has the same scattering of freckles dusting his nose, and the same sharp cheek bones, although his are a little bruised from my pounding.

Standing, I step into his space and hold out my hand. "Hey, man. I'm sorry about yesterday."

His eyes dart from mine to Ava's, as if searching for her approval, then his shoulders relax and he slips his hand into mine. "It's all good, bro." I chuckle at his words while he shakes my hand firmly.

"Todd! You didn't put all the bolts on the door!" I spin to Ava marching toward the door, placing the remaining bolts in place, even though her brother is about to leave.

He mumbles something about her being paranoid. "This is a safe neighborhood, Ava. Jesus. I put two out of the hundred on." He shrugs with a cocky grin.

TATE

Ava's eyes blaze with fire as she stalks toward us holding up her hand. "There's five, Todd. Five. I expect you to use them. They're there for a reason."

"Fine. I'm about to take the five bolts off the door now because I'm going to be fucking late," he snaps, throwing his rucksack over his shoulder on the way.

When the door closes behind him, she rushes to put the bolts in place while I lean against the table with my arms crossed. She spins on her heel to face me, and our eyes lock. "Are you going to tell me what that's all about?" I point toward the door.

"No. What's in the past is in the past, remember?"

I grind my teeth as she repeats the words I said to her last night. Only I have no intention of leaving this shit in the past. If she's in danger, I want to know about it.

"Av—" She holds her hand up.

"Don't, Tate. I don't want to discuss it. If this is going to work between us, we need to move forward."

If she thinks she can keep things from me, she can think again. I own every part of her: past, present, and future. But I stop myself from voicing it, prepared to wait until I get the answers I need.

Because I'm pretty sure someone tried to clip her wings, and when I find out who, I'm going to fucking slaughter him.

AVA

We've spent all day together at the park. The sun has gone down, but with the warmth in the breeze, it feels like a summer day. Earlier, I explained to Tate how I got legal guardianship of Todd last year and how he's such an incredible football player that he goes to a specialized sports school and trains every day. I know he assumes it's on a scholarship, but that couldn't be further from the truth. I work damn hard to get the best for my little brother, and to do so, I gave away a part of myself, one that haunts my dreams.

"Hey, you went quiet. Where'd you go?" He shoves the remaining hotdog into his mouth while watching me closely, propped up on his elbow.

Biting into my lip, I struggle to explain my worries, but instead of backing down, I decide to be honest with him. "I don't want what we have affecting work."

His eyebrows pull in. "Okay."

Mine shoot up in response. "Okay. Just like that?"

A smile plays on his handsome lips, and his eyes sparkle. "Just like that."

"Why do I get the feeling you're playing me here, Tate?" He tugs me toward him, forcing me to tumble onto his chest, then he falls into the grass, holding me against him. My lips so close to his, his breath fans my face, and when he seals his lips over mine, I can't help the whimper leaving my throat as he grinds his cock against my pussy in response.

"Because I'll give you whatever you want, whenever you want it," he breathes out, and I smile.

The shrill sound of his mobile ringing causes his body to sag, so I move to climb off him, but his hand grips my waist to keep me in place while he digs into his pocket.

"Yeah?"

He pinches the bridge of his nose. "Seriously?"

His eyes flick to mine, and I don't miss the flash of disappointment in them. "Mase is better at this shit than us."

I bite into my lip to stifle a laugh. Clearly, he's being called to deal with something he has no intention of dealing with.

"Fine. I'll see you there." He ends the call. "I'm sorry, baby. Shaw had an argument with Emi, and Owen wants us to meet him at a bar." He sighs.

Smiling down at him, I bend and place a kiss on his lips. "I understand."

The hand on my ass tightens, and he grinds up into me. "I want to fuck you so bad right now."

I push down against him, ignoring the fact the park is full of people. "Me too. But your friend needs you. Come on." I jump up from him and can't help but giggle when he has to adjust his firm cock.

"Fucking idiot should just fuck his wife and tell her he's sorry."

We walk back toward Tate's car. "Why, what did he do?"

His fingers lace with mine, spreading warmth throughout my body. How the hell we will keep this PG in the workplace, I'll never know. Every touch from him sends heat to travel over my body and arousal to drip from my pussy.

"I've no idea what he did. But if I was him, I'd apologize anyway." He grins back at me, and I swat at him.

If today is the first of many to come with Tate, I couldn't be more excited about our future. And part of me can't help but hope I'm pregnant, because a life with Tate feels like I'm flying.

FIFTEEN

TATE

Shaw knocks back another shot. "I'm just fucking saying, you didn't even ask the girl what the deal was before you flew off the handle," Mase exclaims, and Shaw scoffs in response. I can't believe I've been dragged over here because the idiot argued with his wife about her chatting to a guy at an event he went to.

"He has a point. I mean, did you even hear any of their conversation before you saw red?" I throw in his direction, ready for this night to be over with so I can get back to my girl. The waitress with barely any clothes on gyrates in front of me, and the motion forces my stomach to flip and my cock shrivel. No way will my body react to her when I have Ava in my grasp now.

I'm done having to pretend I'm fucking someone that looks like her, now I have the real thing.

"She's good for you, Shaw. Don't fuck this up by being

a jealous prick. Besides, you don't have a choice," Mase adds before taking a swig of his beer. I understand where the jealousy comes from; I felt like ripping the prick at the office a new hole when his gaze lingered on my girl too damn long.

Two of the dancers sway their hips as they walk over to our table, and when one parks her ass on Reed's lap, the other struts toward Shaw. Holy shit, this will be good.

I take a pull of my beer and watch the interaction with amusement.

Shaw holds up his hand to stop her coming closer while flashing his wedding finger. The finger I now feel jealous of. Scrubbing a hand over my cropped hair, it dawns on me, I want a ring on our fingers ASAP. The security, alongside her being pregnant with my baby will leave no question in anyone's mind that we belong together forever. "This is a wedding ring, sweetheart. Happily fucking married." Shaw glares at the dancer, and Mase and I chuckle at the venom in his tone.

Reed throws his head back as though what he said is the funniest thing he's ever heard.

"Married men still like their cocks getting sucked," she mock pouts.

Shaw's shoulders broaden. "You're right, they do. By their hot-as-fuck wives."

The dancer stares back at him like he's a fool. But when he pushes his thumb in my direction, panic races through me. "He, on the other hand, is not married."

I tense up. Shaw wouldn't know I'm madly in love and about to propose and fuck a baby into the only girl I've ever felt a damn thing for, because I haven't told them all yet. There's something holding me back. Maybe I need the security of her pregnancy in place before I explain how we became an item and they look at me differently.

The dancer tries to grind herself against Shaw.

"I said, no," he spits. "Jesus. No means no."

The dancer flicks her hair and gives him her back, then rolls herself down to all fours and crawls toward me. She licks her lips, as though she wants to devour me. "Shit," I mumble in a panic and push back in my chair to avoid her, toppling it over as I stand.

"I'm out. I'm not about to get eaten a-fucking-live by that." I point toward the woman on the floor rising onto her knees, and she once again locks eyes with Shaw while undoing the loose ribbon holding her halter top in place.

Suddenly, I'm desperate to get out of the club and as far away from her as possible. "Yeah, me too," Shaw agrees.

I storm toward the exit, feeling like insects are crawling over my skin. No fucking way am I letting another woman touch me. Shaw follows, and Mase throws money at the table as we leave Reed with the two dancers, and he looks like the cat that got the cream when they sit on either side of his lap.

Not too long ago I'd have relished the prospect of fucking two women at once, but now as I climb into Mase's SUV, all I can think about is pulling my girl against my chest and never letting her go.

Every first Sunday in the month, I visit my parents and have dinner with them. More often than not, my best friends join us too.

Growing up together, we're more like brothers than friends, and knowing this has guilt lancing through my chest at the secret I'm keeping.

I side-eye Owen. He's aware of my past with Ava, and when I expected him to be repulsed, he proved otherwise, but that was then. Will he still feel the same way? Besides, I could really do with talking to him about Ava's past. I know she's hiding something, and it eats me up inside we agreed not to talk about it. Owen has all the technology to dig deeper into her life, but can I allow myself to open up to him and betray Ava? Even if it is for her own good.

Casting a glance at Mase, he cuts into his meal, unaware of the turmoil inside of me. I know he'll have my back, but Shaw and Reed will go ape shit at my past decisions, always thinking with a business-level head. It has me feeling like a loser to think about disappointing them. I fidget in my chair.

When my phone buzzes in my pocket, I tug it out, and my chest expands with pride at the photo Ava sent me of her and Todd. They're grinning from ear to ear, Todd is wearing his football jersey, and his face is covered in mud. I can't help but replicate the smile beaming back at me.

> Me: Miss you.

> Ava: It's been 24 hours.

> Me: It's been way longer than that and you know it.

She *knows* I'm referring to the four years we were apart.

> Ava: You have me now.

> Me: I'm never letting you go again. Trust me.

> Me: Love you, baby. See you in the office tomorrow.

> Ava: See you. x

I smile, tucking my phone back in my pocket as I consider what she will discover tomorrow.

The fact Ava took guardianship of her younger brother is a testament to what sort of person she is and how capable of a mother she will be. My blood races at the thought, and I lick my lips thinking of her swollen with my child. Of course, my cock thickens with excitement too.

Fuck, I need her pregnant. I need the family I always dreamed of.

My gaze flicks over the table once again and lands on my mom. She's everything a parent should be, but growing up, I couldn't help but crave more, and it wasn't until I felt the connection I did with Ava, that I realized what that was.

I want a family of my own. One I created, one born out of love and not out of a sense of duty like Shaw's or my parents'.

My sister's voice is distant, but I hear it immediately, and my mom jumps up to greet her. I wasn't even aware she was in the state, let alone coming for dinner. She's been living in Miami, and I haven't heard a thing from her for weeks, so when my eyes land on her, it takes me a moment to register her fully.

My sister is naturally beautiful; she has a Mediterranean look about her that has every guys' head turning toward her. My friends and I have spent years beating any guy who dared to look in her direction.

When she was eighteen, she left town and went to fashion school in Miami. She only occasionally graces us with her presence, always feigning being busy. "Here we fucking go," Dex, my younger brother, grumbles from beside me, causing me to glance around the room in question.

"Laya, this is Emi. Shaw's wife. Emi, this is my sister, Laya."

"I'm sorry. I didn't know you were married, Shaw." Laya smirks back at Shaw, causing him to shift uncomfortably in his seat.

The poor guy has gone from being a bachelor, to being married to his pregnant wife in the span of a few weeks.

"You wouldn't fucking know. You're never home." Owen grunts but refuses to look in Laya's direction.

He's always been a hard ass where she's concerned, and not for the first time, the hairs on my neck prick up with uncertainty about his misguided concern. I've witnessed their glances and the way his eyes linger on my sister, then he dismisses any concerns I have by claiming a brotherly need to protect her.

Laya's jaw tics, and she shakes her head, as if banishing Owen's words from her mind. As if banishing him. "Well, I'm here now and I have news." She straightens her back, standing taller.

Dex sits back in his chair with a shit-eating grin, as if he knows what's coming. Those two always were close. I put it down to their ages, whereas there's a ten-year age gap between Laya and me, and our relationship is one of a fierce need to protect my kid sister from any demons in her past.

"What news? Is everything okay?" My dad's eyes flick over her.

A smile breaks out on her pretty face, and she thrusts her hand out over the table. "I'm married."

The table falls silent as they all stare at her outstretched hand. No fucking way! No fucking way has my little sister gotten married to someone we haven't even met. I dart my eyes around the table because this has to be a joke, right? Everyone stares at her in shock while Owen continues eating at rapid speed, not giving her a second glance.

"And there's more." She bites into her bottom lip with delight. I glance at Owen and don't miss the pulsating vein on his temple. He's about to lose his shit.

More? Fucking more?

"I'm pregnant!"

"Holy shit," Shaw mumbles. Then his mouth falls agape in horror.

"What the fuck, Laya?" I jump out of my seat. Is she for fucking real?

But when Owen's chair slams back onto the floor and he storms from the room, anger boils inside me. Just what the hell is going on with him?

Shaw makes some excuse about leaving with Emi, and Mase follows behind him while I stand staring at the door my best friend charged out of because my kid sister got knocked up by a fucking stranger.

My mom fusses around her, congratulating her, but I

can't find it in me. I need fucking answers. I turn on my heels and follow after Owen.

Stepping behind him as he's bent over, his knuckles are white under the strain of his grip on the balcony railing. His head is ducked low, and he breathes heavily, as if trying to rein in his feelings.

Rage surges through me. It's obvious something has been going on between them, and all this time he's been lying to me.

For years I've questioned his actions around Laya, where she's always been openly flirty with him, he's always played it off as a teenage crush, but looking at his reaction right now, I know there's more to it than he let me believe.

"Have you got something to tell me, Owen?"

He flinches, and his back rises and falls before he sucks in a sharp breath, then straightens and turns to face me. His face is void of emotion, typical fucking Owen, can't read a goddamn thing from him. My fists clench beside me at how he's trying to disguise the fact he has feelings for my sister.

"No," he breathes out, staring back into my eyes with such openness it has me questioning every thought I considered only a moment ago.

"Then why'd you react like that?" I point back toward the house.

He licks his lips, then offers me a shrug. "I'm pissed. She's knocked up and married and we haven't even met the guy yet. Aren't you?"

Of course he turns this around on me. "Yes, of course I'm pissed," I bite out. Pissed is a fucking understatement.

"It has me wondering what she's hiding, she never brought him to meet you all. Right?" His eyes search mine.

This piques my attention because Owen has a goddamn point. Why the hell wouldn't you bring the guy you're going to marry home to meet the family? The father of your baby, no less, and why the hell hasn't he insisted on meeting us? What sort of man is he?

He has to be hiding something.

"I want to know everything there is to know about him, Owen," I snipe out, giving my best friend full permission to delve into my sister's private life and that of her husband's too.

He gulps and darts his eyes away, and once again my suspicion about his feelings toward her rises. "You'll have it. You'll know everything there is to know about him." The venom in his tone lets me know he'll leave no stone unturned where his search is concerned.

I turn to walk away, unable to deal with the niggling feeling bubbling inside me, the same one that's been there for years.

Opening the door, I stop in my tracks and glance over my shoulder to witness his face contorted in hurt. Hurt that tells me there's so much more to this than he's admitting, hurt I can't help adding to, because if he wanted my sister, he should have been man enough to take her, fuck the consequences. Something I myself should have done too. I take my self-loathing out on him. "I'm pleased there's nothing between you and my sister, Owen. Because you don't fucking deserve her."

As I step through the door and into the kitchen, I swear

I hear him whisper, "I know," but I refuse to acknowledge it.

Not when I've been such a hypocrite, not when I should have taken my girl when I had the chance.

SIXTEEN

AVA

I've never been more eager to turn up to work on a Monday than I am right now. The anticipation of seeing Tate has butterflies swirling in my stomach, and I smile at my analogy, considering the whole of my back is painted in them.

Tate spent yesterday at his parents' house but called me last night to talk about the appearance of his sister, one he hasn't seen for months. As much as I'd have liked him to stay over last night, I appreciate the fact he was concerned about his family. It only reiterates the kind of man he is.

As I approach my workstation, Steve leans against the wall. He lifts his head as I approach. "You've been moved," he grits out.

My eyebrows raise. "Huh?"

He points to my now empty desk. "You've been moved." He frowns, spitting the words out.

"Moved?" I glance around for my files.

"Yep. Guess fucking the boss gets you that kind of treatment, right?" He raises a thick eyebrow, and his lips pinch with a sneer.

My jaw tightens on his words, and my eyes flare in rage. How the hell dare he? So, he was fine with me fucking him, my direct manager, but when it's someone above him, then it's too much. And how dare Tate move me without discussing it with me first?

I close my eyes, seething while trying to regulate my breathing.

"You're not even going to deny it are you?" he grits out.

Snapping my eyes open, I stare back at his smug face, giving him a nonchalant shrug. "He has a big dick and knows how to use it. The last guy didn't have a clue."

He opens his mouth to speak, but I turn on my heel, refusing to listen to what was bound to be a rebuttal. Instead, I march toward the elevator.

Only, when I step inside and stare at the buttons, I realize I don't have access to his floor. *Shit.*

My phone rings, and I take it from my purse. Of course the smug bastard chooses now to call me. "I gave you access, come on up." He ends the call before I can question him further, so I turn my attention to the security camera, gifting him with my middle finger.

TATE

I throw my head back on a loud chuckle as Ava gives me the middle finger. My girl is feisty as fuck, and I love it.

"What the hell's gotten into you?" Mase asks, his head spinning in my direction.

"Ava is on her way up here."

"Shit. You want me to give you five minutes to explain?"

I glance at my watch, she's going to need to be fucked into submission, for sure. At least, I hope she does. "Give it twenty." I grin back at him, and he shakes his head on a low laugh. He closes the folder and marches toward the door before turning his head over his shoulder. "Just fucking spray after, will you, I hate it when it smells of sex in here." He scrunches his nose.

"Noted." I gift him with a toothy grin.

No sooner than the door closes does it swing open again. I take my time looking up from the paperwork, my lips twitching with glee at the heat radiating from her.

"What the hell, Tate? You moved my desk without discussing it with me?"

My eyes meet hers, and a flash of softness passes through them before she steps forward and narrows them on me, trying not to act pleased to see me.

"I like you close to me." I shrug.

"Close to you?" She rears back as though shocked at my words when she really shouldn't be. I've made no secret about how much I want her. Need her.

"Yes, close to me. Besides, we're working on the same project, so it makes sense. Your desk is right there now." I point toward the desk on the other side of the door, the one closest to my office.

Originally, I wanted to move her in here, but Mase talked me out of it, mainly because it would raise suspicions among the other guys, and I'm not prepared to answer the questions that move would pose. So I compromised by having her outside my door, this way she's near me whenever I need her and I can see her all the time too.

She glances over her shoulder toward the door, then her raging eyes land on me again. I drop my pen and lean back in my chair, preparing myself for the onslaught about to spiel from those gorgeous lips begging to wrap around my steel cock.

My cock twitches as she steps forward, and the bounce of her tits has it thickening further, to the point of pain. And when my gaze locks onto her nipples, it leaks against my boxers, and my palm itches to punish her for wearing such suggestive clothing.

"I don't need to move up here to work on the project, Tate," she says with her hands on her hips.

I smile back at her. "I know, but I want you to." Her

chest heaves, but I choose to ignore her outburst, and turn my attention to my raging cock, as the fire behind her eyes only thickens it further.

I stroke a hand over it while her face transforms from anger to shock. "Come here, baby." I hold my free hand out toward her. When she doesn't move, I darken my tone. "Ava, be a good girl and come to me." Her pupils dilate and she swallows slowly. I love how submissive she is.

She steps forward, moving around the desk to slip her hand into mine. Not allowing her time to second-guess her move, I pull her toward me until she's standing between my legs.

"Get on your knees, baby."

She licks her lips but doesn't move, as if fighting an internal battle with herself. "Ava, Mase is going to be back in here soon, and I'm fucking that mouth either way. Now you either do it the easy way or I can force you onto your knees after I spank that bratty ass, but you're doing it." My lip turns up at the sides when her breathing hitches.

Her hazel eyes fill with lust, and she lowers herself to her knees, and my cock spurts in response.

Jesus, she's hot. I fumble with my belt buckle as her knees hit the carpet. My heart races with desperation to fill her mouth, and my balls tighten in awareness at the fact Ava, my Ava, is finally on her knees for me.

She hasn't sucked my cock since our reunion, and I've spent every damn day since the first time I slid inside her mouth regretting not creating more memories.

My cock springs free, and I hiss when her palm wraps around the base, watching her closely to witness the moment she discovers the permanent mark of her on me. She tilts my cock toward her open mouth, and I damn near come. Clenching my teeth together, I try to ward off a potential disaster. The last thing I want is to come on her face the first time she touches me, no matter how much I crave to see it.

Her tongue laps at the precum dripping from the tip. "Jesus. Fuck, Ava." My ass rises off the chair in response to her touch, and my grip on her hair tightens.

She freezes, and I stare down at her while the words on my cock register in her head. Her throat works, overcome with emotion, and tears fill her eyes as they lock with mine. "You got a tattoo of me?"

I have to clear my throat of the emotion swimming between us and the enormity of the fact we've both marked our bodies permanently with one another. We both wanted more. Lived for it every day since.

"I did, baby." I gently tuck a strand of her hair behind her ear. "I wanted every woman to know you own me, and every time I fucked my fist, it was you I was thinking of, Ava." Her bottom lip wobbles, and my heart constricts. "You're it for me, Ava. Always have been, always will be."

She swallows hard. "You're it for me too." Our eyes remain locked, my heart thudding against my chest, filling with the love I crave. And when a tear trickles down her face, my cock jumps in response, determined to get in on the action.

"Now, hurry up and suck my cock before I cover your face in my cum. I'm so fucking close already, baby."

Her lips tip up into a smile as she lowers them to shower my cock with kisses, tracing the tattoo of her name with her tongue. "That's it, baby. Lick your name from my cock. Lick away the pain." I groan and thrust up when she takes the dripping head into her mouth. "Fuck." And when I hit the back of her throat, she gags, leaving me with no choice but to hold her head in place so she chokes on me. Fuck, that feels good.

"Fucking, Jesus. Ava." I thrust into her mouth while her tongue circles my cock and around the head each time I withdraw, then slam back inside.

"Fuck. I'm going to come soon, baby." I grit my teeth. "I'm going to come in your mouth so damn soon."

"Mmm," she moans around my cock, and when one of her hands finds my balls, I combust. Wave after wave of euphoria releases into her needy mouth, filling her with spurt upon spurt of cum.

"Holy shit!" I pant out as my fingers grip her hair, and she whimpers in response, which only heightens my arousal. "My slut." I slam inside one more time.

Cum escapes her mouth as she chokes around my cock, and her throat works to swallow each spurt.

My tense muscles slowly relax. "Good girl. Such a good girl." I stroke her hair as my orgasm ebbs away.

My body eases into the chair as I untangle my fingers from her hair, and she pulls my cock from her mouth on a slurp, swirling her tongue around the end to collect the remnants of my cum. Then she places a tender kiss on the tattoo, as if in gratitude, and I twitch in her hand. "Fuck."

My insatiable need to fill her cunt overwhelms me. I tug her to her feet, then lift her ass to sit her on the edge of the desk, ignoring the gasp of surprise to fall from those lips, the same ones that didn't only blow my cock but blew my mind too. Edging my chair closer, I breathe in the scent of her aroused pussy, reveling in the wet spot pooled in her lace panties, as I gather her skirt around her waist.

"Jesus, Tate. You turn me on so much," she pants out.

I slide her panties to the side. "You want me to lick this little cunt clean?"

Her head falls back against the wood, and she moans when I spread her pussy lips, making a V with my fingers, then slide my tongue through her folds. "Mmm, fucking delicious, Ava."

"Please."

I glance up at her, my cock still out and exposed, hardening by the second. "Get your tits out, Ava. Get them fucking out, let me see." She fumbles with the buttons before tugging down her bra and exposing her plump tits to me. The barbell gleams under the office lighting, and my cock drips.

"Fuck, Ava." My eyes roll with each sweep of my tongue, and when she grinds her pussy against my face and locks her fingers into my hair, I can't help but jerk my cock. Using my thumb, I push it into her wet hole, pressing down on the muscle separating her pussy from her ass.

"Oh god, Tate."

"I'm fucking my hand, Ava." She thrusts her hips up, and I drink the pleasure flowing from her as she groans on my filthy words. "It's dripping all over me, desperate to fuck you."

"Oh god, I need that. Please, Tate. I need to feel you," she pants.

I smile into her pussy. "You want my fingers or my cock, baby?"

"Co . . . cock."

I launch to my feet. "Thank fuck."

With her pussy juice coating my chin, I lean over her. "Lick your cum from my face while I fuck you, baby girl."

I line my cock up and surge forward as her hands lock behind my neck, drawing me toward her. Then her tongue lavishes my face and chin. She plucks my lip into her mouth, and I groan at the thought of her tasting herself while my cock stretches her wide. "You taste so damn good, baby."

"Mmm, so good," she agrees, making my hips piston in response.

Her fingers rake through my hair, tugging as she takes pleasure in cleaning me. "You're such a dirty little slut for me, Ava."

"I am." She clenches around me, my words sending her pussy into spasm. "Oh god, I am."

She pushes my head away but doesn't give me the chance to second-guess her motive, because with one hand, she guides me to her pierced nipple where I suck it hard.

The office door opens, and my eyes flick up to see Mase. Ava tenses.

He stands frozen, his eyes locked on the scene in front of him, and the door slips through his hand, clicking shut. My balls pulsate with the thought of him watching me take her and how he'll see how I possess her. Own her.

"Oh fuck." I grunt as I shove my cock deeper inside her.

His lips part to speak but nothing comes out.

Ava tries to move, but I pin her down with a pinch to her hips. "Eyes on me, baby," I pant into her ear. "Eyes on me while I fuck you." A whimper escapes her, and her pussy clenches, then my lips tip up into a knowing grin. She likes the thought.

"I'm going to fuck a baby into her, Mase." My eyes

never leave hers. "I'm fucking this bare cunt. She's going to give me a baby."

I return my lips to her tit, sucking on her nipple with a groan that sends a tremor through her body.

"Tell me you want my cum, Ava," I whisper against her marked flesh.

"Come inside me, Tate." Her husky voice is an aphrodisiac to my already fraught state.

My balls draw up. "Oh fuck." I pull back, then slam inside her.

"Come inside me. Make me yours, to keep." We both know what she means, she wants me to get her pregnant. "Fuck, Ava. Take"—my hips thrust—"every"—I slam inside her—"last"—I push harder—"drop," I roar, falling against her tits, then sink my teeth into her nipple, tugging on the peak and sucking it hard while she convulses against me. Her pussy is so tight around my cock deep inside her. My vision darkens, and I fall onto my elbows, our mouths now so close her breath tickles my lips.

"I love you, Ava."

Then I slam my lips against hers, not wanting the disappointment of her not returning my feelings to ruin the moment.

When our lips finally part, her hazel eyes are filled with affection, and she drags her fingers over my lip. "You're mine, Tate Kavanagh, and I'm yours."

My veins fill with promise, because the look in Ava's eyes is full of every confirmation I need.

She loves me too.

And when I glance up toward the door, Mase is nowhere to be seen.

SEVENTEEN

AVA

After Tate came in me, he put my panties back into place, then helped me button up my shirt before tucking away his cock and zipping up his pants.

The office door opens as he buckles himself back up, then steps up to me and gently tucks my hair behind my ear. My stomach flutters and my cheeks pinken. His fingers linger on the scar on my neck, and his gaze on my eyes has me averting my attention and stepping around him to walk toward the presentation tables. "You almost still had your cock out." I point out, determined not to chance any unwanted questions.

He laughs. "Wouldn't be the first time Mase has seen my cock."

That grabs my attention, so I turn to face him. "You and he—"

Tate scoffs. "Fuck no. I just meant he . . ." He shakes his head. "Doesn't matter, it's all in the past now." I can read between the lines; he's caught Tate in the act multiple times. As if waiting for my response, Tate stands frozen watching me.

"The past is the past, Tate."

His shoulders fall lax and his lips tip into a serene smile, one that fills me with love.

"Besides, Mase is practically a born-again virgin."

I reel back. "Huh?"

"Mase doesn't have sex. Do you, Mase?" He slaps a hand on his best friend's back, both ignoring the fact Mase watched us have sex.

"Don't be a dick." Mase shrugs him off.

"You don't have sex?" I scan Mase; he's hot as hell. Built bigger than Tate, his hair lighter, and his eyes are a mesmerizing shade of green that makes you feel like you're sinking into him.

A throat clears, and I cast my eyes around the room to find Tate glaring at me. "I'm shocked, is all," I defend with a lift of my shoulder.

"Don't be. I'm going through a divorce. The last thing I need is for it to become any messier."

"Oh." I nod in understanding while Mase opens the folders and lifts the ad sketches out.

"When he finally pops his cherry again, we're going to order him a few Indulgence girls." Tate wiggles his eyebrows.

I roll my eyes at his antics, but part of me can't help but smile at the camaraderie they have, and to be a part of this, has me feeling like I belong here—with Tate, his friends, the business. It's so much more than I ever could have imagined.

Tate pulls out an office chair and lifts me into his lap,

and I drape my arm over his shoulder. So much for keeping our relationship out of the office.

"You weren't kidding when you said gold, huh?" Mase quirks a brow as he lifts his head from the display on the table.

"Not at all. We're going for Gold, after all." I pull back my shoulders as I explain my idea for winning the advertisement contract.

A woman painted in glistening gold from head to toe, dressed only in see-through lingerie, walks down a crowded street. When she locks eyes with a man at the end of the street, she walks toward him, and with each step she takes, the street and its inhabitants turn gold, giving off the power of the scent of the product. When they finally meet, her lips lock with his and then his body transforms to gold also.

Not just smelling the gold scent but envisaging it, embracing it, and ultimately, becoming it.

"It's fucking amazing!" Mase exclaims, his face alight with enthusiasm. I cast my eyes over to Tate, but his eyes are locked onto a piece of paper. The grip on the sheet and the tightness of his jaw give away his pissed vibe. His whole body is rigid with fury radiating from him.

I stand from his lap.

"Tate?" Mase questions.

He looks to me. "When were you going to tell me this?" He holds the sheet up in his hand while Mase's eyes volley between mine and Tate's.

I lick my lips, trying to ignore the penetrating heat of his gaze. "When?" he commands again, louder this time. Enough to force me to jump.

"It's been in the contract from the start, Ava insisted on it for us to use her idea." Mase speaks up in my defense.

"It's not my fault if you didn't read the full proposal before Mase signed off on it." I shrug.

His eyes blaze with fire as he swings them toward Mase. "Change it."

My mouth falls open in shock; he cannot be serious. He really doesn't want me to be the model in the advert? My advert. My heart hammers faster. This is what I've worked toward; I deserve this. Anger manifests inside me. I need this.

"I can't, we signed off on it. You signed off on it." Mase glares back at him, looking pissed on my behalf.

"I'm doing it, Tate." I jut out my chin. There's no way I've come this far for it to be taken from me in the heat of jealousy.

"Over my dead body!" he booms. The vein on his forehead pulsates, and his hands are balled into fists.

I shake my head. "And I'm telling you, I'm doing it." I stand my ground, glaring back at him just as fiercely.

"Fuck!" he roars, swiping the contents of his desk onto the floor. He storms from the room, slamming the door on his exit.

"Shit. He didn't read the contract," Mase mumbles.

"I'm doing it, Mase." My eyes lock with his, and he must see my determination because he gifts me with a supportive nod that has me flooding with relief.

Staring back at Mase Campbell, I come to a conclusion: He is loyal, supportive, and he loves hard, but something from my own experiences tells me there's more to him than what we all see.

And I don't think he even realizes it yet himself.

TATE

I storm into the restroom like a bull, almost taking the door off its hinges. The moment I saw her name as the model on the advertisement, jealousy surged through me like poison. I've never felt such rage, so much pent-up fucking anger.

My head feels like it's going to explode, and my veins pulsate with a need to cause damage, with a need to take away my anger. I breathe through my nostrils, the thoughts of other people viewing what is mine makes me want to tell the guys to fuck the contract, let Griffin the prick have it. Because it isn't worth feeling like this.

I duck my head to splash my face with cold water, feeling the need to calm down. Maybe that's the best idea I've had. Maybe I can get them to tell Ava they pulled the advertising proposal while I remain silent so she isn't pissed at me for something she's clearly passionate about.

The door behind me opens, but I stay hunched over the sink while I go over my plan.

When I hear her name, my ears prick up and my body stills.

"I swear, Ava is filthy in bed. She has the type of experience any man would be grateful for, and I intend to use it." The blood pumps wildly through my veins pounds in my ears, as the anger that was only moments ago ebbing away returns tenfold.

"You're so lucky to have fucked her. She's so damn hot," the second voice adds. My hands curl on the counter before me.

"Don't I fucking know it. And now that prick has moved her upstairs," he grumbles.

"But you have her number though, right?"

"Of course, I have her number. I told you we fuck regularly." My body tightens and my heart stops for what feels like an eternity. "Until recently that is," he tacks on, and my heart thumps rapidly once again.

Raising my head from the stooped position, I stand tall, glaring through the mirror at the two sons of bitches who thought they could talk bad about my girl. My eyes lock onto the prick who claims to have bed her, Steve Drayton. The prick who spends his days salivating over my woman. Another reason I moved her desk.

The fucker has seen what's mine and the thought of him seeing her naked has me wanting to obliterate him into a bloody pulp.

The other guy meets my glare in the mirror, and his face pales. "Leave," I bite the word out toward him, and he gulps before turning on his heel and fleeing while Steve's eyes widen.

The door clicks closed. "Look, Tate—" I slam my fist into his face, and his bone crunching beneath my knuckles brings me no comfort, so I pummel his stomach over and over as he hunches over in pain. Ignoring his groans and whimpers, I deliver multiple blows—each one harder than the last.

He falls to the floor, and when the sniveling piece of shit moves to stand, I grip the slimy fucker's hair in my hand and drag him toward the urinals. His legs splay out in each direction as he struggles against me.

"If you ever talk shit about my girl again, motherfucker, I'll force you to eat it. Understand me?" I lift his head and tug it up and down in a nodding motion. His face is splattered with blood, and his nose sits at a crooked angle, but the fire inside me has yet to subside. I take pity on the little pissant and drop him, then press his face into the floor with the sole of my foot.

"If you ever so much as look in Ava's direction again, I'll fuck you up so bad you won't be able to piss or swallow." I glare down at him. "Do you understand me?"

His head attempts to move in agreement under my aggressive step.

Taking in the way his drained body slumps, I realize he's had enough. But I can't quite help how feral I feel when it comes to Ava. I have a fierce need deep inside me to protect her, while selfishly keeping her only as mine, away from prying eyes, past and present. The only eyes to ever settle on her again will be mine. I'm her future, and I'm determined to prove it to her.

Stepping over the blubbering prick, I stride out of the restroom feeling lighter than when I entered.

I might have taken my aggression out on Pissy Pants Steve, but Ava will receive a punishment much more fitting.

EIGHTEEN

AVA

Dropping the hot bread onto the plate, I blow on my fingers, retrieve the plate, then place it down on the table. Todd grabs a slice as soon as the plate touches the wood, and I smile at my little brother's eagerness.

"You act deprived of food," I chide.

"I am," he sputters as he bites into another chunk.

I scoff. "Please. You sure as hell don't look deprived. Plus, your big sis looks after you." I beam back at him and bat my lashes.

He opens his mouth to respond but is halted by the doorbell. My heart skips a beat, and my blood turns to ice. Todd must sense my apprehension because he stands. My little brother has become my defender this past year. I fought so hard to get custody of him, and now he fights just as hard to protect me.

Todd swipes his hand over the security screen, then his shoulders relax, and he begins unlocking the door. "It's fine, it's—" He doesn't get chance to finish before Tate pushes through the door.

The moment our gazes collide, all the uncertainty about earlier drains away from me. Remorse coats his features as he steps toward me, and when his arms band around me, drawing me against his chest, I melt against him, breathing in his fresh sandalwood cologne. "I'm sorry I stormed out," he whispers against my ear.

He draws circles on my back, reminding me of our first night together and bringing a wave of emotion I wasn't prepared for. "I'm proud of you for having your wings, baby." I cough, trying to disguise the sob lodged in my throat.

A loud clapping echoes the apartment. "Fantastic that your lovers tiff is over. Now, are you going to eat, or did big sis cook this all for me?" Todd tilts his head toward the table.

I giggle against Tate's chest.

"Did you cook?" I raise my head to meet his blue eyes, and the storm from the office has evaporated from them.

My fingers dance along his neck and over toward his nose that I give a bop. "I'll have you know, I'm a good cook."

"You're so fucking perfect." He takes my hand and kisses my fingers delicately.

"Christ. You two are ridiculous," Todd groans with his hand on his forehead. "Whatever you did. Apologize to her later, when I'm not here, will you?"

"Oh, I will." He winks, and a promising smile graces his face. One that sends a rush of need coursing through my body.

TATE

Watching Ava interact with Todd fills me with warmth. It's the exact same way I act with my best friends who I class as family.

"So, Tate, who appears to be dating my sister, tell me about yourself." Todd's familiar hazel eyes meet with mine.

With my jaw on edge, I try not to verbalize the bite I feel when I speak. "I don't appear to be dating your sister. I am dating her. In fact, she's going to be my wife." I stare back at him, hoping he can see the sincerity oozing from my body.

Ava chokes on her water, sending a spray of the liquid across the table. I ignore her cute reaction and hold Todd's eyes, knowing how important it is to have him on board. "I love her. And I know she loves me. She's engrained deep in here"—I tap my temple—"and most importantly, in here too." I tap on my heart. "I refuse to live another day without her." I puff out my chest with pride and stare back at him.

Todd's eyebrows shoot up and his mouth falls open. Whatever he thought I was going to say, that wasn't it. "I'm going to live every day to make her happy, Todd. Because I never want to know the feeling without her again." He swallows thickly on my words. "Ever," I tack on for emphasis.

Todd leans back in his chair. "I'm happy for you guys. Ava deserves to be happy." He nods in Ava's direction while she beams back at me—the smile so wide it encompasses her entire face and my heart skips a beat.

We all sit together eating spaghetti Bolognese, a side salad, and some fucking delicious bread Todd said Ava made herself.

"I have a game this Saturday, will you be there?" Todd asks Ava with hope in his eyes.

"Sure, I told you I wouldn't miss any." She points her fork in his direction, and the smile encompassing his face is childlike, and my heart aches for the kid.

"I'll come too," I jump in.

"You will?" Ava's eyes widen in surprise. "I told you. I'm all in. That means with Todd here too." I tilt my head in Todd's direction, and his shoulders seem to expand with the grin on his face.

"Really? That's amazing." He beams back at me with gratitude. "Thanks, Tate." It's like I just gave him the world, when, in reality, I'm coming to watch a football game. I remember how that felt before the Kavanaghs took me in—lonely and unloved. It only has me more adamant to show him and Ava everything I can offer them. The fact the kid wants me around has me wanting to step up even more. Determined to care for both of them.

"I'm looking forward to it, Buddy."

He shoves more spaghetti in his mouth, the grin still on his face, and I chuckle when just as much falls from his lips as what made it in his mouth. Ava squeezes my thigh, and her gaze lingers on me while I continue eating and acting unfazed by how grateful they both are.

When Ava stands and begins clearing the plates, I grab her wrist. "Go take a bath or something, we got this." I tilt my head toward the mess we created.

She bites into her bottom lip, and my cock takes notice. "Ava," I growl, and she jumps. Leaning into her ear, I whisper against her, "If you don't go now, your brother is not only going to hear us fuck. He's going to witness it too." She swallows deeply, probably remembering Mase watching me fill her earlier today.

Her eyes widen. "Okay," she breathes out, her eyes filled with lust.

Her ass sways as she walks away, then I listen for her bedroom door to close before I turn on my heels to face Todd.

"So, what's with all the locks?" I throw my hand out toward the ridiculous number of locks on the door. There's no way with the security system in this apartment building she needs the additional locks. But it was niggling me all the way through dinner, and with how long it took Todd to unlock the door for me to see my girl, I was about ready to burst through it.

He sighs. "She dated this guy once, and I'm pretty sure he still has a thing for her." My spine straightens at his words. The way he leans closer and lowers his tone tells me how bad this situation is. "She's always jumpy. I know it was a bad relationship." He shakes his head. "She panics when the doorbell rings, you've seen how she acts when I don't use all the locks. He did something to her." His words are coated in sadness, and I want nothing more than to pull him to me, tell him everything is okay, and I got them both now.

"I think he hurt her."

I grind my jaw from side to side, pissed that I'm just hearing about this. "Has she reported him to the police?"

Todd rears back. "Fuck no. She's a foster kid." I nod in understanding. Foster kids have a hard time in society and often feel like the authorities are against them instead of for them, especially if they've been let down in the past. Something I know nothing about, where Ava is concerned. That's a conversation we need to have. "Besides, she would have worried about it affecting custody of me, she said so once." Todd's tone is softer than ever, and he doesn't even try to disguise the vulnerability he feels. And for the first time when I look at this broad-shouldered kid, who is stacked with muscle and easily passes for someone in their twenties, I see a scared teenager. One desperate for an opportunity to be happy with his sister.

Dragging my hand over my jaw, my shoulders lower and I give in, tugging him toward me, giving him no choice but to accept my embrace. "Don't worry, kid. I got you, and I've got your sister. I'll watch out for you both from now on."

We remain in a bro hug for way longer than would be deemed acceptable with my friends, but as his hold on me tightens, I know he needs this, but I need it too.

My demons of being the kid with no family hit me square in the chest, and I promise Todd here and now, "I'll always keep you safe, kid."

NINETEEN

AVA

I take my time in the tub, relaxing beneath the bubbles while the guys tidy the kitchen. As usual, I stop my mind from drifting into the darkness and instead concentrate on how I feel having Tate and Todd together. It's like someone pulled the scene out of my dream and made it a reality.

How Tate spoke about me with such confidence in our relationship made me want to scream from the rooftops that I love him, but something is holding me back. Maybe it's because my happiness feels so temporary, like something will go wrong and take it all from me. If I utter the words I know he wants to hear, then will everything around us suddenly change? It's almost like I don't want to tempt fate. I'm the happiest I've ever been, and I can't do anything to risk it.

So, for now, I'll hold those words close, and each time he uses them, I'll use my touch to show him how I feel.

"Hey, baby. Are you ready to get out?"

His jeans are stretched over his thick, muscular thighs, his feet are bare, and his white T-shirt strains against his broad shoulders, and my thighs clench at how gorgeous he is.

He holds out a towel for me, so I rise from the bath, allowing the suds to drip down my body while I take my time lifting one leg, then the other out of the tub. I love how my body is such a turn on for Tate. His eyes fill with lust, his Adam's apple bobs, and his nipples peak beneath his shirt. I bite into my bottom lip to stifle a smile.

He wraps the towel around me, then bends and scoops me into his arms. I can't help but squeal as he carries me into my bedroom. He throws me up in the air, and my ass bounces on the mattress, causing the towel to unravel around me. My legs open in invitation, and when he releases a growl, I almost combust. He tugs his T-shirt over his head and drops his jeans, releasing his thick cock.

He kneels onto the bed and lifts my knees to expose my lower half. His eyes penetrate me, and heat travels over my body like a wildfire, then he slowly licks his lips. "Fuck, Ava. I wanna fuck your ass so bad, baby." He glances from my exposed holes up toward my face, as if seeking approval.

Jesus, I want to feel him there, to have him take over everything, and for the bad memories to be eradicated beneath his touch, so I gift him with a confident nod.

"You let anyone else fuck it?" His eyes snap up toward mine.

I swallow deeply, hating the word I have to murmur. "Yes." His eyes close in response, and I hate myself for it. Then he sucks in a sharp breath, as if collecting himself.

When he reopens his blinding-blue eyes, I see the fire and determination behind his gaze. His sharp jaw is locked, and the muscles in his forearms flex against our touch.

"I'm going to erase every fucking memory of anyone else touching my girl, do you understand me?"

Without giving me a chance to respond, he spits on my pussy and then does it again. The spittle drips down toward my ass, and my heart races.

"Ta-ate?"

The grip on my knees tightens as he raises his head from between my open legs. "You have to feel me, Ava." He wants me to feel the aggression behind taking me, and where I thought that would be something I wouldn't want, I find myself holding my knees open for him and spreading myself wider. I give myself over to him. If he can use me to exorcise his demons, maybe he'll exorcise mine too.

TATE

She spreads herself wide, and her pussy is dripping with my spit. Taking hold of my cock, I drag it up and down my spittle, loving her moans each time my tip comes in contact with her clit.

"Fuck, Ava. You're so damn responsive."

"Mm. More, Tate."

I chuckle at how needy she sounds. "You want me to fuck your ass, don't you?"

"Yes. God, yes." She nods.

Dragging my cock over her tight little ass, her eyes flare wide with uncertainty. Whatever fucker she screwed here before will be gone once I've fucked her.

She's mine.

I flatten my palm on her pussy and use my thumb to circle her clit, pressing down with each sweep of a circular motion. Her lips part, and my cock pulsates and drips precum over her hole. "You're my little slut, Ava."

"Yes, yours."

"Are you going to let your man fuck your ass?"

She throws her head back when I press on her clit harder. "Yes."

"My needy little slut needs her ass pumped with cum, isn't that right?"

"Ohhhh." I circle her clit again, releasing the pressure when her legs tremble. "Yes," she pants.

With one hand on her pussy and the other gripping my cock, I push the slick head against her tight hole, slowly inching inside. "Fuck, baby." I bite into my cheek, and every muscle on my body is pulled tight, as I try to refrain from hurting her.

"Please, Tate. I want you to fuck the memories away." I don't read too much into her words, all I hear is she wants me to get rid of every thought of any other man that has entered her here. Damn fucking right I will.

I rear back, and this time, without care, I slam my cock to the hilt into her ass.

"Fuckkkk!" she screams, but I ignore her and draw my cock back out, slamming inside her again and again.

"That's it, little slut. Take all of me."

Slam.

I pull back out. "I'm going to use my cum to wash away anyone else." *Slam.*

I slap her cunt hard, then press the heel of my palm against her clit. Her body tightens beneath me, and her legs tremble. "You filthy little slut." I spit on her tits, and when I slam inside her again, I fall forward. Leaning over her, I open my mouth and lash my tongue over her swaying tits like a man possessed, covering her in my spit. "Fucking slut." I groan as my balls draw up.

"Yes." Her nails dig into my hair as I piston in and out of her stretched hole. When she convulses around me, my cock erupts, firing spurt after spurt of my hot cum deep inside her ass while biting down on her tit. Marking her so boldly, the copper of her blood tangs in my mouth. Fuck me, that's hot.

My body falls heavily against her, drained but satiated. Exhausted but full of life. My balls empty but my heart complete.

"I fucking love you, Ava."

TWENTY

AVA

After coming inside me, Tate pulled himself from me and insisted on watching his cum drip from my ass before going into the bathroom to grab a warm washcloth to clean me up. Then he took a shower so if I want to suck his cock, it would be safe for me to do so. I couldn't help but giggle at his cheekiness.

We lie in bed on our sides, staring at one another, not a word being said, just a feeling of fulfillment floating between us.

"Tell me about your family, Ava."

My body stiffens, and Tate must sense the change in me, because he pulls himself closer, then drapes his arm around me and uses his thumb to draw circles on my back. My throat is suddenly dry and my mind a frantic mess as the panic inside me rises.

With his free hand, he brushes my hair from my face. "It's okay. I'll tell you about mine." He swallows and his eyes remain on me. And I swear I love him a little more for doing so. For taking the pressure from me, for not pushing, only guiding.

"When I was seven, my mom overdosed." My heart plummets because that's not what I expected to hear. Tate has a family, an important, wealthy, kindhearted family. "I found her." My hand finds his free hand, and I link our fingers together, solidifying our support for one another. "I was placed in foster care with the Kavanaghs." My eyebrows shoot up at his admission. "I was a little shit and acted out a lot. They put me in a boarding school." My body vibrates with anger, and a carefree laugh slipping from him tells me being at the school didn't bother him. "But it was the right thing to do, Ava. I was a little shit."

I shake my head, refusing to listen, annoyed with the Kavanaghs for essentially ditching their son in a boarding school. "You were a small boy that needed help, Tate."

He drags a hand through his hair. "Ava, they sent me to the best fucking boarding school. I had therapists, came home every holiday. And I was able to meet four incredible best friends that became like my brothers. They became my family while we were at school, and I pretty much got to bring them home every school break. They love my parents as much as I do."

"How bad could you have been?" I raise an eyebrow.

Tate winces. "I mean. I was about to set my mom's cat on fire. That was after I used it as a target for the staple gun." He winces. "Luckily, I had shit aim."

I can't help the laugh that bubbles up inside me. "You're kidding?"

"I'm deadly fucking serious, Ava. I was fucked up." He places a tender kiss on my hand. "Don't worry, I'm now the ambassador for the Cats Protection Service in New Jersey." He beams, his eyes seeping with truth. "I felt guilty, ya know." He gives a small shrug, and my mouth falls open in shock. *Jesus, he's serious.*

"Tate, that's really fucking bad."

"I know. Just saying, boarding school was a good thing for me." I nod in agreement, because Tate got so much out of what the Kavanaghs did for him, and I shouldn't have judged. I should be grateful for them helping him become the man he is today.

It's obvious he always wants to impress people, make his family proud, and he hates to see anyone hurt. He has a naturally protective instinct, and I love him for it.

"Tell me more about the guys." I nudge him in encouragement.

"Okay, so you've met Shaw. He's a stress head, he's been forced to marry a Mafia princess because he knocked her up." My lips part in shock, but he continues. "Mase, who you eye-fuck at every opportunity." He gives me a playful pinch, and I roll my eyes because we both know that's not true despite him finding me checking him out that one time. "He's married to a viper. She once tried to fuck me, then told Mase I tried to fuck her." My body coils tight, and Tate chuckles. "Don't worry, baby, I had it on security footage. Anyway, he's been trying to divorce her. It's finally moving along but something tells me she's working on something, she's too quiet this time around." He sighs, his jaw ticking in irritation.

"You'll make sure he's okay." I stroke his arm.

"We all will." He swallows hard, and his body bunches tight. "What happened at the office. . ." My lips move to tell him I only want him, but he rushes the words out.

"You're mine, Ava. I never want another man touching you. You understand me?" Relief floods me. As hot as it was knowing Mase was watching, it's not something I want to happen regularly. Not with so many of my demons always lurking in the back of my mind.

"What about Reed?" I ask, changing the subject.

Tate's body relaxes. "Reed is a lawyer. He has a stick shoved pretty far up his pompous ass, but he's one of us. He'd do anything for us and the business. He's fucking ruthless and demanding, and I kinda look up to him." My heart melts at his words. "He's also fucking loaded. But always seems to want more." He rolls his eyes.

"Then there's Owen, he deals mainly in the security side of the business." He scratches the side of his jaw. "A few times I thought he had a thing for my sister, Laya. But he insists it's just brotherly affection, him being overprotective due to us all having shitty homes, ya know." Agitation coats his features, his jaw grinds from side to side, his temple pulsates and his fists clench. It's clear he's still unsure of his best friend and sister's relationship.

"You don't believe him?"

Tate sighs. "I want to. I just have this feeling niggling inside me that there's more to it."

"Did you try asking him?"

"Yeah, when I was at my parents'. Laya told us she was married and pregnant." My eyebrows raise in shock. "He flew off the handle and stormed from the room. I went and asked him if he had anything to tell me. He said no. Shrugged it off as being concerned about her." I don't point out that he didn't really ask Owen if it was more than a platonic relationship he had with Laya. I'm not convinced he's ready for the truth behind that question, so maybe that's why he posed it the way he did to Owen.

"How would you feel if something had happened between them? Before her marriage and pregnancy, of course."

He scoffs loudly. "Pissed. He's my best fucking friend."

I stifle a giggle at his antics.

"Anyway, stop with the deflecting questions. I know nothing about before I met you at my parents' house. Tell me about you." His thumb begins the soothing circular motion again. My past before meeting Tate is easier to talk about than the one after, so relief floods me.

"Me and Todd, we've always been close. My parents were alcoholics, so I always looked after him. I enjoyed playing mom to him." I smile thinking about how I used to bathe Todd and take him food shopping with the change from my dad's pants pockets when he was passed out. Maybe this is why having a baby doesn't faze me. I loved caring for Todd and reaping the benefits of receiving his love back.

"You're gonna be an amazing momma." He beams back at me, filling my heart with a surge of love and hope.

"Then, one day, my dad took us out in the car." I swallow back the memory. "He'd been drinking of course. They both had." Anger pumps through me. Who the hell gets behind a wheel of a car drunk out of their head with their family? I shake my head at the memory. "I didn't say anything because my dad would get mad if I mentioned the drinking. So I stayed quiet. All I remember is the car drifting into the other lane and a huge truck headed straight for us."

"Jesus." Tate exhales, and sympathy oozes from his

eyes as his face etches in concern. Emotion clogs my throat. "When I woke up, I was in the hospital and all I wanted was to know that Todd was okay." Tears cloud my vision, and I chuckle on a sob. "He'd been screaming the children's ward down for me. I've never been so pleased to hear his whiney voice than I was that day." Tate laughs too.

"My parents passed away," I say with ease. "After they released us from hospital, they told me we were going into care." My voice catches on the lump in my throat. "They split us up, Tate." Tears spill from my eyes. "They took the only thing I had left in the world. They took him from me."

Tate pulls me against his chest, and I cling to him so tightly my nails bite into his skin.

"I've got you now, Ava. Both of you. And I'm never letting you go. Either of you." He presses a firm kiss to my head while hugging me with such love and affection I feel like my heart will combust. But no sooner does the love flood me than it gets replaced by the gut-wrenching pain that's followed me around for years, bringing with it a force so strong it takes my breath away.

I choke silently against the warmth of his chest while the tips of his fingers draw the tender, lazy circles on my spine, completely unaware of the storm brewing inside me.

Because when he finds out what happened after I met him, there's not a shadow of doubt in my mind that he'll take my heart with him.

Leaving me abandoned once again and my wings broken beyond repair.

TWENTY-ONE

TATE

Ava's soft hand in mine has me feeling territorial as I guide her through the crowd to watch Todd's football game.

We move to the top of the bleachers and sit in the center, the perfect view to watch the game.

The crowd around us is in full swing, with chants and cheers as the game begins. Watching Todd has my chest swelling with pride at how far he's come in his short life, and it's all thanks to his sister. Her hand rests securely on my thigh while my arm is draped over her shoulders. I glare daggers with a snarl at every guy that looks her way, yet she's unperturbed, as if she doesn't even realize the attention she draws.

Her wavy hair is pulled into a ponytail, elongating her gorgeous neck. I lick my lips, reveling in my bite mark, so every fucker knows she's owned, or maybe she should have my name tattooed there?

Her T-shirt is stretched over those glorious tits, and every time she claps, they bounce against the fabric and the piercing becomes more evident, and my cock jumps alongside them.

I lick my lips, trailing my gaze to the center of her thighs—the same thighs that shudder against me when she comes and lock tightly around my head when she thrusts her pussy into my mouth like a naughty slut begging for my tongue.

My hand travels over her shoulder, and I wrap my fingers around her neck. She turns to face me, I lick my lips, and her eyes widen, as if sensing where this is going. With my free hand, I stroke over her thigh, and she squirms as the hand on her neck pulls her lips toward mine. I part her lips with my tongue, seeking access, and lavish hers with my own.

"Mmm," she moans, spurring me on as my fingers rub the apex of her thighs. She stills beneath my touch, and I smile into our kiss, not caring about the spectators around me. It's dark, they're enthralled in the game. While I pop open her shorts, she lifts her ass to help me.

Pulling back from our kiss, my cock drips with appreciation at the heavy look of lust in her hooded eyes. "Watch the game, baby. Watch the game while I finger-fuck you." Her breath hitches in response. I drop my arm from her throat and tug her closer, then rest my arm over her shoulder once again.

Slowly, she turns to watch the game, then her eyes flick over the crowd, as if checking to ensure we're not drawing any attention to us. She settles back against the chair, tensing when my hand slips into the waistband of her panties, stretching them against my thick hand. She opens her legs slightly to gift me further access. "Good girl," I breathe into her ear, earning a shudder. Her slick pussy folds are like goddamn heaven on my fingers. I continue my delving into her little pussy hole, and a groan catches in my throat at how wet she is. Pumping my finger inside her, I use the heel of my palm to grind it against her clit. "Such a little slut for me, letting me finger fuck you at your brother's game," I hiss into her ear, and the fabric of my jeans rubs against the tip of my swollen cock.

Her chest rises, and she grinds down on my hand, pushing my finger further inside her with each pump. "You're my slut, Ava." I nibble on her neck, embracing the goose bumps that skitter out over her bare skin. "Mine." I sink my teeth into her neck, tugging on the skin. Her body coils tight, and I shove another finger into her sopping pussy, curling them, rubbing on that sweet spot that has my girl digging her nails into my arm. "That's it, little slut, come with my fingers buried deep inside you. Come, while I fuck you with my fingers."

Her pussy convulses as I use my thumb to circle her pebbled clit. "Your nipples are begging for my cum, Ava." Her breathing escalates. "Begging to be covered in my cum."

My eyes dart toward the field, and Todd runs for a touchdown, the crowd on the edge of their seats while my girl pushes against my hand, biting into her lip as I double my efforts.

Her mouth falls open, and a loud "Yessss," screeches from her lips at the same time the crowd erupts from their seats.

"Touchdown." I grin against her ear with a low chuckle, earning a playful slap on my shoulder.

AVA

"Todd played amazing." Tate grins as I buckle myself into the SUV.

"How would you know? You spent most of the game finger-fucking me." I smirk at him before pulling down the visor and checking my wayward hair. I puff it out, and with a huff, push the visor back up.

"Not going to lie, I'm pretty fucking happy he's staying at Denny's tonight." He winks at me, sending a flutter of butterflies to take flight in my stomach. "And I can still smell your pussy on my fingers." He lifts his fingers to his nose.

I wrinkle my nose up on a soft laugh. "You're disgusting, Tate!"

He throws his head back on chuckle. "What, you're my favorite flavor!" I squirm in my seat at his words, and I have to admit I love his taste too.

"My cock is rock-fucking hard and I have a wet patch." He glances down toward his cock, and I stifle a giggle. It's pitch black in the SUV, so he won't be able to see a damn thing.

"Poor, baby," I jest. "Do you want me to help ease your pain?"

His eyes flick to mine before darting back to the road. "If you're asking me if I want you to suck my cock, baby, that's never a question."

I unclick my seat belt and take great delight in the hitch of Tate's chest and the jolt of his body, as if realizing what I'm about to do. "Fuck," he groans while popping open his jeans. "Come and suck this cock beautiful girl. Let me feed my little slut." His words fill me with warmth and a sense of ownership. No matter how derogatory they may sound to some people, they couldn't be any more powerful to me. I'm his.

Leaning over the center console, I push his boxers down for his cock to spring free. He's right, it is wet, soaked, and my mouth waters to sample his reaction of me. "You're so wet," I rasp out as my fingers find his velvety length and trail over his tattoo.

"Yeah. I nearly came in my jeans." His eyes fall heavy, and he licks his lips while I slide my free hand over his cock and down to play with his balls. "Fuck, that feels incredible, baby." He grunts when my fingers slide over the tip of his cock, taking the precum with them. I trail my tongue from the bottom of his cock up and keep my eyes on him as I suck his swollen head into my mouth. "Holy fuck," he grits out, pushing his hips up to force more into my mouth.

One hand weaves into my hair while the other holds onto the steering wheel. I bob up and down, lavishing his cock with my tongue, and the sloppy sounds fill the SUV as he bucks up into me.

My hand continues to stroke over his balls, tugging them and dragging my nails over his heavy sack. "Fuck, baby. You suck me so good." I moan around him, reveling in the fact his muscles contract, as if trying to ward off his orgasm, drag it out. As I withdraw him from my mouth again, I push my tongue into his slit, then glance up to see his lips parted and his chest rising. "Fuck, that's it, little slut, lick that slit out. You're a hungry slut, aren't you?"

He pushes my head back onto his cock, and I gag from the force, but the pressure of his palm holds me in place. "Fuck, yeah. Choke on it."

My panties fill with arousal, his filthy words and aggressive actions turning me on further. Leaving my palm on his balls, I slide two fingers further down. His body tenses. "Ava?" I suck harder on the head of his cock, forcing his chest to rumble in pleasure.

"Relax, Tate." I meet his eyes, and he swallows hard.

"I haven't . . ." Vulnerability flashes in his eyes before he quickly masks it.

While pressing on the soft skin between his balls and his ass, he relaxes slightly. "Fuck," he hisses out.

Not giving him chance to think about it, I push a finger into his ass, and his body lifts from the seat. "Holy fuck!"

"Mmm, you like that?" I ask, swirling my tongue around his engorged head.

His eyes flick down to mine while I pump lazily into his hole.

He licks his lips. "Shut the fuck up and suck, you filthy little slut." He pushes my head back down, hitting the back of my throat with his cock. I slowly edge another finger into him. "Fucking Jesus." I pump the fingers together in and out, stretching the muscle surrounding his hole. "Fuck. You're such a slut for me, Ava," he grits out. I pump harder, and he slams up into me. "Such a fucking filthy slut. Fuck. Don't stop." The hand in my hair pains my scalp. The car swerves.

My eyes widen, yet his firm hold doesn't allow me to move. He thrusts up into my mouth again and again. "Holllly shit!" A tsunami of hot cum floods my mouth and drips down my chin. "Holy fucking shit," he repeats while swerving the car and slamming on the breaks so hard my body shoots forward, but his arm wraps around to secure me against him. I release his cock with an audible pop, and when I glance up, I smile at him resting his head against the headset, then his lazy eyes meet mine and his thumb catches the cum dripping from my chin. Love seeps from his eyes, and I swear my heart swells so wide I feel like I'm floating.

"You look so beautiful covered in me, baby." He smiles down at me.

TWENTY-TWO

AVA

It's been two weeks of bliss; Tate barely left my side until yesterday. He had to fly to New York on business, something he wasn't happy about doing. He said he didn't want to be away from me for another day and insisted I go with him.

But when I explained Todd had an important game, one I didn't want to miss, understanding flashed over his face.

He knows how much it means to both of us. Besides, he will only be gone for a few days. I tell myself this multiple times a day.

As soon as the whistle is blown and Todd's game is finished, he rushes toward me with muddy streaks on his face. I squeal as my younger brother picks me up and spins me in a circle. "Can you believe it?"

He places me down on unsteady feet. "Call Tate, I want to tell him." He nods toward the phone in my hand.

So, I video call Tate, and when he answers on the first ring, my heart swells.

"We did it, Tate. It was fucking epic!"

Tate blows out a deep breath. "Thank fuck. Congratulations, Buddy."

"Denny's dad said we could go to his club. Can we go? You're invited too, Ava." I glance at my brother's excitable face and can't help but nod. "You're the fucking best, sis!" The happiness oozes from him, and I beam with excitement for him and the night ahead. "I'll go and take a quick shower, then we can head home, get changed, and head over there, okay?"

"Yes, go." I slap a hand on his shoulder, pushing him away, and he jogs toward his waiting teammates.

When I turn back to face Tate, his face has transformed to pissed, his expression stoic and cold. "I don't want you to go out." The words drip from his lips in warning, and my jaw sharpens in response. There's no way I've spent my life being trapped to have someone tell me when I can and can't go out.

"I'm going," I grit out.

He drags his hand through his hair, his chest heaving. "I don't want you to, Ava. I'll take you out when I get home."

He doesn't get it, this is for Todd. "I'm going out tonight, Tate."

"Ava, I swear to Christ if you go out tonight without me—" I press end.

I'm going out tonight, whether Tate likes it or not.

Steeling my spine, I march toward my car, determined for it to be a night to remember.

TATE

She ended the fucking call. I called her back eight times before launching my phone at the wall. Then I worried I broke it. Which I had. Such a dumb prick. Luckily for me there's always a spare phone in our sister branch office.

After making some quick calls, I bypassed Owen, who I usually run to if I have an emergency, but instead went straight to our guy at the hangar, telling him to have the jet ready.

I can't believe how reckless Ava is being, knowing she has an ex she fears terrifies me, and the fact she still hasn't given me details on this ex has sickness rolling in my stomach. And she's going out, with a bunch of teenagers, to a fucking club. Without me.

My car pulls up outside the club, and I head straight toward the security guy. He lifts his chin, expecting me. "They're on the second floor, the girl is on the dance floor," he tells me. Fury manifests inside me, my shoulders bunch tight, and I crack my neck from side to side trying to ease the tension accumulating there. She's here dancing without me.

I stride through the doors, and it's like a weight hits me square in the chest, forcing me to reel back on the balls of my feet at the atmosphere surrounding me. My feet vibrate beneath me with the heavy bass of the music, and my senses fill with the sights and smells of the club, but what hits me is the fact I don't want to be here. There's no buzz or excitement that normally fills my bloodstream, there's nothing.

Until I see her. She dances close to Todd, her hips sway and her face is flushed, and for a moment, I can't breathe. She's like an angel. That sweet, innocent face of hers is full of happiness. But her body stiffens, and my eyes narrow when I realize someone is speaking to her. She shakes her head, and he turns with a nod, walking away, and it's only now I see it's Steve from the office.

Darkness fills me as my nostrils flare and my jaw aches from my gritted teeth. My feet move in her direction, and when I reach her, Todd grins, causing Ava to spin and face me.

Her cheeks flush, and she bites into her bottom lip while I take her hand in mine and move us through the crowd, ignoring her protests. I guide her down a corridor, then push open the fire exit, pulling her through it.

"What the hell, Tate?"

"Me? You're the one talking to that sniveling little prick, Ava." I spin her to face me.

She studies my face. "Then you saw me tell him I wasn't interested, right?"

My shoulders sag in relief but still, the thought of him sniffing around her infuriates me. "I don't like him around you."

Her head jerks back. "How can you even say that?"

This time, it's my eyes that widen in surprise. She's shocked by this? After she slept with him, she thinks it's okay for her to speak to him?

"I don't want you talking to him again," I demand.

A mock chuckle leaves her throat, and I glare back at her. "You do realize I have to deal with a tirade of women you slept with on a regular basis, right?"

My face falls and my body jolts. What the hell was I thinking? I breathe through my nose as reality sets in. I virtually parade women around my company that I've slept with all while I'm hung up on the one guy she's fucked from the office.

She crosses her arms over her chest, and I know she's about to hand me my ass, and I sure as shit would expect nothing less from my girl. "If you don't want me talking to Steve, then you do realize I expect you not to speak to any of the women you've slept with."

"Done," I counter without needing the time to think. If it means her attention is solely on me, then I don't need to consider it.

She reels back on her heel, and her jaw falls open. "Done?"

I beam back at her, pleased with her reaction. "Absolutely. I've no need to associate with them any longer. Have you slept with anyone else from the office?" I ask, dragging my palm over my jaw as I begin concocting a plan.

"No. But Tate, these women work at your company."

Her gaze roams over my face, as if trying to search for my thoughts.

Her words appease me. Knowing she hasn't slept with anyone else in the company, the possessive part of me swells with pride, and my cock throbs with a need to be satiated once again. So much so, my eyes leisurely trail over her body, and she fidgets from foot to foot.

My pupils dilate and my cock jumps at the sight of her skimpy red dress and the way it molds to her every curve. "Turn around, Ava. I'm going to fuck your pussy."

She sucks in a deep breath but wastes no time in spinning around to face the brick wall while I fall to my knees at her feet.

I push her dress up to her waist and tuck it into her panties while I push them to the side, allowing me access to her bare ass. Kneading her firm globes, I hiss when my cock spurts in my pants, begging for release, but I ignore it and concentrate on preparing my girl.

My tongue slides up the crack of her ass as I push my face into her. "Oh god," she breathes out, and my cock thickens to the point of pain. Slowly, I lower my zipper and allow it to spring free, unable to take the pain any longer and knowing it would only become worse with each swipe of my tongue. She pushes back against my face, encouraging me with a whimper, and then my fingers curve around to spread her arousal and circle her clit. "Oh god." Lust spills from her heavy moans of approval when I push my fingers inside her leaking pussy. Her fingers scratch against the brickwork, trying and failing to clutch onto something as I drive my tongue into her ass, flicking it over the tender bud of nerves.

"Fuck, my little slut likes to be fucked against the wall. Don't you, Ava?"

"Mmm."

"Such a slut for me." I slap her ass cheek, and she jolts, then a chuckle slips from my wet lips.

"Just for you," she confirms with heavy pants.

"Damn fucking right, just for me." I stand to my full height, gripping her hair in my hand, and tug her head back sharply so our gazes clash while I line the head of my cock with her pussy hole and surge inside her. "My slut," I confirm with our eyes remaining locked.

Her pussy pulsates and I pull my hips back before slamming them forward again and again.

Ava's face falls against the rough wall, and I kick her legs open further, raising her ass to give me a different angle to drive into.

My hand slaps her ass cheek, then I follow it up by palming her red globe before delivering another brutal slap that has her moan vibrating to my balls.

"Oh god, Tate. So good," she pants as I brutally fuck her against the wall. "So good."

I spit on my fingers, then move my hand toward the crack of her ass, and the sound of my punishing hips and our heavy groans fill the air of the alleyway.

I swirl my fingers in my spittle, then without warning, I surge two into her tight ass, she raises up on her tiptoes at the intrusion, and I fucking revel in it. "That's it, slut. Take them for me."

"Ohhh. I'm . . ." Her pussy squeezes my cock, my balls draw up, and when I rub that tender spot with the tip of my cock while driving my fingers into her ass at a rapid pace, wetness floods us both. Her pussy latches onto my cock, milking it for every drop of cum that spurts from my throbbing slit.

"Fuckkkk, Ava," I pant out in awe. My vision blurs, and my head swirls as my footing wavers, but her legs give out, so I hold her against my chest and our orgasms collide with a violent manifestation of pure euphoria.

As my breathing regulates and my hand trails over her beating heart, the enormity of what just occurred hits me, and I can't help but grin with pride. "You just squirted on me."

"Huh?" She looks over my shoulder with lazy eyes.

"Hold your dress up, baby. I'm going to clean you up."

She does as I command, her face falling against the wall again, as if struggling to find the strength to hold herself up while I pull my cock from her pussy and tuck it away. I kneel on the ground, taking in the stream of my girl's arousal.

Sticking my tongue out, I trail it up from her ankle, over her leg, along her inner thigh, and suck on her pussy lips, cleaning her.

Sen-fucking-sational.

TWENTY-THREE

TATE

"Tate, you need to get your head out of your ass. We need this contract. Besides, Ava has worked hard on this," Mase implores from across the boardroom table.

It's been three weeks since I moved Ava onto this floor where I can see her through the one-way glass, yet she still feels so far from me.

When she told me about her family, I hated her pain, but I was relieved when I dug a little deeper to discover that although her parents were drunken dicks, they weren't physically abusive. Yet something eats away at me at the fact she hasn't mentioned the guy she dated who scares her so much she's paranoid about her security. I bypassed Owen and contacted our security team; they've given me full access to her mobile phone records. When I discovered she blocked Steve after our first hookup, I was over the damn moon. No wonder he quizzed her in the club that night that sent me into a jealous, possessive rage.

And when she spoke up, arguing she has as much reason to be pissed if not more than me, it felt like someone had stabbed a knife in my chest. I was left with no other option than to relocate Steve's ass, along with thirty-three women, leaving our human resources department with the task of finding us new employees I haven't fucked.

But I can't help the sickening feeling that swirls in my stomach that tells me I'm missing something important. Something huge.

"If it was your woman modeling for the world to see, you wouldn't want her to do it either," I counter.

"I wouldn't give a shit," Mase grunts back. Of course, he wouldn't. I doubt he even loves his wife anymore. Hell, he'd probably cheer with joy if he had proof of her infidelities.

"Do you want the guys to know the reason you want to pull the contract? Because that's what's going to have to happen, Tate." I grind my teeth at the realization. "Not to mention, Griffin, the cock-sucking thorn in our side, is going to be over the fucking moon if we pull out as his competition. He'll see it as a win, that we got scared and handed it over on a gold fucking platter to him. Pun intended." The muscles in his neck protrude on his every word. It's not often Mase gets angry, but I've seen him in action before. I've seen him lose control once and it scared the shit out of me. There's a reason he's so stacked; he needed to vent his pent-up aggression out on something, and that something became a punching bag at the gym.

"I don't like the thought of other people seeing her like that," I admit, hating how vulnerable and lame I sound right now.

Mase's face softens. "I get ya, brother. But we need this contract, and with Ava on board, we have it in the fucking bag!"

My chest puffs out with pride at the mention of my girl's name.

"Like it or not, Tate. You're going to have to suck it up."

I fall back against my chair, letting my head drop backward with a thud as I groan dramatically.

"You're such a damn child!" Mase throws a ball of paper at my head as my office door swings open.

Shaw and Reed park their asses around the table while Mase runs through the plan for filming the advertisement.

"Why the hell do we have new staff?" Reed huffs out.

"Like a lot of new staff?" Shaw quizzes, looking from me to Mase.

"We needed a fresh new approach, a new mindset." I grin, mimicking Mase's words he not so long ago used on me.

He pinches the bridge of his nose, then tilts his head back toward the ceiling.

Reed doesn't miss the odd action.

"Don't worry, Reed. I'm sure there's plenty of new pussy available for you to tap."

"Mmm, I guess so," he muses.

"I think a shakeup is a good idea," Shaw adds, and all our eyes dart toward him at his sudden change in attitude. Ever since he married Emi, the guy has taken dedication to another level.

"So, Tate, are you going to the fundraiser for the Cats Protection next Saturday?" Reed asks in his usual stoic voice.

This piques my interest, and I raise my head. "That's next Saturday?"

"Yep." Shaw grins back at me with mirth, no doubt remembering the numerous tales of the poor kitty my parents had, and the guilt that has followed me around since.

I drag a hand through my hair on a loud groan, as much as it has me feeling better putting my money to good use, I hate having to go to functions where I'm expected to give speeches about something I've no actual interest in.

"Aw, of course he's going. He's going to be purrrfect up there, telling the city how much he lovveeed his parents' pussy." Shaw smirks at me, then bats his lashes, and I recoil in horror at my friend's antics.

"They're like fucking rats. The city is full of them." Reed picks invisible lint from his suit.

"You could be Tate's plus one?" Mase suggests, struggling to stifle a grin. I ignore his jibe, and my cock leaps with excitement at the thought of taking Ava to the event with me.

Reed's eyes shoot up, and he stares at Mase as if he's a piece of shit. "I have allergies."

"Of course you fucking do." Shaw rolls his eyes. According to Reed, he's allergic to almost everything. The thing is, we've never witnessed any reaction to these so-called allergies.

"Actually, I have a date," I announce with pride.

Shaw reels back in his chair, and his eyes narrow. "A date? Like a hookup?"

I grit my teeth. "She's not a fucking hookup."

Shaw's mouth falls open in shock while Reed's eyes

TATE

volley from mine to Mase's. Knowing full well if I had told anyone about my date, it would have been him.

Mase clears his throat, breaking the line of questions before they start. "Okay, so does everyone understand what's happening on set? Reed, you can sort the contracts, right?"

"Of course." Reed waves his hand like he's swatting a fly.

"Good. That's it for today, then, guys." Mase closes the file.

"How's Thirsty Thursday going?" Reed fires out while his eyes remain locked on me.

For the past year, we've had a bet on who can get a blowjob every Thursday, and the winner is the one to maintain it the longest. I take the title as the winner.

"Swimmingly," I counter with a grin.

Mase chokes on the chips he's stuffing his face with while Reed throws his head back on a chuckle.

"She swims in your cum. I like it." Shaw smirks.

Damn fucking right she swims in my cum. I wouldn't have it any other way.

"You do realize the point of the bet was to get her to swallow it, right? Hence the thirsty part," Reed drawls while swiping through his phone.

"It's not possible for her to drink it all. Unlike you, I have a very heavy load." I grin back. And hopefully a very fertile one too, but I'll keep that to myself for now.

"Fuck's sake." Mase's nose crinkles.

"I have enough that I need two women to satisfy and swallow me." Reed lifts his head from his phone, a smirk playing on his lips.

"That's because you're not satisfied, dip shit. You pay

199

two women to please you while me and Shaw have found the perfect women. We don't need more than one."

His eyebrows furrow, and he scrunches his face up. "I'm not even going to apologize for your choices in limiting yourself to one person."

This time Shaw scoffs. "Man, when you find that woman that can give you everything you need, you'll understand."

"Impossible," he breathes out before going back to swiping on his phone, probably choosing tonight's two lucky women.

Shaw turns toward me. "Tell us more about this girl of yours, Tate."

Absolutely fucking not. I push back in my chair, ignoring him.

"Where the hell are you going?" he questions.

"Swimming." I wiggle my eyebrows, and he rolls his eyes while I stride toward the door with one thing on my mind.

Filling my woman with my cum and ultimately, my baby too.

TWENTY-FOUR

AVA

Tate's gaze travels over me again, and the heat from his stare is so intense it consumes my body with a surge of arousal. It feels like he's eating me alive, like his mouth is drinking me in and his heart is beating purely for me.

"You look fucking sensational, baby."

Air escapes my painted lips in a subtle pant of need.

He leans over the bar and pulls out a bottle of champagne then he pops the cork, causing me to startle and the bubbles to flow over the rim. He lifts the bottle to his lips, and I watch on as his throat bobs, the motion erotic as the liquid spills from his mouth and down his chin. He gasps as he lowers the bottle, and our eyes lock in a haze of magnetism, then he swipes his hand over his mouth, and heat gathers inside me at the intensity behind his hooded stare.

"Fuck. You wanna paint my cock with those red lips?"

He strokes his hardened cock, and it jumps in his pants against his touch. "You wore red lipstick the first night I met you. A nice little red dress. Did you dress like this on purpose for me, Ava?"

My panties are damp with arousal, and my heart hammers as heat travels up my neck. I lick my lips and gift him with a small nod. "Fuck," he groans and jerks his palm over his hard length.

Unable to take it anymore, I move to the floor of the limousine, and his hand on the champagne bottle tightens till his knuckles turn white. He sucks in a sharp breath when I unbuckle his belt with fervor. Then he takes another swig of the champagne, watching my every move as he does so. With one hand, I slip inside his boxers, stroking over his velvety skin, and I use my other hand to explore his tense muscles beneath his shirt. When I glance up at him, his eyes are hooded and heavy with lust, and that alone has me wanting to please him all the more.

I stick my tongue out, deciding to torment him by creating a show of swiping it along the string of precum dripping from the tip and down the vein that protrudes the length of his cock. "Fuck, Ava." His knuckles whiten on either side of him as he grips onto the car seat, as if restraining himself.

While I caress his body with one hand, I use the other to jerk his cock up and down, teasing the head by sucking it into my mouth on each upward stroke. Tate hisses between his teeth when I drag my lips over his taut, solid skin, purposely leaving lipstick along the way. "Fucking Jesus."

He takes another pull from the champagne bottle.

"Mmm, you taste so good, Tate."

"Fuck, yes. Lick me, Ava. Suck me into your filthy mouth like my good little slut." Glancing up toward his face as I take his length into my mouth, I moan around him, embracing the unadulterated awe on his face while he watches me. His lips part as I work him in and out of my mouth at a rapid pace.

"Open your mouth for me, baby." His cock slips from my mouth with a pop, strings of saliva and precum drip from my chin, and I open my mouth as he commands.

He tips the champagne into my mouth, letting it spill down my chin. "I'm going to fuck your mouth now, baby." Without warning, he rams his cock past my lips, and I choke on the bubbles fizzing down my throat and the intrusion keeping me from swallowing. His hips thrust forward again and again.

"Fuck, that feels incredible." He pulls out. "Again," he pants out. I open my mouth, and this time, he leaves the head of his cock on my tongue and spills the liquid onto both of us. He hisses through his teeth before he slams back inside, and his eyes roll with rapture.

"Drink us both down, baby." His hips piston against me. "Mmm, fuck, I wanna come so bad."

I moan around him, desperate to take him all.

"Fuck, I wanna fill you with my baby. Fill your little pussy so bad. You want that, don't you, my little cum slut?"

"Yes," I gargle around his soaked cock.

He moves in a flash, tugging me back by my hair. "Climb on my cock, Ava. I wanna fill you up."

I rise while Tate swiftly pushes my red dress up to my waist, then his thick fingers push my lace panties to the side while stroking over my slick folds. As I straddle his thighs, he sucks my arousal from his fingers. "Fuck, you're delicious."

His hands grip my waist, and he slams me down on his cock, not giving me a choice but to accept him, every thick, solid inch of him. "Oh god, Tate," I pant out as he stretches me to the point of pain.

"Fuck, yeah. I'm going to fill my little slut with my baby." He lifts me, and I have no choice but to comply. "Fill you with so much goddamn cum, I flood you." He pants. "Forcing you to swell with my baby."

Pleasure builds inside me, my pussy clutches him deep inside, and with each slam on his cock, the head hits against that perfect spot. My hands tangle in his hair, and I pull him toward me in a messy, passionate kiss where our tongues fight for dominance.

I pull back first, breathless.

"Fuck, Ava. I taste good on you." He groans when his lips find mine again. My hands cling onto his shoulders as our fucking becomes frantic—me slamming down on him, him thrusting up into me—and when my pussy convulses, my body tenses and a surge of pleasure from my toes travels up my body. "Tate, I'm . . ." My orgasm hits me, rendering me useless while Tate chases his release. His cock pulsates into me and his face hardens with determination before it falls lax under his release, it sends another wave of pleasure through me while his cum drips between us.

Tate takes my face in the palms of his hands. "Fuck, I love you, baby." Then he slams his lips against mine.

A reminder of how satiated I feel, not only physically but emotionally too.

Tate leans over the seat and grabs the cork, and my eyebrows furrow.

"Lift your ass up, baby."

Slowly, I lift, releasing Tate's cock. His fingers scoop up the excess cum. "Fuck, I hate the thought of wasting it." He speaks low, as if to himself. Then his fingers press into my hole. "I'm pushing it back in."

Tate's eyes fill with lust, and he smirks, then I feel something being pushed inside me, and my pussy pulsates around it. "I'm plugging my cum inside you, baby."

I pull back to search his face, and my eyebrows furrow.

Tate chuckles. "How does it feel?"

My pussy clenches around the intrusion. "You put the cork inside me?"

He swirls a lock of hair between my fingers. "I did." His gaze holds mine, as if waiting for me to argue. "I want you pregnant, and I like the thought of my cum inside you all the time." He places a gentle kiss against my lips.

"You're mine," he reiterates.

All I can do is nod when his tongue swoops into my mouth, tasting the champagne mingled with his possession.

TWENTY-FIVE

TATE

I guide Ava through the crowds of guests, stopping occasionally to shake hands with donors or volunteers. The fact her palm is in mine as we head toward our table fills me with a sense of pride. Add in the fact her pussy is full of my cum and her panties drip with it, and I'm more feral than any animal in this room.

Locating our table, I pull out her chair for her, and she gifts me with a serene smile that warms my heart. Feeling eyes on me, I look up to find the guy sitting opposite Ava staring back at me with such intensity, I jolt. Narrowing my eyes, I scan over him. He's young, maybe early twenties? Bright-blue eyes that hold an edge of insanity to them, and he strokes a fluffy cat that sits in his arms, reminding me of the James Bond villain. Not wanting to cause issues, I gift him a chin lift, but his eyes drill into me like he has a problem with me.

"Hey, I'm Tate. Good to meet you." My ass finds my

seat beside Ava, and I tug her toward me, enabling me to drape my arm over the back of her chair.

The dude's face remains stoic. "I know who you are." His voice is deep with a threatening edge to it that forces me to take more notice of him.

Casting my eyes around the table, I realize everyone else is unaware of the weird interaction with the dude, as they're all enthralled in their own conversations.

A server brings champagne over to the table. "Ma'am, would you care for some champagne?"

Her cheeks flush red, and she fidgets in her seat. "Please," she whispers out.

I grin from ear to ear at her uncomfortable situation while the server pours her drink, then she raises the glass to her lips, taking a small sip. I lower my voice so only Ava to hear. "Ask him for the cork too, baby, Then I can slip that one in your tight little ass. Keep you nice and filled with my cum."

Ava chokes on her drink and I throw my head back on a chuckle. She elbows me, then I squeeze her shoulder and place a kiss on her heated cheek.

The feeling of being watched causes me to dart my gaze around the table, and I freeze when the guy stares back at me with calculating eyes. I scrub a hand over my neck, unsure of how to break the weird tension rolling off him in waves.

Ava clears her throat. "Your cat is cute. What's its name?"

His eyes flick toward Ava before coming straight back to me. A rush of reassurance runs through me, as it's clear his problem is with me and not Ava. "Pussy."

My mind whirls in confusion.

"You named your cat pussy?" Ava grins back at him with glee in her voice. "That's genius." Her face lights up with excitement, and I mirror her infectious smile.

The dude's lips tip up at the sides before he quickly masks it. "That's because I am a genius." He stares back at me, as if waiting for some sort of argument, and honestly, I have no fucking clue what is happening here. I'm lost as to what his problem is.

A server places our food in front of us, and the dude puts the cat on the table, letting it eat from a small plate. Fuck, Reed would break out in hives over this shit. Good thing he didn't come.

The dude's eyes remain focused on me.

Maybe I should just ask him what his problem is?

I lean over the table. "Listen, man, do I know you? Because I'm getting some vibes from you that I did something to offend you."

He smirks and legitimately looks like a serial killer. "You call yourself a cat lover. But you have no cats. You're an ambassador for a charity you have no interest in. You've consistently donated the same amount of money every year, despite the inflation our country is undertaking. You're a fraud."

My head rears back in shock. Oh shit, he's really into his cats and I definitely offended him. Ava's fork remains halfway to her open mouth. Then she flicks her eyes toward me. "You should increase your donation."

I nod in agreement, having not even considered inflation affecting the charity too.

"And you should take more interest in the cats or give the ambassador title to someone who warrants it." She points her fork in the dude's direction, causing his shoulders to swell. Clearly, the little prick wants the position. But I nod along to Ava's suggestions, impressed with how she read the situation so quickly and acted on it. Lifting my drink, I take a swill, smiling at how I'm about to get out of future events I have no interest in.

"And you totally need a cat," she adds.

I choke on my drink, sputtering it into my meal. What the fuck? My eyes dart to hers, and her eyes hold mine with sincerity.

Jesus, I'm getting railroaded into buying a fucking kitty when the only pussy I want is my girl's.

"I will assist you with the placement," the dude chimes in. "I have a knack for finding the perfect cat for the correct owner."

"Thank you for being so helpful." Ava smiles back at him, and she practically purrs with fucking excitement. My lips tip up at my analogy.

An ear-wrecking boom breaks out from the stage as some idiot hits the microphone. "We'd like to welcome one of our devoted ambassadors to the stage, for him to give an insight into his passion for our charity. Let's welcome Tate Kavanagh." The guests burst out into claps of support while my stomach sinks, reminding me why I hate these fucking events.

AVA

Tate walks onto the stage, and I grin to myself. He's no fucking clue about cats, whatsoever.

"He's no fucking idea about cats, has he?" the guy from across the table says.

I flick my eyes toward his and bite into my bottom lip, not wanting to confirm or deny his words.

"At least he isn't an animal abuser. Did you know that a lot of serial killers start off hurting animals?" I grimace on his words and shake my head while focusing back on the stage.

Tate drags a hand through his hair, and my heart aches for him. "So, I started showing an interest in the protection of cats, when, er . . . when I was a child." He moves from foot to foot. "I was placed in foster care."

Blood pumps through my body with nervousness as my pulse races with each word he utters.

Tate drags his hand down his face. "And what happened was . . . Well, I, erm . . ." The crowd glances to one another in confusion.

He tilts his head toward the ceiling in what is undoubtably the most awkward speech I've ever witnessed. "See, it was all a misunderstanding really . . ."

My whole body feels like it's being drained of blood. *Please don't tell them*, I implore with my eyes in a panic.

"I was in a bad place and I . . ."

"Jesus fucking Christ he's going to ruin his career." The dude whose name I still don't know pushes back in his chair, the screech echoes around the room, and all eyes follow his movements as he strides toward the stage with an air of confidence.

He steps up and stands beside Tate, then takes his microphone from him. "What Tate Kavanagh"—he spits his name like vitriol—"is trying to say is, his love for felines started when he was placed in foster care and found love and sanctuary in the support of his family kitten. And now, he'd like to show how much he appreciates such loving animals by gifting a substantial donation to the charity. Everyone, please show your support to our highest donation so far this year, ten million dollars from Tate Kavanagh himself."

Tate's mouth falls open in horror while the dude whispers something in his ear, then the crowd stands, and the room fills with applause at Tate's generosity.

When the crowd dies down, Tate heads toward me and downs the rest of his drink as he drops into his seat.

"Can you believe this shit?"

"What did he say to you?" I point toward the dude walking back in our direction with a smug smirk on his face.

"He said I owe him and be ready for when he calls in the favor," he grits through his teeth.

While my mind works as to what kind of favor he could ever ask Tate for, he takes a seat, then mine and Tate's eyes meet his.

"My name is Reece O'Connell, good to meet you both." He smirks.

TWENTY-SIX

AVA

I throw my head back on a laugh when Stacey Dover, a volunteer at the cat sanctuary, tells me about how one of the cats is a nightmare and everyone keeps returning him. He even has the nickname Chaos among the staff. Although, they try to disguise the fact and instead call him Blinky to prospective owners, hoping the cute name draws them in.

"I'm going to go back to the table, I'll catch up later."

"It was nice to meet you," I tell her as she leaves while I cast my eyes around the room. Taking in Tate at the bar, I relax and take another sip of my almost empty champagne.

"Nice to see you again, *Pet*." His voice sends a tremor of fear over my entire body, my blood freezes, and my mind goes blank, unable to cope with the recognition of his voice. I close my eyes, trying to control my breathing.

"That's right, breathe slowly. You know how much your panic angers me."

My eyes snap open, and when they find him standing close to me, I will my feet to move, but they can't. My entire body has shut down.

His fingers pinch into my hair as he pushes it off my shoulder, and my eyes close at his contact. The pain of his touch sears so deep into me I can no longer breathe. I whimper when he grazes the scar he was determined to leave behind. As if I could ever forget him.

The mental scars are far greater than the physical ones left behind.

My legs feel like Jell-O, and time has stopped. His gray eyes bore into me behind my closed ones. I can feel them, feel him, smell him, and I hate it. But I'm too paralyzed to move. Someone help me, please. I whimper but it doesn't reach my ears, and I realize, I didn't say it at all.

"Does my pet need punishing?" His thick thumb grazes my lip and vomit threatens to expel from me as I revolt against his touch.

"Mmm. You belong to me, you do realize. I still own you, Pet," he drawls.

"Get your fucking hands off her!" The connection and fear is gone when Tate pushes Griffin away from me.

And finally, my eyes open as his warmth embraces me.

He really is my savior.

TATE

I turn from the bar with our drinks in my hands, but when I see Griffin Snider close to Ava, I freeze.

My first reaction is one of betrayal. My stomach sinks at the thoughts of her speaking to him—the enemy. Does she still work for him?

But then as I watch transfixed at his movement and the way her body pales, freezes, and appears locked in some terror-like trance, I push the drinks into an oncoming waiter's hand and storm across the dance floor.

His thumb grazes her bottom lip, and her body shudders, her eyes close, and her face contorts in pain. I slam my palm into the prick's chest.

"Get your fucking hands off her!" Then I pull her against me, wrapping my arms around her while my heart beats rapidly, desperate to punish the scum that dared to touch her.

My gaze roams over Griffin, and the smug bastard straightens his jacket, then his eyes bore into mine. The gleam behind them is unnerving, a sadistic edge to his features I hadn't recognized about him until now. No, they're not just sadistic, they're dangerous, calculating, and demonic.

"It appears someone let Pet out of her cage. Tell Tate, how you scream when I discipline you. When I tear you apart." The sick words roll off his poisonous tongue in a taunt as ice slithers through my body at the insinuation behind his words.

What the actual fuck?

His words replay in my mind as I realize he hurt my girl. Fire burns through me, melting the ice in an instant as I step forward with my fist clenched by my side, preparing to unleash on the scum who dared to touch my girl with his sleazy hands.

But when her trembling fist tightens in my shirt, I stop myself. Her entire body shakes in my arms, and her heart races at an unbelievable pace, and I know I've no choice but to get her out of here. I bend and whisper into her ear, "Come on, baby, let's get you out of here." She whimpers brokenly in response, my heart constricts at the sound, and I lift her into my arms, not caring how it looks to anyone else as I hurry toward the exit while squeezing her against me.

Vowing to put a fucking bullet in the prick's head.

Because he doesn't get to touch what's mine and live.

TWENTY-SEVEN

AVA

Tate lifted me into the limo and asked the driver to take us to my apartment.

He placed me on the couch while he sat opposite me, watching me, waiting for an explanation, no doubt.

With his eyes on me, he drags his hands through his unruly hair as he sits forward on his elbows watching me, and concern mars his handsome face. I can't respond to a single thing right now. It's like my body has locked down, like I'm empty inside, unable to do anything but clutch my knees to my chest and rest my head against them.

Tate's legs bounce and he rubs the back of his neck as he blows out another breath. "Ava, baby. You're really scaring me."

The pain behind his voice makes me lift my head. It swims with emotion, fear being the biggest.

Not fear of Griffin, I can handle that. I'm used to it.

But fear of losing Tate if he hears the truth.

"I don't want to lose you," I whisper so low I hope he doesn't hear.

He kneels on the floor and takes my face into the palms of his hands, the tremble in them a sign of his concern. The warmth of his touch spreads over my body, like a drug treating an infection, pushing away from evil.

"I love you more than anything else in this world. Nothing you say will make me feel any differently about you. I swear it." His eyes implore mine as I shake my head. "But I need to know, baby. I need to know your demons so I can conquer them for you."

My heart fills on his words, and for the first time tonight, tears run down my face, splashing against his hands along the way.

"I told you, you'd only ever cry for me, Ava. Your pain is mine. Now let me be your cure too."

I nod in agreement while my mind goes back in time.

"I was seventeen when I first met him." I swallow hard. "I'd won a school prize for my design work and after I accepted it on stage, I was called to the principal's office."

Tate sits beside me, then drapes my legs over his lap, allowing him access to draw the soothing circles on my thigh.

"The principal introduced me to Griffin, owner of Flawless, and of course I knew the company name. But I didn't know him. He said Griffin had offered me a three-year design scholarship to work in his company." I choke. "I was over the moon, Tate. I got offered a scholarship at a prestigious company, me, a foster kid. One desperate to get her little brother back. I finally had the one thing I was striving toward, I had hope."

I swipe away the tears. "They said there would be

additional terms and conditions of the contract I'd sign. That the summer after my eighteenth birthday I would start working with him. It included living accommodations, food, everything." I shake my head at how naïve I was. "When he said I'd receive a two-million-dollar bonus if I completed the three years, I didn't care about the details of the contract." I shake my head in disgust with myself. "Can you believe how fucking naïve I was!" I bite out in anger.

My eyes meet with Tate's. "I sold myself to him. I sold myself to a monster, Tate."

Tate's body tenses. The circles stop.

"What the fuck do you mean you sold yourself, Ava?" he grits out.

A lump of emotion forces me to choke on a sob, not on his words but because his hand has stopped moving. My eyes flick back up to his, begging for his touch and understanding.

His shoulders drop. "I'm sorry, baby. I'm not mad with you, I swear it." His thumb gifts me with the soothing motion, and I relax.

"I would never leave you, Ava. Just know that."

My blurry eyes meet his. "Tell me, baby. Tell me what he did."

I close my eyes and take a deep breath.

My fingers find the scar on my neck and graze over it, finally feeling the freedom of being uncollared. Tate doesn't miss the action, and his jaw tics, as if understanding.

"I was his pet."

His head rears back. "His what?"

"His pet. I was his pet and he collared me." I choke.

"He put a fucking collar on you?" Heat radiates from him, and his body stiffens.

Struggling to spill the words, my throat goes dry. "A metal collar. It was tight, too tight, and it bit into my skin." I wince, my stomach churning as I relive the terror of realizing the drastic mistake I made when I walked confidently into the spare room at Griffin's apartment only to discover the hell I would have to endure to get my endgame. My brother. A whimper escapes me, lodging in my chest as I swallow it back down.

Tate grinds his jaw and presses circles into my thigh, as opposed to breezing over the skin. But he's still there.

"Shhh. I'm here, Ava. Always." He speaks softly, as if hearing my thoughts.

"I had to stay naked in the apartment all the time." Shame burns away inside me, and wetness coats my chin as my tears stream from my admission, the embarrassment. "I'd only ever been naked with you." The pain behind his eyes forces me to close mine to block out the hurt seeping into him, bleeding from me.

"I slept in a cage, Tate." My stomach revolts as I choke the words out, a flash of pain hits my chest at the thought of my own horror and the way the chains were used against me, constricting my air flow until I panicked that I was about to die. How could one human abuse another in such a vile way against their will with blackmail and a promise for a better life? "He'd humiliate me. He only called me Pet. I had to eat from a bowl on the floor." I grimace, turning my head to the side, as if that will help block that memory.

"He kept me in a cage," I admit in a broken whisper.

His nostrils flare in response, and he exhales deeply before repeating the action, then nods at me to continue.

"I had to call him Sir. When he . . ." I struggle to say the words, to get past the pain inflicted on not only my mind but my body too.

His body tenses, as if realizing my words, so I glance up at him, away from the reassuring circles.

"Did he?" He swallows hard. "Did he?"

"Yes. A lot. He . . ." I swallow hard and take a deep breath. "He raped me a lot, Tate."

He breathes in through his nose, his chest heaving and his body vibrating.

While my tears spill and my conscience bleeds, he continues his circles.

And because the circles haven't stopped, because his warmth still seeps into me, because he's still here listening to me, I admit the thing that scares me the most. "He let others too."

His body stills.

The circles stop.

"Others?" he spits, and I wish he could take it back. Wish the circles would continue. But they don't, and I can't breathe as panic takes over me. I want him to want me. I'm losing him, like I always knew I would, and all I want is for him to need me like I need him. I want him to fix my broken wings with a promise of forever. Flying so high, no one can reach us.

As my body is racked with turmoil, he lifts me, placing me on his lap. And those circles, the ones I so desperately need, grow bigger and bigger, stronger and stronger against my back.

Over my tattoo with the cage, the broken butterflies

waiting to be uncaged, and finally the ones that are fixed, freed, flying high.

"I got you, baby." He kisses my head as I cling to him.

"You're mine."

My heart soars free.

TATE

My heart thunders, causing my chest to vibrate in a hate-filled rage, the beat so strong it fills my ears with the whooshing noise as I try and fail to slow my raging temper.

While I knew there was something more to Ava's past than she was allowing me access to, I never thought of anything like this.

Her reliving her abuse made me want to vomit, but I shoved the feeling down. Deep down. I needed to be there for her.

I'd give anything to turn the clock back, expel her demons from her life. But I can't, and knowing she holds this past inside her, feels like hell already. How can I take away her pain? How the fuck do I put this right for her?

All I can think about is the horror my girl lived through. "You're a fucking warrior, Ava. Absolute fucking warrior, and I'm proud to have you by my side." I tilt her chin up so she can see the truth in my eyes. "So fucking proud, baby."

Her lip wobbles and her reddened eyes fill with tears, then her shoulders relax as I hug her tightly against me, vowing to protect her forever.

I lick my dry lips as I prepare my next question. "How many men hurt you, Ava?"

"I don't know." Her grip on my shirt tightens, as if panicked, and I hate that she feels this way. "A lot, Tate." She squeezes her eyes closed in pain, and I hate it. Fucking hate it! I suck in a lungful of air, trying to regain control of my body as fury burns at my veins, and the sensation forces my head to feel like it's about to explode.

"He made a lot of men take turns on me." A cry catches in her throat while my stomach rolls at the thought of what she went through, is still going through. "They laughed at me." Her hands tighten on my shirt. "They laughed when I cried." My heart breaks for my girl; how fucking dare they do this to someone?

"They laughed." Her choked sobs fill me with fury I struggle to mask. I grind my teeth, trying to rein in the need to storm from the room and hunt the fucker down to burn him to ash like the fire burning my veins.

I'll fucking show them. I swear to Christ I'll force them to pay.

Using my thumb on her spine, I circle it around her smooth skin, knowing she finds the motion reassuring, but also needing something to ground me too. Determined to stay strong for my girl.

I want nothing more than to tear the apartment apart and unleash the anger building inside me, but I force myself to sit and listen, determined to be there for her. All the while, I'm plotting each and every fucked-up thing I will do to the twisted bastard.

A humorless chuckle escapes her, and she swipes the tears again. "I'd had sex once before. I was just a teenager, ya know. A fumble in the back of a car. But that summer, with you." She opens her eyes, our gazes collide, and I suck in a sharp breath at the intensity behind her hazel orbs. "I wanted to give myself to you. Experience something I wanted. And I wanted you."

My mouth fills with bile, and I slowly swallow it back. My eyes brim with tears, and my heart shatters to a thousand pieces as the enormity of our summer together weighs heavily on me.

She knew she was walking into hell, and I fucking let her. When I knew something wasn't right, instead of doing the right thing and questioning her, I let her endure it.

I'm the reason she's been through hell. I'm the fucking reason she has demons and my poor girl's wings were broken. Tears spill down my face, and my lungs tighten as I struggle to breathe.

I was a coward. Too scared for repercussions, not fucking man enough to be what she deserved.

My stomach threatens to revolt, and I'm unable to move, my whole body no longer working as I crumble under the guilt.

This time, Ava's touch reassures me. Her hand moves to my cheek, and her palm circles my face, repeating the motion I used on her. How the fuck is she so strong? How the hell is she still by my side when I don't deserve her, when I let her down. My chin quivers at the thought. Failed her.

"You didn't know, Tate. Please don't hate yourself." I could drown in the pools of her tears, yet after everything she's been through, her feelings are washed away in concern for me. My heart stutters at the thought.

I swipe away her tears with my thumb. Looking down at my girl with her tear-flooded cheeks, her pained expression, and her wilted demeanor, I make her a promise.

One I intend to keep. "I'll slaughter the monster. I'll chase away the storm, and when it's all over, we'll fly together."

TWENTY-EIGHT

TATE

I left her in bed sound asleep. After instructing my security team to stand guard at her door, I ordered my driver to take me to Shaw's house.

My leg bounces all the way here, and when the security finally opens the gates, I will the car to drive faster.

The enormity of the situation has my heart racing. It's not lost on me that I need help. As much as I'd like to kill Griffin, I need to be careful and strategic. We don't know who else is involved, and with that in mind, I race toward Shaw's house.

No longer caring about disappointing my best friends, now it feels so minute and pathetic. I'm ashamed to not have admitted it was an issue before now.

When my girl was strong, I was weak, but not now.

Now I will be everything she needs and so much more.

The car barely comes to a standstill before I open the

door. Like an idiot, in an attempt to rush, I trip up the steps to their mansion.

I slam my fist against the door in desperation as I try to rein in my rage by breathing through my nose.

Shaw barely opens the door before I push past him; not giving him a chance to greet me.

My eyes lock with Shaw's, and his Adam's apple bobs while his gaze travels over me in concern.

His wife, Emi, stands in the kitchen doorway with her mouth agape. No doubt taking in my messy hair and scuffed clothes.

"I'll go and make us coffee," she announces, gifting Shaw a soft smile before turning toward the kitchen.

"Tate?" My head snaps toward Shaw, who tilts his head toward his living room.

As soon as he sits down, I throw myself down on the couch. "I can't do it anymore," I admit, licking my lips at the words about to spill from me. The secret I kept from my best friends sits heavily on my shoulders. I shouldn't have, not when Ava has been so strong. Straightening my spine, I raise my head with a new resolve and meet his eyes.

"I didn't know how old she was. I fucking swear it." My lip quivers as I prepare to go back to the beginning of how our story began.

"Do you need an attorney?" Shaw chokes out.

He opens his mouth to speak but the front door banging against the plaster has me halting the words on the tip of my tongue.

As Shaw walks away to deal with Emi and her brother, Luca, I take a deep breath and pull out my phone, sending a message to our group chat.

TATE

Me: I need help. I need you all at Shaw's house. ASAP.

Mase: On my way.

Owen: I'll be there.

Reed: Okay.

I sit back in my chair and lace my fingers behind my head while staring up at the ceiling as I wait for my best friends to arrive. Knowing I have backup on the way and that I'll have the support of them behind me, gives me hope but doesn't ease the guilt flowing inside me.

"Let me get this fucking straight. She just turned eighteen?" Reed asks again, and I pinch the bridge of my nose.

My eyes snap up toward his. "Yes. Does it fucking matter? After everything she's been through, you're bothered about me fucking her?"

Reed's body recoils, and he stares at me blankly. "You're clearly misunderstanding. I asked her age because I'm weighing up his offenses. I want to get the fucker on every damn one."

Shaking my head, I lock eyes with him. "I don't want him going to prison. I want him fucking dead!"

"I can help with that," a voice comes from the doorway, and all our heads turn in his direction. Standing there watching over us is Shaw's brother-in-law, a poignant member of the Italian Mafia, Luca Varros.

When Shaw explained his brother-in-law had unexpectedly showed up not long after my arrival, he didn't go into detail, but given his booming voice, whatever he had to discuss with Shaw and Emi, he wasn't happy about it. I was just relieved he didn't shoot Shaw again. Luca's known for a short temperament and a clicky finger.

"We're fine. We'll deal with it," Shaw snaps, glaring back at him.

They have a silent argument, staring each other down before eventually Shaw gives in, shakes his head, and turns toward us.

"Thanks for the offer, Luca." Owen stands and holds his hand out, and I watch in shock as he slides his hand into Luca's, as if knowing him well.

Just what the hell does our security do? And who the hell do we deal with?

My eyes volley from Shaw's aggravated ones to Reed's nonchalant ones, then on to Mase, who gives me a shrug.

"Very well. But when the time comes to dispose of him, I have a basement where you can take your aggression out on him, away from prying eyes." He stares back at me with sincerity, giving me no choice but to stand and shake his hand in thanks, then he gives me a nod before turning and walking away.

Spinning back to face the guys, I motion toward the door. "Fuck, he is intense!"

Shaw scoffs loudly. "Intense?"

"He's a good ally," Owen chimes in.

"Fuck yes," Mase agrees.

"Don't worry, Tate. We've got you." Reed's words force a pain across my chest, and I can't help but rub my fist over the offending area, my heart.

TWENTY-NINE

AVA

Soft kisses are peppered down my spine, and his scent wraps around me, bringing me reassurance and comfort.

"Tate?" I breathe out, even though I know it's him.

"Yes, baby."

"I need you." I push my ass against him for emphasis.

"Thank fuck." He lifts the covers and climbs out of the bed, removes his boxers to reveal his solid cock, then climbs back in. I flip to my back, lift my top over my head, and throw it to the floor while his hands scramble to tug my panties off.

Seeing the look of desire marring his face and the way his eyes are full of lust, leaves no question that Tate still wants me, and my heart skips a beat at the thought.

"I love you, baby." He lowers himself onto his elbows, his lips a hairbreadth from mine, and his eyes drip with love, and I find my heart constricting to tell him how I feel but for some maddening reason, I can't. As if sensing my struggle, he takes the option from me, crashing his lips down on mine before descending to my neck, where he sucks and nips at the flesh, and my hips pump up in encouragement. His cock brushes against my slick folds before he slowly slides his thickness into my dripping pussy. One of his hands grips my throat while he uses the other to hold my hip in place as he glides in and out of me. Each stroke feeling better than the last.

"You're mine, Ava. You own me and I own you."

My pussy seizes his cock, and his lips part beautifully. Then, as if not able to help himself, he tugs my piercing into his mouth and sucks hard while holding my gaze. My hand finds his hair and squeezes it tightly. My orgasm engulfs me, and my body shudders beneath him while his climax sends a rush of pleasure through me again. "Fuck-kk," he grits out as his cock pulsates deep inside, and his warmth spreads through my veins.

He pops off my peaked nipple, then scrambles down the bed, tugging my legs open wider, and I'm shocked when he begins lapping at my pussy. "Oh god, Tate. That's hot."

"Yeah? You like me licking your cunt after I just filled you with my baby?"

"Oh god!" I cry while my clit throbs under the stroke of his tongue. My hips thrust up to meet his face. Sweat coats my skin as I greedily chase another orgasm.

"Fuck. I wanna lick my cum out of your pussy, baby."

"Oh god. Do it." My chest rises with anticipation at the thought of him tasting our pleasure together. "Do it, Tate. Please. Lick your cum out of me."

His tongue works faster, thrashing around, and his

moans of pleasure vibrate through my body. When he raises his head and the arousal coats his face, I almost come.

"Open your mouth, baby. I'm going to feed you our cum."

His head travels lower, and he laps at my pussy hole with a loud primal groan that sends pleasure skittering through me, then my legs tremble with such force, he tightens his grip. "Lick it out," I encourage.

I can feel his breath escaping his nostrils as he pushes his face harder against my pussy. "Holy fuck!" I scream as I convulse around him.

He rises onto his knees, his face wet and dripping, then hovers above me while I open my mouth. He spits a stream of cum onto my waiting tongue while he jacks his cock in fast strokes. White coats his lower lip, and I itch to suck it into my mouth. "My perfect little cum slut."

Moving to kneel on either side of my head, he fucks his fist with fervor.

There's something incredible about watching Tate fuck his hand with aggression. The way his taut muscles struggle to move, sweat drips from his forehead, and the lower V constricts with each pump.

"I want to face-fuck you so fucking bad." He shakes his head, as if dismissing the idea, and I hate it. Hate the thought of him being scared to use me how he wants because of guilt?

"I want it. Give it to me." His lips part on my words as his fist pumps quicker, then his precum drips in ropes onto my chin. "Force me to choke on your cock, Tate."

"Fuck!" he snaps, then grips my chin, parting my mouth. Sliding the head of his cock over my tongue, he pushes himself down my throat, and the action forces me to garble, but I breathe through my nose and allow him access. "Holy fuck. Jesus, Ava." The reverence behind his tone causes my clit to throb with need, so I rub my clit in time with his deep thrusts. "Fuck, little slut, you need to come because my cock is filling you, don't you?"

I moan around him, and he powers into me, forcing my teeth to graze his skin, but he doesn't flinch, just continues his onslaught. "I'm going to feed you again, don't worry. But don't swallow, okay?"

My eyes narrow, but I nod. Then he drags his length back over my tongue, leaving the tip resting inside my mouth, and repeatedly pumps himself in his tight grip. "Fuck. It's coming," he pants out.

Pressing down on my clit, I come while his warm cum fills my mouth, and with each repeated lash, it trickles down my chin and onto my neck.

With his chest still heaving and my mouth open, he sticks two fingers into the cum, moves my hair aside and paints over the scar on my neck.

The scar of ownership is now marked with his mark, and the feeling of his warmth seeps much, much deeper.

THIRTY

TATE

I glance around the studio again. My body is wrung tight, full of tension. Her soft hand grazes my arm. "I need to do this, Tate." Ava lifts her chin with determination, and pride fills me at the sight of my beautiful girl painted head to toe in shiny gold.

As she stands there in a color representing strength—and with defiance in her eyes—she refuses to bow down. She fulfilled her dream to gain guardianship of her brother, she came to our company as soon as her contract allowed her, and now, she stands with us. A force to be reckoned with as we go toe to toe with her tormentor, and she wants to be the one to take down our competition. She wants to be the one standing in gold when she wins us the advertising contract and show him she's still standing.

"I'm proud of you, Ava," I breathe against her ear, relishing the shudder that skitters across her skin as my words breeze over her.

"Thank you." She smiles back at me. I grip the back of her neck and pull her toward me, sealing my love with a tender kiss.

A throat clears beside me, startling Ava. "Where do you want me?"

My eyes travel over the guy almost a foot taller than me and twice as wide. His bare chest is chiseled, his muscles the size of boulders. And then it dawns on me, he's the male model. "Not a fucking chance!" I spit out.

"Absolutely fucking not." I waste no time in pulling my shirt from my pants and unbuttoning it. "I'll do it. Mase? I'm doing it. Send this guy home!"

I ignore the dude's shocked reaction and Ava's giggle as I motion for the make-up department to come over and help prepare me.

"You're insane." Ava grins.

"Yeah, for you!" I admit while the chaos of my actions sends the team into a tailspin.

AVA

I stand on the sealed-off street with the camera crew surrounding me. I'm wearing a thin, see-through dress and equally seductive underwear while being covered in shiny gold body paint. Breathing in deeply, I wait for the action call.

This feeling is euphoric; it's like giving Griffin a big fuck you. Showing him he didn't break me, not even close.

As the slate claps down, motioning us into action, a thrill of pride straightens my shoulders and I walk down the street with an air of confidence. My hips sway as I strut toward Tate, and our eyes latch onto one another's, the pull between us magnetic. Unbreakable.

I ignore everything happening around me and keep focus on the target in front of me—the man I love. My heart skips a beat and a desperate need to tell him so urges me on.

He stands from his table on cue and waits for me to approach, and when I do, the electricity between us sizzles. It engulfs me, like nobody else exists but us.

My heart thuds with every step, and when I finally reach him, he takes my hand in his, bringing it to his lips; at this point in the advert, his body will become gold at our touch.

When the slate claps down, letting us know filming has ended, Tate brings his lips to mine. "Look at you fly, little butterfly. You soar so beautifully."

He sees me.

My heart stutters and my vision turns hazy under his words, and at my stunned reaction, he tugs my lip between his teeth and sweeps his tongue against mine, and his hand tangles in my hair.

"How the fuck are we going to get through five more takes today?" Mase sighs beside us, and we both pull back on a chuckle.

"We'll manage. We're going for Gold, Mase." Tate winks toward Mase, who rolls his eyes at his cheesy joke.

Biting into my lip, I watch as Tate walks away to be painted in gold, his ass fitting his boxers perfectly, and I can't help but moan in appreciation at the sight of my man.

The man who would do anything for me. I need to tell him how I feel before something goes wrong.

THIRTY-ONE

TATE

My eyes roam around the room, and my body fills with warmth. To have Ava here, among my best friends, completes me, and even Todd has come along to Shaw's house for an evening of Emi's incredible food. We seem to be swapping our bachelor nights out for family-oriented ones, and I, for one, couldn't be happier about it.

Todd took off to Shaw's gym, so I make a mental note to ensure when I buy us a house, it's one equipped with a state-of-the-art gym, just for him.

Emi places little Eleanor on a playmat on the floor, and I watch transfixed as my girl lowers herself from her seat to sit beside her. Eleanor lifts her head up and smiles in Ava's direction, she smiles back widely while stroking over a tuft of her curly hair.

"Are you planning on having kids, Tate?" Shaw's voice snaps me out of my gaze, and I turn to face him while he nods in Ava's direction.

"Absolutely." I stare back at him with certainty. "The sooner the better," I admit.

Reed leans over the table. "You're not using protection?"

"I never have with, Ava. I'm kinda hoping she's pregnant already."

Reed's eyebrows raise in shock, then he shudders. "Jesus, that would be my worst nightmare." We all laugh at his words. It would be his worst nightmare. I can't even imagine how he would cope with the mess and chaos a child would bring.

"I want this too." Mase reaches his arm out toward Ava and Eleanor. "Always have," he admits meekly. I take in my friend; his face is solemn and disappointment laces his tone.

Owen slaps him on the back so hard his body jolts. "You need the right woman. You'll find her."

I break the mood that's quickly becoming depressive for Mase. "Yeah, but first, he needs to enjoy himself. You need to order a bunch of Indulgence girls and fuck your way through them. Get some experience outside of your old mundane sex life before you find the right girl to settle down with."

"I couldn't agree more." Reed smiles, which is a rarity for him, and based on the glances we give one another, we're all thinking the same.

"How about you, Owen. Do you want kids, the family thing?" Shaw poses the question, and Mase looks over at Eleanor with longing.

"Of course. I don't care how I get it either. But I'm determined to." He takes a drink of his beer.

"Meaning what? You'd knock any girl up for a kid?" Reed stares at him dumbfounded.

Owen's eyes snap toward his and he holds them, the sharpness of his stare has me realizing the seriousness behind his words. "No. Of course not. What I'm trying to say is, if she's already got a kid, I'm fine with that. I'll take hers on and bring them up as my own. That's what I mean when I say I don't care how I get it."

My friend's words hit me hard and prove the kind of man he is. He's admirable and loyal, whoever ends up with my best friend will be lucky to have him.

I just hope she's as deserving.

"Any news on him?" I bite out, referring to Griffin.

Owen stares back at me. "No. He's disappeared. I have a team on the lookout for him and in the meantime, security is aware and monitoring Ava's every move."

"He couldn't just disappear. He's planning something, I can feel it." My chest heaves under my admission. "I just want to keep my family safe, Owen."

His stare never wavers. "We won't let anything happen to them, Tate."

"None of us will," Mase adds.

Their words should reassure me but an unsettled feeling lodges in the pit of my stomach that I can't seem to shift.

AVA

Helping Emi dress Eleanor, I giggle at the cute little bubbles she blows in my direction.

The nursery is pretty and pink, she has a closet full of clothes, wicker baskets overflow with toys, and she has the prettiest frilly comforter. And most important, she has parents that love her, cherish her, and would do anything for her. My heart swells thinking about being able to provide this for my own child.

Being able to give everything Todd and I never had.

"It's really nice to have a friend. Thank you for coming over."

Her words are sweet, like her, and as I take in her wavy hair and dark eyes, I see a little sadness behind them, I can't help but wonder what her story is, what her demons are. Because we all have them. Some people hide them better than others, some break, and some wear them with pride.

"I lost a sister, so it's nice to have interaction with

someone similar in age to me," she adds, then glances away as her cheek pinken.

A lump lodges in my throat. "I'm sorry." The words don't seem enough, so I offer the only thing I have to give, friendship. "We could swap numbers and do this as a regular thing?" I suggest, her head darts up to face me.

Her eyes glimmer with hope, and I practically feel the excitement radiating from her. "Really? That would be amazing. Although, I have Eleanor and . . ." She places a hand on her stomach, then quickly moves it away.

"It's okay." I shrug. "I love babies."

"You do?" Then she laughs. "You might feel differently if you were expecting one." She sighs. "Honestly, my boobs hurt. I get horny all the time, and I wanted to eat at such random times and weird things too. That's when I felt like eating of course, early on I couldn't stomach anything at all. Which upset my brother; he's a controlling jerk and expected me to eat every meal that was placed in front of me, whether I threw my guts up or not." She scoffs, making me laugh.

As she continues telling her experience of pregnancy, my pulse races, I zone out, and a sudden need to speak with Tate overwhelms me.

"Ava, are you okay? You've gone a little pale."

"I need to speak with Tate." Her eyes flick over me, and she nods, as if understanding.

"Come on, you can talk in the spare room." She lifts Eleanor to her hip, and I follow behind her.

Opening a bedroom door, I walk inside, and she bypasses me and goes into what I imagine is the bathroom before reappearing a few seconds later. "Everything you need is in there. I'll go grab Tate for you. Take as long as you like." She winks and closes the door behind me while I spin around the room in confusion.

THIRTY-TWO

AVA

Biting my nail, I open the door to the bathroom, and there, sitting on the counter, is a pregnancy test. My blood races at the sight, and I stand frozen, unable to move. Transfixed at the white packaging of the stick that determines my future, our future.

"Baby, is everything okay?" Tate's voice slices through the room in concern, and I spin to face him. His gaze travels over me, as if looking for something wrong, then when he finds nothing, he casts his eyes over my shoulder. The moment his eyes lock on to the pregnancy test, his body stills and his breathing increases.

"Are you?" He licks his lips. The way his eyes are full of expectation and hunger causes me to squirm under his scrutiny with need.

"I don't know yet," I whisper while placing my hand over his beating heart. The heavy thud grounds me, and when he places his hand over mine, I know I'm grounding him too.

"We should use it now," he says, and our eyes remain locked.

Taking a deep breath, I step back and turn to the packaging. Giving it a quick read, I get the gist; you pee on the stick and wait two minutes for the result.

"Do you want to . . .?" I wave my hand toward the door, asking him if he wants to wait outside.

His eyebrows furrow and his nose scrunches up. "Fuck no. I want to be here. It's my baby too."

I stifle a giggle at his response. "We don't know yet . . ."

Tate shrugs. "If there isn't one in there now, there will be soon. I want to watch you swell with my baby so fucking bad, Ava." His palms find my stomach, then he pops open my jean shorts, and lets them pool at my feet.

My panties dampen even more as he drops to his knees. His hands trail up my legs to my hips, and he takes the top of the thin lace panties and slowly drags them down to my ankles. Then he helps me slip out of them and the shorts, shoving them to the side with a grunt as if they offended him.

When he stands, his cock is rock hard, a steel length pressed toward his waistline that has my mouth watering. Heat radiates from his muscular body, and I want nothing more than to relieve him of his discomfort.

He takes the test from me and points toward the toilet while he scans over the instructions.

I sit down, waiting for him to pass me the test. He opens his mouth and bites into the packaging, tugging it with his teeth, and the act somehow feels seductive, reminding me of the way his lips tug at the flesh of my skin, or the way his teeth sink into me to mark me.

When Tate kneels between my legs, my heart races. His thick palms trail up my legs languorously slow, as if he's taking in every second as much as I am.

His touch sends a skitter of goose bumps over my body, and I fidget under his heady gaze. "Open up nice and wide, baby."

I straddle the toilet, a little stunned at how a simple pee on the stick is turning into something so much more.

Tate licks his lips, then with one hand holding my thigh open, he uses the other to place the stick between my legs. "Go on, baby. Pee on the stick." The warmth of his breath hits my waist.

His eyes are locked on my pussy, and I tangle my fingers in his hair, needing to feel the connection.

My bladder opens slowly, releasing a small trickle. "Good girl, such a good girl for me, Ava." I whimper, and my bladder fully opens. A fast stream leaves me, no doubt splashing against Tate as much as the stick, but he doesn't so much as flinch.

"Such a good girl," he coos, stroking over my thigh as the steady flow ends.

He leans over and pulls some toilet tissue off before returning to face my pussy. I move to take it from him, but he bats my hand away and wipes me gently.

"Tate?" I breathe out.

He clears his throat, stands to his feet, and gifts me with his hand to pull me up. I follow him over to the counter where he places the test. Turning on the tap, I rinse my hands. Tate presses his chest to my back and takes my hands in his, soaping us both up while our eyes lock on one another's in the mirror.

"What made you think you might be pregnant?" he whispers against my ear, sending a shiver down my spine.

"Emi, was telling me some symptoms."

"Have you missed your . . . you stopped bleeding? That's a sign, right?" I chew on my lip to stop myself from laughing at his ridiculous and almost clueless question.

Shaking my head, I reply, "I'm not regular anyway. But I haven't bled since we first had sex."

His pupils dilate and his heart thuds against my back.

"Before you, I had two periods, and it was months since the last time I had sex. And I always use protection."

He swallows against my face. "You belong to me, baby."

My body melts against his when he removes my hands from the water and dries them with the hand towel.

"My tits ache a lot," I murmur.

His hands lift my top over my head, then drop it to the floor. He presses his hard cock against my ass, and I push back against him in encouragement. Then he unclips my bra and lets it fall away.

Our eyes remain locked in the mirror as his large palm skirts over my stomach, caressing it in circles. His pupils are blown wide, and his lips part as his tongue sneaks out and flicks over his top lip before tugging it into his mouth. I sigh when he palms my heavy breasts tenderly and his thumbs give a gentle flicker over my peaked nipples. "Will you feed our baby from your tits, Ava?" My clit throbs, and arousal drips down my thigh.

"Oh god," I push back against him.

"Will you feed me too?" He presses my tits together,

but his usual brash roughness is banished with a feeling of tenderness, a feeling of wonderment as he explores my nipples.

"Yes," I breathe out heavily.

"Such a good girl, for me. Will you still be my slut too?"

Pleasure builds inside me, and once again, I push against the heavy ridge of his cock.

He chuckles. "Fuck, you need my cum, don't you?"

Then he tweaks my nipples. "Yes." I moan, throwing my head back onto his shoulder.

Tate moves quickly, unbuckling his jeans, then kicks my feet apart and lifts my ass slightly. The head of his cock sits at my pussy hole, and I watch in the mirror as he grips his fingers in my hair, wraps it around his fist, then tugs my head back so I hit his shoulder. He slams into me, and my body jolts at the sudden intrusion. He powers into me while placing tender kisses up my neck, a contrast to the way his cock powers inside me.

"Beg me to fill you," he grits out. "Beg me to fill your slutty cunt."

"Ple . . . please fill me with your cum." I moan as pleasure zings through my veins like electricity.

"You're so fucking wet, baby. So wet for my cock." His teeth nip at the flesh of my neck. With one hand wrapped around my hair and the other toying with my piercing, I freefall around him, my pussy seizing his cock in a smoldering grip.

"Fuck, that's it, little slut. Come for me. Come on my cock." I convulse.

He bites into his cheek while my orgasm takes over; it's

obvious he's trying to hold back, and I thrive on his attempt to restrain himself.

"Give me your baby, Tate. Fill my hole with your cum."

"Motherfucker!" he bellows as his cock throbs deep inside me. I close my eyes at the impact of his orgasm and the way he pinches my nipple while forgetting the tenderness. The way he bites into my skin sends a wave of rapture through me, sending me floating so high, I never want to land.

"Fuck, I love you," he breathes against me. I palm his cheek, hoping the love seeping from my eyes, boring into his, will be enough to appease him. His lips tip up at the side, and he chuckles, as if amused by my inner struggle.

Then he pulls his cock from me, and his cum slides down the inside of my thighs. I watch through the mirror as he sinks to the floor. "I need to clean my pregnant girl up," he murmurs, and my heart stutters on his words, hoping above all hope I am pregnant. His wet tongue glides over my leg, lapping at our combined juices, and the vibration of his groan of approval causes me to clench my thighs. Tate chuckles, using his thick palms to spread me open further. I bend over the counter while he spreads my ass cheeks and presses his face into me, dipping his tongue into my pussy, then gliding it over my ass.

"Fuck, Tate."

He smiles against me. "We taste delicious together, baby."

I groan when his hands fall from me and he moves to stand. "Don't worry. I'm going to spend all night tasting you." His hand finds my stomach, and our eyes lock on one another. "Let's get dressed." He nods toward the white stick resting on the counter, then zips himself up and helps me into my clothes. We don't speak as the atmosphere between us feels metamorphic. A peacefulness that is simmering, about to spread into something so immense my body vibrates with anticipation. Tate reaches for my chin, tilting it up to face him.

"Are you ready?"

My tongue feels heavy, and I struggle to formulate words, and the tremble in his touch only adds to my heightened nervousness. He wants this so bad— me and our baby.

I only hope I don't disappoint him.

"I'm ready," I blow out with as much confidence as I can muster.

"I love you." He pecks my lips and turns, grabbing the test from the counter with shaky hands, his body stills, and I suck in a sharp gasp waiting for the result. And when he spins to face me, his expression almost brings me to my knees.

Pure unadulterated exhilaration.

I'm stunned to silence.

"You did it, baby." He takes my cheeks into the palms of his hands. His grin so wide my whole body revels in it.

Our lips meet and our tongues tangle.

I've never felt so damn happy, loved, and cherished.

So, when he pulls back from me with such happiness in his eyes, why does a sickening feeling wash over me?

I grip the counter with one hand, and Tate is completely unaware of my internal panic as he beams brightly at the test in his hand.

Closing my eyes, I breathe through my nose, but for the first time while in Tate's presence, I see Griffin staring back at me with his sinister smile.

My hand finds my stomach, already protecting the little one growing inside me.

Will I ultimately be able to protect my baby too? Panic swirls deep inside me with the familiar feeling of dread. The feeling that something is brewing, that something awful is going to go wrong and ruin it all.

Ruin us, and finally break my wings beyond repair.

THIRTY-THREE

TATE

The past few weeks have been fucking blissful, and I couldn't be happier. The advertisement for the Gold contract is in the fucking bag. After seeing it, we all agreed it's our best work yet, and it's all thanks to Ava.

In a week's time, we'll present the advertisement in the bid to secure the contract.

Ava and I went to the doctor together earlier and discovered she's almost nine weeks pregnant. I dropped her off at her apartment to relax, then tonight I will take her out to dinner, where I plan on showing her the portfolio of the house I purchased for us.

We spend our nights together at her apartment, usually reading the baby books and fucking, then I feed her, and we fuck some more.

She hasn't told me she loves me yet, and honestly, she doesn't need to. I can feel it in her touch, the way her eyes linger on me, and the way her heart beats faster in my presence. Every small detail of her I drink in and analyze. If I could go back in time and say when we first fell in love, it would be the night we met.

That's why I struggled to let her go, struggled to have only one night with her, not when I could have more, and went on to. The hole left behind in my heart that day I left my parents' home was never filled.

Until she stood up in front of my colleagues like the warrior she is and fought for what she believed in.

There is no way I am letting her go again.

Ever.

But never in my wildest dreams did I expect it all to be so easy, for all the pieces to fit together so perfectly, they fill that hole and make it complete.

Make me complete.

And nothing will change that.

SHAW

"You're certain?" I ask Owen as he drags the palm of his hand across his face with a heavy sigh.

"I am."

"Fuck!" Mase throws down his pen, then jumps to his feet at the information Owen provided us with.

"Motherfucking fuck!" He slams his fist into the wall, shocking us all with his aggressive outburst, completely unlike him. When he turns to face us with his chest heaving and blood dripping from his fist, he exhales loudly. "How the fuck are we going to tell him this?" he spits. His face is etched in worry and, no doubt, pain, given how he's rubbing over his knuckles with a wince.

"It's a fucking mess," Reed agrees.

Owen stares ahead at the laptop, his shoulders bunched tight at the evidence before us. "It's going to hit him deep, but he needs to deal with it."

My stomach flips while I consider how my best friend will feel about being betrayed. And not only that, but how he will deal with the aftermath with a baby on the way too.

What I do know, we have his back.

We will all support him by doing whatever it takes.

TATE

My office door opens and my head darts up when all my best friends fill the room. Owen locks the door behind him, causing my eyebrows to furrow.

I watch on as each of them pulls a chair around my desk. My eyes flick over toward Mase, and sympathy oozes from him before he quickly glances away, and a slither of unease rushes through me. Just what the hell is happening?

"Is Ava okay?"

"She's fine. Security informed me five minutes ago she was still in her apartment," Owen replies coolly.

But his words do nothing to appease me, because why the fuck would he be checking up on my girl?

"Why are you checking up on her?" I bite out, and Shaw winces.

Anger floods my veins that my friends know something I don't.

"Is this to do with Griffin?" Blood pumps wildly through me at the mention of his name on my tongue.

"You're not going to like what I show you." Owen nods toward the laptop, and the air is stolen from my lungs at the sight before me.

THIRTY-FOUR

AVA

After seeing our baby on the screen, Tate took my hand in his and placed delicate kisses over my fingers in gratitude.

The love swimming between us was on the screen for us to see. Our future, the one we've both always dreamed of.

He returned me home and filled me with his cum before promising to sign off on a contract and finish work early to take me out to dinner. The passion behind his eyes sent a flurry of excitement through me.

So I spent the afternoon pampering myself. A lazy bath first, where I shaved myself bare before washing and blow drying my hair and moisturizing with the cherry lotion I know sends Tate wild.

When the apartment door clicks, my body jolts, and I swallow thickly at a sudden nervous ball gathering in my chest at knowing Tate wouldn't be home just yet.

Taking a deep breath, I tell myself to stop being so stupid, that my paranoia has reached ridiculous heights, especially with the security Tate put in place for me.

I tug my arms through the sleeves of the bathrobe and step out into the living area, coming to a standstill when Tate's blue eyes meet mine and the intensity behind them is damning.

My chest tightening restricts the air trying to flow through it, and my legs feel like Jell-O at the glare of hatred radiating toward me.

"T-Tate?" My voice is trembly and weak, a complete contrast to the usual me.

Venom spills from him, his fists are balled tight beside him, and he looks past me, as if unable to look at me.

"Tate?"

Every cell of him vibrates with anger, so I take a step back. For a split second, hurt flashes in his eyes before he masks it with a well-practiced ease that has me wondering what else he could be hiding from me.

"Did you think I wouldn't find out?" he spits, tilting his head away from my searching eyes.

"What are you talking about? What's wrong?" I step forward, but he holds his hand up to halt any further movements.

"As if you don't know." He lifts his head to face me with fire behind his stare. Rage pulsates from him, hate even, causing me to choke on a sob trapped in my throat.

"I . . . I . . ." Words escape me as my mind whirls with what could be wrong. What I should know but clearly don't.

But he doesn't see it. Whatever he thinks he knows, he believes it, and that has pain lancing through my heart, tearing into it with such strength I struggle to remain standing. My palm finds it to reassure myself that it still beats. And it does, thudding heavily under his scrutiny.

"I'm not sure."

"Not sure? Not fucking sure, Ava?" he bellows. My lip wobbles in response; he's never spoken to me like this. Never. This isn't the Tate I know, this isn't the man I've fallen in love with.

This man, I don't recognize.

I broaden my shoulders, prepared to fight for answers, prepared to fight for my man. "Tate. Tell me what's happening."

His tongue creeps out over his top lip, as if calculating his next move. "What's happening is, you got found out."

I reel back on the balls of my feet, but he doesn't give me time to process what could be happening before more venom spills from him. "What happened is, Flawless sent their advertisement in." I nod, following what he's saying. "A replica of our fucking advertisement, Ava."

Panic floods me at the thought of them receiving the same advertisement as the one we have created. "That's not possible," I mumble, stupefied at how this could've happened.

"Oh, I can assure you it did happen. And I can also tell you, they won the fucking contract before they even saw ours!" he spits.

My head swirls, trying to create sense of it all. How the hell did this happen? Every person on that set is tied in with an NDA.

"You know what else we discovered?"

"We have a mole," I add, knowing this is the only way for them to replicate my idea. My mind starts working through the faces of colleagues, searching for something they might have done or said that should have raised suspicion, but I find none. I open my mouth to tell him so . . .

"Save your breath, Ava. I know it was you." I suck in a sharp, sickening breath at his accusation, rendered powerless to confirm or deny. I stand there, breaking slowly inside at the thought of him even considering I could do this to him. To us.

My head falls forward in defeat.

I thought I was building a future. I thought I finally had my family. I thought my wings were finally fixed.

It was all a myth—a cruel, twisted, plan to give me hope. When ultimately there is none. Ultimately, I was born to always be broken.

"Owen used our security to trace where the files were sent from. You know what I discovered?"

I shake my head as tears stream down my face in hopelessness. His cold eyes bore through me.

"Here."

"No!" I shake my head in refusal. "I didn't. I wouldn't." I sob and step forward, but Tate steps back, taking a chunk of my love with him.

"We're done, Ava. Fucking done. You betrayed me." He drags a hand through his cropped hair. "You betrayed my friends, they're my fucking family, Ava."

My body jolts, because I'm his family too, aren't I? "I swear I didn't, Tate."

He grits his teeth. "I fucking trusted you!"

"Tate, listen. There has to be—"

He shakes his head while looking down, and a rage toward him fills me at how easily he can discard me. How easily he thinks I could betray him. Does he not know me at all?

His promises of loving me forever, that I'm his.

We're his.

I step toward him, preparing to fight him. Force him see.

He continues to step back, and I step forward, a battle between us I intend on winning. With tears spilling down my face, my chest aching, and my heart in tatters, I intend on fighting for us. Because whatever Tate thinks he knows, is a huge mistake, and I won't allow that mistake to ruin not just our lives but our baby's too.

"Ava," he warns.

I shake my head, refusing to listen.

"Enough, Ava," he snaps when I stand before him, toe to toe.

"Look at me, Tate," I plead.

He shakes his head and closes his eyes, blocking me out.

"Look at me and tell me you believe I could do this," I demand.

He doesn't move, nor does he open his eyes.

I place my palms on either side of his face, bringing my lips a hairbreadth from his. "Please look at me. I swear I didn't do this."

His eyes snap open, a tear drips from his eye onto my hand, and the coldness of its touch sends a shock through me I wasn't expecting.

"Don't make me do this, Ava." The pain behind his words causes me to pull back and fully take him in. "Don't force me to say the words you don't want to hear. Enough, it's over."

Determination sets in my blood, because I haven't been through hell and back to have all my happiness end here, on a lie. I was locked in a cage, endured torture of the worst kind, so I fought for a better life and fucking succeeded, I flew.

There's no way I will back down to a lie.

I straighten my shoulders. "I love you."

His body jolts, and a slow tremor works over him. His eyes glimmer with love and empathy, and that gives me hope, but when he straightens his shoulders, exhales, and takes my wrists roughly in his hands, then pushes me away, I know he's not about to back down either. He's about to fight too.

"You realize I could take this all away from you, right?"

I step back, unsure of what he means while my gaze searches his. He speaks with such disconnection as he stares into the distance.

"All of it," he tacks on, as if I'm not understanding his words. And truthfully? I'm not.

"Someone with your background, your history?" he spits like poison, which has my willpower crumbling. My chin quivers, and I hate how small I feel right now. That he'd use it all against me. "I could take it all. No baby should be bought up in a home that isn't safe."

I startle, and my whole-body stills. Paralyzed.

He steps forward. "I'm going to take what's mine from you."

My eyes flick up toward movement at the door, and I watch his retreating back as he walks through it.

Taking everything I had with him.

Our future.

As if in slow motion, my legs give way and I lower myself to the floor. Devastation engulfs me, and turmoil racks through my entire body at the heartache of his cruel words.

He's going to take my baby from me. I struggle to suck in air.

I'm not safe. My lungs restrict the airflow.

We're not safe. I can't breathe.

And I need to get as far away from here as possible.

Pain sears through my chest at the thought of losing him. "But I love you," I admit loudly through stuttered breaths.

THIRTY-FIVE

TATE

My legs give way as soon as I reach the end of the corridor. The room spins around me, and as I fall to the floor, my hand clings to the excruciating pain in my chest. It feels like something is being torn from me, and I'm unable to do anything to stop it. Tears burn my eyes, and my whole chest feels alight with flames of bitterness that she finally said those words. The very words that brought me to my knees.

Her distraught face flashes in my mind, and I squeeze my eyes closed, willing away the image of me letting her down again. I didn't want to do that to her, rip out her heart the way I did, and it kills me that I did it, but I had no other choice.

Of course, my girl wasn't backing down. She had no intention of doing so, and I couldn't be prouder of her, but knowing how strong and determined she is, left me with no other option.

Vomit fills my throat, and I choke it down while dropping my head to the floor as I try to stifle the wail threatening to spill from my lips. My hands grasp my hair as I silently sob into the floor.

Mase grips my shoulder and gives it a gentle squeeze.

My red-rimmed eyes meet his. "She finally said it. She finally said she loved me," I choke out in devastation.

TWO HOURS PREVIOUSLY . . .

"You're not going to like what I show you." Owen nods toward the laptop, and the air is stolen from my lungs at the sight before me.

Our advertisement video is being played out, but it's not Ava and me as the actors in the scene. No, it's people I don't even recognize.

"What is this?"

"It's Flawless's new advertisement," Shaw adds, making me rear back in my chair at the revelation, because what the fuck? That sick fucker Griffin has stolen our advertisement.

"Their winning advertisement," Reed tacks on.

Panic rises in my chest. "What? We have a mole?" It's the only explanation.

"No mole." Owen drags his hand over the scruff of his jaw.

My eyes dart around the guys, knowing I'm missing something.

"I traced where the files came from." Owen's stare

finds mine, holding me still at the power behind his words. "They came from Ava's apartment."

A chuckle escapes my lips. "She wouldn't do that. There's been a mistake," I bite out. The fact my friends think of her this way is ridiculous.

"You're right, she didn't do it," Shaw agrees, and the tension eases from my shoulders at his support. "Her brother did," he adds. My spine bolts straight and my eyes widen. Shit, Todd. What the fuck have you done, Buddy?

"There has to be more to it," I implore them all to see past his mistake. Whatever he's done, I can fix it.

"There is. You're right." Owen's Adam's apple bobs in an unusual gesture. He never shows emotion, so that singular action sends anxiety rippling through me with fear of what's to come next.

"He was being blackmailed." He licks his top lip.

"Blackmailed?"

Owen nods. "By Griffin."

His name on my friend's tongue feels like acid burning my skin and sends a fury through me like no other. I'm going to slaughter the sick fuck and enjoy every fucking minute of it.

"Tate?" Mase's soft voice breaks my sidetracked mind.

"Yeah."

He sits forward, and his eyebrows draw together. "What we're about to tell you is pretty fucking bad, man. But what we want you to do is even worse."

My nostrils flare on an intake of breath, and my body vibrates, so much so my knee bounces, hitting the desk.

"Tell me," I grit out, trying to fight the feeling of sickness welling inside me.

Mase opens his mouth, but Owen holds his hands up.

"Just so you know, there's no other way to resolve this unless you're willing to do it the right way." He means the legal route, and like fuck will I give him the chance to slither out of everything he's done.

No, he'll pay for his sins in hell. But first, he'll pay for those sins at my hands, and I'll deliver the piece of shit to the gates of hell. In pieces.

"He sent Todd videos and threatened to publicize them. Ruining both her career and yours," Shaw blows out.

My pulse races as I struggle to rein in my temper. "What kind of videos," I snap.

"The bad kind." Shaw grimaces.

"Of Ava?" My heart skips a beat in terror, and my mouth goes dry.

"Yeah, buddy, of Ava," he confirms with a softness that somehow feels alien to him.

My body tenses, each muscle coiled tight to the point of pain, and I suck in air thinking about what's on the video, and then a new reality hits me. One where I consider the fact my four best friends might have seen it, seen her.

"Have you seen it?" I fire out at them with malice behind my words.

They shake their heads, barring Owen who speaks up. "Only me. Only because I found it."

My shoulders ease slightly under his confirmation.

"I want to see." I turn to Owen. "Show me the fucking video," I demand.

"Tate, I don't think—"

I stop him. "You saw her. You saw my girl." My heart hammers. "And she fucking endured it. All because I was too fucking scared of my goddamn feelings and the repercussions. Now show me the fucking video!" I bellow, and all the guys jump.

Owen takes his memory stick from his shirt pocket and presses a button, transferring the files from him to me. Then he reaches inside his pants pocket and pulls out a set of AirPods. "You're going to need them." He tilts his head toward the guys, and my blood freezes, knowing I'm not only going to see something bad, I'm going to hear it too.

Placing the AirPods in each ear, I click on the file and watch as the screen fills. I grip the arms of my chair, sending pain radiating into my knuckles when I see the horror of the scene.

Ava is locked in a cage in the corner of a room with nothing inside, barring a metal-framed bed and sheet-covered mattress. Her despondent eyes latch onto the camera, and she stares straight at it, as if seeing into my soul. Seeing what a coward I was not to stand up for her. Not to act on the trepidation in her words when she told me she was okay. When I knew she was anything but.

I can't look away from her harrowing eyes, the way she stares is as though she's speaking to me, telling me her truths, her horror while I sit in my lavish office and fuck nameless women trying to eradicate her memory.

My vision blurs, but I refuse to cry. I don't deserve the privilege, not when my girl is so strong.

A noise sounds as if a bolt is unlocking, and terror flashes in her eyes, forcing my heart to pound against my chest so loud, I hear it in my ears.

"My pet is coming out to play." Griffin appears at the door. "And I brought my friends to play with you," he taunts. Terror washes over her face and she attempts to back away from the entrance of the cage.

My body shakes with rage. I want to scream; I want to cry. I want to turn back fucking time and put it all right. Sweat drips from me as bile churns in my stomach.

"Tate?" Owen tries to speak to me, sensing my unraveling, but I shake my head, refusing to give in and not see what she had to endure to get to where she is today.

Three more men enter the room, and my stomach plummets, taking my heart with it. And when he tears her from the cage and throws her onto the mattress while wrapping the chain around his fist, I swear a part of me dies.

A gut-wrenching sob escapes me when the first man steps up to take her. She barely breathes, and if I didn't know better, I'd have thought she wasn't conscious anymore. This frustrates the bastard, and he whips the chain back, her scream in agony echoes off the walls. I feel like my chest is being torn in two, like someone is reaching inside me and crushing my heart bit by fucking bit.

My fist finds my mouth as I blink back the tears and wail into my knuckles when they violate her. One by fucking one.

And when they flip her over and slap her face with laughter, a surge of violent fury expels from my body. Then I jump up from my chair and swipe the screen and the contents of my desk to the floor, pushing her screams away by throwing the AirPods from my ears to the carpet.

"Is there more?" I sniffle, swiping away the snot. "Is there fucking more?" I roar.

Owen's sad eyes meet mine, and I know there's more. "Yeah, brother. There's more."

My friends watch me trash my office, lifting the boardroom chairs and flinging them against the wall. Turning over the table and smashing the projector. I destroy it, all of it, while they sit by and let me, and when I finally bow over the desk and sob in defeat, I lift my head and face Owen.

"What do I have to do?"

The guys' eyes volley from one another's in nervousness.

"You have to break her heart."

And that's when I die a little more.

THIRTY-SIX

AVA

I stuff my clothes into my rucksack like a crazed woman, struggling to see through the haze of my tears, and my hand constantly swipes them away, but they seem to multiply.

"Ava. What's wrong?"

My heart thumps heavily as I spin and face Todd. His face falls at my appearance, and he rushes toward me and pulls me into his arms. I cling to his shirt like it's a lifeline.

"Do you want me to call Tate?" His chest heaves with his own panic.

I clear my throat. "No. We need to leave." Pulling away from him, I spin and begin stuffing more things into the rucksack.

"Leave? You're making no sense, Ava."

Ignoring him, I move around the room, grabbing a photo of me and my brother from my nightstand and shoving it into the bag.

"Ava. You're fucking scaring me," he yells, stilling me on the spot.

Taking a deep breath, I raise my head to face my brother. "Tate thinks I sold the advertisement to Flawless. He thinks I betrayed him, Todd." His face falls, and a shudder racks through his body.

"Oh shit," he mumbles.

"He's finished with me. Ended us. I've never seen him so angry, Todd." My lip quivers. "He's not the man I thought he was." I hold my brother's gaze, hoping he can see the sincerity and devastation in mine, the enormity of the situation.

Todd drags his hand over his hair. "It's all my fault. It's all my fucking fault, Ava." My eyes bounce over his face as he unravels in panic. "I'm sorry, so fucking sorry."

"Wh-what are you talking about?"

"I sent Griffin the files." He swallows hard. "I sent them because he was going to post videos of you, Ava." He glances away, as if pained. When he brings his eyes back to mine, my heart sinks at the guilt and sadness behind them. "The videos of the things you did. To help me." He swallows hard and shoots his eyes away while the feeling of disgust rears its ugly head.

A whimper catches in my throat at the thought of my little brother knowing these things and potentially seeing them. My body shakes uncontrollably, and before I can register what's happening, he pulls me against him, hugging me so tight I can barely breathe. "I'm sorry you had to do those things." A tear from him falls onto my face. "I'm sorry you did those things for me." He swallows. "I wanted to protect you. Like you protected me."

His body jolts, as if realizing something, and he pulls

away from me. "Maybe. Maybe we can explain to Tate. I'll tell him the truth, Ava." He nods furiously. "Yeah. Yeah, I'll do that."

A mocking laugh escapes me as I shake my head. "I'm pregnant, Todd." His gaze snaps up to meet mine. "I'm pregnant and he threatened to take my baby away." I choke on a sob burning in my throat. Todd's eyes widen, his jaw sharpens, and he stands taller.

Then he broadens his shoulders as if preparing for battle. "What are we going to do?"

"I refuse to be caged again, Todd. We have to leave." I swallow back the emotion my words bring. "I want to be free."

His nostrils flare and he nods firmly in agreement as I stuff my purse into my rucksack. "Don't take your bank cards, Ava. They'll probably try and find you."

"You're right." I throw the purse out.

"What are we going to do about cash, Ava?"

I walk into the closet, and Todd follows. Keying in the digits to the safe, I wait for it to open, and reveal an array of jewelry. I grab them, ignoring the feeling of dread that rushes through me thinking about what I had to endure to receive them, all treats for being a good pet.

"There was no way I was leaving that hell without something more."

Todd's eyes light up, and he bends, placing a soft kiss against my forehead. "You're a fucking warrior, Ava."

We spend the next hour packing, preparing to leave my life behind in a bid for the freedom I always dreamed of.

I push away thoughts of Tate, those sparkling blue eyes and the security I felt in his arms and remember his words that drive me forward. *"I'm going to take what's mine from you."*

I'm done letting people take from me. I didn't escape one hell to replace it with another.

Butterflies were meant to fly, Ava. And you're going to fucking soar.

THIRTY-SEVEN

TATE

My leg bounces. "We have eyes on her, don't worry," Owen reassures me.

"I just want her safe." The blood in my veins is filled with trepidation. Every time I close my eyes, I see the look of devastation on her face. She uttered those fucking words I longed to hear. She finally fucking said them, and I ripped her heart out.

"She's in the elevator now." My eyes dart to his in question, silently asking if they're both safe? Owen sighs. "Our guy is in there too, Tate." All I can do is nod because my body is strung so tight it feels like the life has been drained out of me, even my voice has been taken. Proof I'm nothing without her. He points to the screen. "See. He's a bellboy."

Owen eyes me skeptically, and my body doesn't relax like he probably expected on his words. It won't relax until I have her in my arms again.

The elevator pings, then Ava and Todd step out and casually stroll past the security guys dressed as guests and head toward the hotel room.

This hotel room.

As soon as Owen located the hotel Todd booked through a burner phone, we raced ahead, putting every measure in place along the way. Our men followed them to the hotel and have been behind them every step of the way. Owen upgraded her room to the penthouse suite and booked every room on the floor to give us privacy for what's about to go down.

When the guys told me I had to break Ava's heart, I insisted there had to be another way, but they explained the lengths that Griffin had gone to keep Ava under his watchful eye. The outside of her apartment building was connected to his personal security system, as was her apartment. Owen was confident it had been bugged, just like her cell phone. We figured out he always had access to the advertisement files but waited for the right time to blackmail Todd for them, knowing it would put Ava in the firing line. He knew how much we had fallen for one another, how we discussed having a family, and worse, he probably knew she was pregnant, and that had a whole new feeling of terror washing over me.

There was no time to plan anything other than feigning a breakup with Ava, no matter how devastatingly difficult it was to do. I needed an excuse to leave that apartment and have Griffin think we were over, enough for him to be made aware my security had been pulled. When in reality, we were using them tenfold now, with the help of Luca Varros, a connection Griffin is unaware of.

The guys told me I needed to break her heart enough to

give her no choice but to run, to appear vulnerable. Ultimately, I was using my girl as bait, and it fucking killed me to do so.

My beautiful girl, with her broken wings, was flying.

Without. Fucking. Me!

AVA

Anxiety ripples through me as we stroll toward the hotel room. Knowing we were being upgraded made the tension in my body ease, but only slightly. Though everyone knows security on the penthouse floor is always top notch.

"We'll be safe up here, Ava," Todd reassures as we walk down the corridor toward our suite.

He swipes the key card, and the door opens wide enough for me to step inside, then he follows behind.

The door clicks shut with a heavy thud.

And my heart sinks.

Blue eyes that swirl with guilt and sadness meet mine, and he launches himself up from the bed toward me. I stand rigid from fear, and my heart constricts in my chest as panic wells inside me.

"You son of a fucking bitch!" Todd bellows from behind me and flies toward Tate.

Strong arms come from behind him, holding him back, and Owen grits his teeth as Todd thrashes about in his arms. "I'm going to fucking kill you. You piece of shit," he spits.

As Tate approaches me, I step back. My lips part to beg him to stop, but his determination means my back hits the wall.

I close my eyes as I try and block him out. How can he look so torn when he ripped us apart.

Warm hands encase my face. "Look at me, Ava."

I shake my head, trying to rid myself of his touch and his soothing words.

His forehead presses against mine. "Please, baby. Please look at me."

Turning my head from him, I try to shake him off, but he stands firm. "Please?" The gut-wrenching pain in his voice has my eyes snapping open.

"I can explain everything. Can you let me explain?"

His blue eyes are filled with tears, rimmed red, and I hate it. Shocking myself, I reach out and swipe away the wetness dripping down his cheek. "Please," he implores with such emotion I'm rendered useless to fight against him.

"We don't have time, Tate. Griffin is in the parking lot," Owen booms from across the room while still tackling a red-faced Todd.

Fear grips me, and my body feels like it's floating. "Shhh. It's okay, baby. It's all part of the plan. I got you. We're going to get that piece of shit. I swear it."

Tate scoops me into his arms, and I melt against him, unable to do anything as my entire being is paralyzed in fear. "Fuck, I missed you so damn much." He kisses the top of my head as my mind whirls. *Just what the hell is happening?*

He kicks open another door and places me on a bed. Mase and Shaw are here along with a guy in a black suit I don't recognize. He barely spares me a glance, but his presence sends a shiver of terror through me, his black eyes so dark, so deep, I feel like I'm drowning in a sea of blackness.

"He's with us. Don't worry," Mase whispers, leaning over the bed to reassure me.

"Can you calm the fuck down and help us?" Owen chides as he struggles to enter the room with Todd lashing out at him.

"Give him a fucking sedative and be done with it," the devil in the black suit drawls out.

This stuns my brother, his struggle quickly forgotten. "What's happening?" he demands, glancing round the room.

"Well, we needed to come up with a plan to . . ." Mase begins.

"Fuck's sake." The guy pinches the bridge of his nose in annoyance. "Cut it short. We're using your sister as bait. We will get the sick fuck in the room and then torture him until he wishes he was dead." I reel back against the headboard. *Bait?*

"Then I'll bring the fucker back to life and do it all again." He smiles sadistically, causing Todd's eyes to bulge in horror.

"Show time!" Owen announces with a grin.

THIRTY-EIGHT

TATE

Owen gets in the bed, covering himself with the sheets, pretending to be Todd, while I close the blinds and run the shower. We set the scene and wait for the sick fucker to show up. My back is pressed against the tiled wall, waiting for him to step into the room. The moment the door handle presses down, I know it's him. I sense him. It's like the grim reaper has stepped into heaven to destroy the life of the innocent. He steps forward, unaware of my presence. It takes everything in me not to pounce, and my muscles are bunched so tight it's painful. My hands are balled into tight fists and blood drips from my lip as I struggle to hold back the roar threatening to escape me. He strolls toward the shower as if it's just another day, and that seems to anger me more, but when he reaches inside his jacket and pulls something out, I jolt, expecting to see a gun in his hand. I zone in on the device he's holding and shock strikes through me, realizing it's a taser.

The sick fuck was going to taser my girl in the shower.

He opens the shower door, letting the steam escape. Not giving him chance to focus, I rush from behind with a hefty roar. Slamming him against the tiles so hard his face crunches. The taser skitters to the floor as he tries to push me back, and his feet slide in the water as the spray beats down on us both.

I grab the showerhead, and he dodges the head but it's the hose I intend to use. My hand works quickly, wrapping it around his fucked-up neck, relishing the panic encompassing his face and the way his eyes widen in fear.

"That's it, you sick fuck. You're going to wear your own goddamn collar." I rear my head back and spit in his bloody face, tightening the hose until he sputters, his face reddens, and blood vessels pop among the white of his eyes. "That's it, fucking choke."

"Tate." Owen grips my shoulder in warning. "Take it easy, brother. We want to inflict pain on him for a long time. We want him to suffer his own personal hell, you hear me?"

His words surge into me, and my grip loosens to allow the twisted bastard a moment to breathe. He exhales loudly, the panic evident on each erratic breath.

"What the hell is that?" Shaw spits from behind Owen.

I glance over my shoulder, unable to take my eyes fully away from the scum in the palm of my hand.

Shaw stares at the device near his feet. "A taser," I confirm.

"A fucking taser? He was going to taser her?"

"Yeah," I grunt out, unable to comprehend the sick

piece of shit's motives. Sickness penetrates me when I consider this might not be the first time he's used one on her.

Well, he's about to discover my idea of punishment is far greater than his. I'll take everything from him.

Every.

Single.

Thing.

"Bring it with us."

AVA

No noise travels through the room, and I bite my fingernail waiting to hear something, anything. But not even a murmur.

When the door finally opens, all our spines straighten and Tate appears. He's soaked, his lip is bleeding, and he swipes at it with the back of his hand. Seeing him with blood on his face panics me, and I mewl in discomfort.

His solemn, blue eyes meet mine. "It's okay."

"Is the subject ready, bagged, and prepared?" Luca asks, stepping forward.

I now know the man filled with darkness as Luca, and he's Shaw's brother-in-law, a member of the Italian Mafia.

"Yeah, he's sedated and in the trunk."

"Unnecessary." He lifts his hand. "I can have anyone disappear without question, but so be it. I'll have him delivered to my basement. Owen will give you details." He turns to face Owen, who gives him a swift nod. All the while, Tate's eyes remain locked on me. Heat travels over my body at the intensity of his stare, filling me with warmth again, and I want to embrace it so badly, but I refuse to after how he treated me.

"Come." Luca clicks his fingers, and Shaw's mouth falls open in mortification at his action, but when Luca glares in his direction, as if begging for argument, Shaw's shoulders drop in defeat.

"I'm not leaving you with him," Todd spits, spreading his arm out toward Tate.

Tate's jaw locks and he grinds it from side to side. "I just want to speak with Ava for five minutes. I want to explain."

With my heart thudding rapidly against my chest, I glance at Todd and give him a quick nod. He rolls his eyes and leaves the room with a heavy huff.

As soon as the door closes, Tate's feet move in my direction. But I hold my hand up to stop his approach. "You can tell me from there."

His feet still, his breathing stutters, and his eyes fill with sadness. "Ava, I swear there was no other way."

"Explain," I bite.

"We needed to act quick, the guys came to my office and told me about Todd handing the files over . . ." I open my mouth to defend my little brother, who thought he was acting in my honor not knowing Tate already knew about the trauma I suffered—still suffer. "I know. Believe me, I fucking know, Ava. And you know what? I didn't fucking care about the advertisement, and neither did the guys. It's just fucking money, Ava. Just an advert, but you. You and our baby, you're fucking everything to me." He taps his fist against his heart. "Fucking everything, Ava. It killed me saying the shit I said."

"Not as much as me!" I scream back, my pain etched in every word.

His head sags forward, and silence suspends between us, the hurt transcending the air. When he finally raises his head, I see the guilt coating his face, the damage and devastation vibrating from his skin, his body reflecting his actions. "I know that," he whispers.

A tear drips from the end of his nose onto the floor. "I know that," he repeats. "I don't want to lose you, please tell me I haven't lost you, baby." He kneels to the floor. "I don't want to live without you, Ava. Not a single fucking day. You hear me, not a single fucking day." Staring into his tear-filled eyes, I feel the veracity behind each word, the tangible truth penetrating the air. "I fucking love you," he declares louder, every organ in my body pumps to life on his words.

"I love you," he whispers, as if in defeat, before dropping his head.

The room is silent, barring his heartbreaking sobs.

When he finally regains some composure, his gaze searches mine. "He'd been tracking you. The apartment was bugged." I jolt, a gasp clogs in my throat. "He's been listening in, probably knew about the baby too." My hand finds my stomach in a wave of protection.

"We needed him to think we broke up. That you were vulnerable and had no security. I had no choice, Ava. I had to break up with you, use you as fucking bait, baby," he spits like he still hates the thought.

"I thought you threw me away," I sniffle in admittance.

His gaze snaps up to mine. "Never." Determination mars his tone.

"You made me feel expendable." My heart races and

my hands shake. "You said . . ." My palm rests over my stomach protectively.

He rears back on his heels and closes his eyes. "Please don't say it, Ava."

But I can't help it. I need him to hear what he said to me and feel what he did. "You said you'd take my baby away, Tate."

He jumps to his feet, shocking me. Then, in flash, he hovers over me, my head pressed against the pillow as he cages me in with his elbows resting on either side of my head. His tears drip onto my face, and I want nothing more than to reassure him, to show him I love him.

"You know I'd never do that to you. Never, Ava." His tears drip onto my face. "Tell me you believe me, please, Ava. Tell me you know I'd never do that."

My chin wobbles, and my feelings for him leave me conflicted, but past the haze in his eyes, I see the love for me and our baby. I see it all. That he had no choice, that his wings were broken too.

"I believe you."

His body sags in relief, his forehead weighs heavily on mine. "Forgive me. Please," he breathes out. "Please, Ava." His soft lips find mine, his warmth spreading through me like a wildfire, filling my body with the hope I'd lost, filling it with the love that was stolen, fixing my broken wings.

I palm his cheek, and he tilts his head against my touch.

"I love you, Tate."

His body stills and a shudder takes over him, forcing his eyes to close behind the power of my confession.

Without thinking, I move my freehand beneath his T-shirt, exploring every ridge of his muscular body. His cells come alive under my touch; goose bumps spread over his naked flesh, encouraging me on. My hand travels down to his belt and I flick it open.

"Ava?" I pull my gaze back to his.

"Show me how sorry you are, Tate. Show me how you love me."

His jaw slackens and he moves quickly, fumbling with his belt while I shuffle my shorts down. He pulls his hard cock from his boxers, the head soaked, bulging, and full of need. "You need my cock, baby?"

"Yes," I pant as my hands travel over his body lifting his shirt over his head, exposing his taut muscles and that delicious V.

He pushes my panties aside. "I fucking love you, Ava." He pushes the head of his cock toward my entrance.

"Love you so fucking much it hurts." He pushes the head inside, and my spine arches at the intrusion. "Fuck," he hisses through gritted teeth. "So fucking good."

"So good," I agree as I meet him thrust for thrust, lifting my ass for his hand to squeeze while the other tugs my camisole top down to expose my bra. "Oh fuck. I thought I'd lost you."

I push my bra down, exposing my tits, knowing how much he enjoys them. "Thought I'd lost you, baby," he mumbles into my tits as he places dozens of kisses around my nipples.

"Tell me you love me again." He slams into me faster now. "Tell me." He powers inside me, banging the headboard against the plaster wall and causing the bed to creak.

I drag my hands down his back, and he hisses at my nails scorching his skin. Marking him like he marks me.

"I love you, Tate."

"Fuckkkk." His cock expands and the power of his orgasm sends my pussy spiraling, contracting around him while his warmth fills me.

"Thank you," he whispers before his tongue tangles with mine.

We float, flying in the realms of pleasure.

Together.

THIRTY-NINE

TATE

It's been seven days since we returned home to my apartment. Ava and Todd agreed they didn't want to return to her apartment since Griffin had been there at some point and bugged the place. Ava said she felt defiled all over again, and her words made me want to vomit.

She's distant from me. I feel the disconnection, and understand it, but I want nothing more than this forcefield she's placed around us to come down.

Stroking over her hair as she lies with her head on my lap, I can't keep it in any longer. "I bought us a house." She turns over so she's facing me. "Before all this happened, I bought us a house. It's big. It's got a huge yard for bump."

Ava chuckles. "There's no bump yet."

I grin back at her. "There will be soon. I remember Shaw calling Eleanor that." I lick my lips. "And I can remember thinking, how the fuck did my best friend get so lucky? He was staring at Emi, and I knew he loved her before he did. That's when I realized, I'd been lucky too, and I let you go." She swallows deeply, and I trace my finger along the column of her throat. "So when we discovered you were pregnant, I knew right then and there I was calling our baby bump. Besides"—I lift a shoulder—"you're my baby." I smirk back down at her, loving the tenderness flashing over her face.

"So, yeah. I bought us a house." I grin with triumph.

"I need to end it, Tate." My shoulders tense, and my heart skips a beat. "I need to end him," she clarifies, as if aware of my oncoming meltdown.

I search her face for answers. "I feel like I can't move on." A tremble takes over her voice. "Like something is holding me back. Like he's holding me back, and I want to move forward. I need to move forward, Tate."

"Ava, I don't want you to see him," I admit.

She shakes her head. "I see him every night when I close my eyes. In every corner of the room, I feel like he's watching me." Her chin wobbles, and I hate it. Wishing I could do something to stop it, reassure her he's never coming in contact with her again. Never going to hurt her again.

"I want to see the life fade from his eyes," she grits out with such courage, I second-guess my plan to end him myself.

"It was me that went through the pain, Tate. Day after day. Me that suffered at his hands and others'." I flinch on her words. But the small voice inside my head speaks up, reminding me Owen is already tracking the people that hurt Ava, tracking them and passing all their information onto Luca Varros. We'll owe the man at some point, but I don't fucking care. I want each and every one of those men found and slaughtered in the worst way possible.

"I want to be the one to end him." The fire behind her eyes and the strength in her words has my chest puff out with pride.

"I'll call Owen, let him know."

Her body relaxes against mine. I only hope I made the right decision and we don't cause more damage to her already fractured mind.

FORTY

AVA

Tate cups my face in his hands. "Are you sure about this? If you want to stop at any time, you can, you understand that, right?"

"I won't want to stop," I reassure him, but the tension etched on his face doesn't disappear. I heard him on the phone last night telling Owen's he's concerned what I'm about to do will affect me mentally and emotionally. As if it could affect me anymore than it already is.

The door to the basement opens, and the first thing to hit me is the putrid smell. A waft of copper fills my nostrils, and I force down the vomit rising in my throat.

"Can you imagine Reed in a place like this?" Owen jokes as he leads us down the stone steps. I chuckle back, whereas Tate zones out. His hand tightens in mine as we descend the stairs.

A loud clap echoes around the room. "Ah, fucking

finally," Luca spits out, then he glances at his watch. "I have a thing about punctuality and you're late."

"By seconds," Owen chides back, glancing at his own watch in confusion.

"I had him cleaned up. We'll leave you to it."

I scan the darkness of the room, and the eeriness doesn't fill me with terror, and that thought alone solidifies why I'm here. I'm used to the scene laid out in front of me, a replica of the room I was kept in for two years. Apart from the short time I was allowed out to work on projects for the company like I was any other colleague, then returned to my cage like the abused pet he saw me as.

I turn and face Owen. "Can you get him out?"

He tilts his head, then walks over to the cage. "Wakey wakey, motherfucker." He bangs against the bars with a heavy chain.

"Fucking piece of shit," Tate grinds out.

I stalk toward Owen and Griffin. The calmness in my veins feels almost surreal, there's not a slither of fear or trepidation inside me.

His bold eyes meet mine, and where they used to terrify and haunt me, they no longer hold the same cruel force they once did. They hold nothing. Their power relinquished.

"Dinner time, Pet," I bite out.

Owen drags him across the floor. His naked body dropped against the side of the cage while he moves to hook his metal chain on the wall. Like he did me.

Griffin snivels, "Ava, I—"

Tate stiffens beside me at the sound of his voice, or maybe my name on his tongue. I'll fix that. But not just yet.

I hold up my hand before he goes further. "Ah ah, Pet," I bite out, "no speaking unless I say. Now, you know the rules." His eyes widen in horror as I point toward a metal bucket he would have been using to pee in. A bucket I know all too well.

"You sick fucker!" Tate spits, and Owen clenches his hands beside him, as if struggling to rein in his own anger.

"I can't . . . I can't do that, Ava. Please . . ." He sniffles, dripping snot onto the floor. Now, that really won't do.

He scurries back against the wall before tugging on his chain with one hand.

In this light, I can see his other hand is broken, flopping at a weird angle. His feet are swollen and dripping in blood, and I count his missing toes, three on each foot. His skin is covered in open welts and marks I know well, as I received the punishment myself. They're marks of the chain being whipped against your skin, heavy and painful, that tear through your flesh with ease, driving into you so hard you bite on your tongue, choke on your blood.

"What do you need, baby? Tell me what you want me to do." Tate's warm palm draws circles on my lower back, bringing me back from my memories with a violent shiver.

"I want him to choke on his piss. To drown in it," I whisper.

Tate's spine jolts beside me, as if aware it's a punishment I would have suffered.

With his body wrung tight and his hands balled into tight fists, he strides toward Griffin. He grips him by his hair, forcing him to wail with his heavy-handedness, and drags him over to the metal bucket.

Griffin is unable to stand, as his knees are swollen and deformed, broken.

Owen glares daggers in Griffin's direction, then spits on him as he gets dragged past him. And when Tate dumps his heaving body at the side of the bucket and glances at me for approval, I give it with confidence and I raise my chin.

Tate sneers, stamps on one of Griffin's hands to hold him in place, pressing down heavily with his boot, then he takes a hold of Griffin's head and pushes it into the bucket, giving him no choice but to choke on his piss.

Watching Tate drown him in his piss, I feel nothing, no triumph, revenge, nothing. I simply want this to play out, I want him to experience what he did to me. If only for a short while of the measly time he has left in his life.

Tate pulls him up, and he sputters and gasps and begs before Tate plunges his head down again. "Choke, you sick fucker," Tate bites through his bared teeth. "Fucking choke, you sadistic fuck."

When Griffin appears to be losing consciousness, his body no longer fighting against Tate, he quickly pulls him back. Dumping him to the side of the bucket, he then kicks it at his head, spilling the contents onto his naked body.

The clanging of the bucket hitting the floor forces me to jump, a memory seared so deep inside me, I reel back on my heels.

Griffin startles too, and as if remembering the same thing, his eyes dart toward the wall, mine follow.

A wall of instruments hanging from hooks, and I lick my lips at the sight of the device I'm about to use. I march toward it, snagging it from the shelf.

"I want him attached to the wall with his legs spread wide."

Owen nods while Tate scans over me in concern.

"I knocked the bucket over once," I explain while walking toward Owen, who hooks Griffin to the wall, stretching him so tight he winces against the restraints. "He made me pay. I made sure not to knock the bucket over again."

Tate seethes, his nostrils flare—the heat radiating from him feels catastrophic, like a volcano ready to erupt, with such devastation the ash it leaves in its wake will be the only thing left.

Just how it should be.

Nothing.

"The chain attached to his neck needs to be pulled tight and hooked onto the top hook. He needs to choke, to feel like he's being hung as he struggles. The collar will bite into his flesh, scar him," I warn Owen, who quickly works as per my instructions.

Tate vibrates beside me and runs his hand over his hair, then paces back and forth. "Swear to God if you weren't doing this, Ava," he grinds out.

Walking over to him, I place my palm on his face for reassurance, our eyes meet, and our worlds collide. I ground him, and his shoulders slacken. "I know," I admit. He'd do it for me in a heartbeat. "But the greatest thing you can give me right now is the power I never had." His chin wobbles, and he presses our foreheads together, and our eyes bleed love for one another. No words needed for the strength he instills in me by that simple gesture.

"Thank you." I blink back the tears and turn to face my tormentor.

TATE

Ava sashays toward him with the taser in her hand. Knowing what that sick, demented, twisted fuck did to her, pains me. My heart and soul have been ripped out, torn to fucking shreds at the hands of the warped bastard.

My girl, my warrior, walks toward him with such strength it almost brings me to my knees. She flicks open the taser and Griffin begins to shake, incoherent words drip from his slimy tongue, my lip quirks up in jest at the fear taking over his body, rendering him speechless.

"Tut tut, Pet. You need punishing." She sparks the taser up and then surges her arm forward, horror engulfs my chest when she aims at his balls.

"Fucking Jesus!" Owen blows out in shock while I stare in awe at my girl.

Griffin's body goes rigid, straining against the metal of his bindings, and when he falls lax, she drives forward again.

She tilts her head to the side to speak without taking her eyes off Griffin. "Hose him down," she calls out.

"Wait, won't the water . . ." I'm about to tell her she might get electrocuted.

"No. These little devices are special, isn't that right, Griffin?" She lifts an eyebrow, and the hate I feel toward the man multiplies.

Owen douses him in water and steps back. The shock of the cold liquid drenching him causes him to shudder and regain consciousness. She moves quickly, sparking the device up in her hand before taunting him with it, waving it in his face. Owen chuckles at the brutality behind her action, she then surges it into his balls again and I swear I can smell burning flesh.

When his screeching stops and his wrung body falls lax, Ava's shoulders sag in disappointment, then she turns to me, and my heart aches with a need to comfort her. I pull her toward me and draw circles on her back as she clings to my chest.

"I want him to suffer more, Tate."

I lick my lips and tilt her chin up as I step back and part my feet in determination. "He will."

"We can cause him to suffer, Ava," Owen confirms while coming and standing beside me in a sign of unity.

"You're drained, baby. Let me deal with this." My heart hammers against my chest, hoping she gives me the power of approval to dispose of the sick fuck.

"I want him dead. Gone. I want to be free." A lone tear descends down her beautiful face, and my finger catches it, then I draw it into my mouth, sucking away her salty taste.

"What did I tell you?" She looks at me in confusion. "You only cry tears for me, Ava. I own these tears." I use my thumbs to swipe them from her pretty face.

"You do." She smiles back at me.

"Let me finish this for you, baby. Let me set you free, and finally we can soar together."

"Okay," she breathes out, taking all my tension with her.

"Can you take her back to the apartment?" I ask Owen with a tilt of my head.

"Of course."

I step forward and place a kiss on her forehead. "Go shower and wait for me in bed."

She gifts me with a nod before turning her head over her shoulder. "Tate?" My eyes meet hers. "Make him suffer."

My lips tip up at the side. "Oh, I intend to." She smiles back at me and ascends the stairs, and when the door to the basement closes, I finally turn to face him.

"Now motherfucker, prepare to scream." His eyes widen at my venomous tone. "Pet," I spit out.

And then his bladder bursts.

My body aches from inflicting pain on the sick fuck who hangs from the chains like a piece of meat waiting to be carved into portions. After spending the past couple of hours whipping him with chains, tasering his body, and pummeling him until his bones break, I take him in, his battered body hangs limply, bleeding profusely over the floor but still it doesn't feel enough, still I want more from him. I want him to suffer like Ava did, feel her pain and more. So much more.

"It doesn't feel like enough, does it?" A voice from

behind me breaks my thoughts, and I swipe away the sweat from my forehead to glance at him over my shoulder.

He leans against the wall with a toothpick hanging loosely from his lips, his bright-blue eyes look familiar, but I can't quite place them.

I turn to face him. "My name's Finn O'Connell. I believe you met my nephew at an event a few weeks ago."

The intense dude from the table opposite me springs into my mind, the one that saved my ass on the stage that night, and I realize now the reason that the bright-blue eyes with a hint of manic staring back at me are so familiar. "Reece?" I reply.

I watch him closely as he pushes off the wall, flicks open a penknife, and flips it in his hand with a chuckle. "That would be him. Kid loves his Pussy." He smirks. My lips tip up in response.

He walks toward the wall housing the torture instruments. "Luca sent me down here. He knew you'd want him to suffer, knew you'd want more," he throws over his shoulder.

The man empties a bag of something resembling salt into a barrel, then connects a hose to the tap at the bottom of the barrel before walking back to the instruments.

"Ah, my specialty." He picks up a large hunting knife and swirls it round in his hand, the metal gleams in the light and it only makes him look all the more deadly.

"Anything in particular you want help with?" he asks as he strolls toward me, the untied combat boots he wears clonk against the concrete floor and through the trail of blood.

"Yeah. I want him to understand the true meaning of"

—I walk toward Griffin and tug his head up by his hair, giving his gaze no choice but to find mine—"being torn apart." Griffin's eyes flash in fear and understanding of my words, the very words he spoke to Ava.

"Excellent." Finn's eyes light up in a deranged glee. Then in a move so quick I barely have chance to step back, he slices the skin from Griffin's bare stomach.

"Ahhhhh!" Griffin roars back to life.

Finn throws his head back, then spits at him. "Piece of fucking shit."

Watching Finn O'Connell, I realize he has demons too, his words repeat in my mind. *"It doesn't feel like enough, does it?"* Something tells me this man uses punishment to expel his guilt too. His wedding ring flashes and a surge of pain sears into my chest, and I know his guilt comes from not being able to protect his woman.

A renewed energy flares inside me as I stride toward the wall holding the devices, determined to expel evil for the sake of all women and children that have suffered.

Carrying the drill over toward them, Finn turns his head and gives me a chin lift, then puts up a finger, stopping me from going further.

He bends down and picks up the hose before pressing on the handle and dousing him in salt water. Griffin's body springs to life on a gut-wrenching scream that fills my blood stream with pride.

His body wrestles against the chains, fighting and failing as he writhes in agony.

"Pleasssse," he begs.

Finn switches the hose off and glances over at me. "Start at his feet, and be sure you do his cock before he passes out. They don't tend to live past that when they bleed out this much," he spits in disgust. "I want the fucker to suffer."

I nod and step forward, pressing the tip of the drill to his ankle. I preen at the pleasure leaving my body when he begs me to take pity on him.

Darkness takes over me as I prepare to make him suffer. Prepare to tear him apart.

I'll slaughter the monster. I'll chase away the storm and when it's all over, we'll fly together.

FORTY-ONE

TATE

ONE WEEK LATER...

My hand rests on my thigh, her fingers entwined with mine, and I couldn't be happier. I turn into the driveway of my parents' home. "Jesus, Tate. Your parents really are rich, right?" Todd leans between the front seats of my SUV in awe.

When I gave my mom a shortened version of how our relationship began, she swatted me across the back of my head, telling me how dumb I was to let her go in the first place. She told me she believes love has no bounds, age being one of them. She didn't know I ravaged the recently turned eighteen-year-old in her spare room, multiple times. Just that I met her here. I'm not so sure she would have been so on board with it if she knew the whole truth.

After dismembering Griffin, Luca assured me he would

dispose of him in an acid tank. I stayed while I watched his body parts sink inside, knowing he was gone for sure and no evidence would be left.

Worry gnawed at my chest about how Luca would call in his favor: Would he blackmail us with proof of me killing him? Or worse, use Ava. Owen reassured me our company operates the security system running through Luca's properties, and all footage of us even being on the premises has been wiped clean.

I trust my best friend; the guy is a fucking genius and loyal to the bone.

"Your mom hasn't aged." Ava smiles as she gestures toward the steps where my mom rushes toward the SUV.

I bring Ava's hand to my lips and gift her fingers with a gentle kiss.

"Come on, let's go meet the parents." I smile and push open my door. "Again," I add with a wink.

AVA

"Remind me again why we're not staying in your old room." I smirk at Tate as he stalks toward me. "Because I want us to sleep in that room." He points over my shoulder, and I turn to face the room in question. The room I slept in on our first night together. I bite into my lip as wetness gathers in my panties.

Meeting Tate's parents as his girlfriend was a little embarrassing after meeting them as a foster child. But they welcomed me with open arms, both excited over the fact that they're going to become grandparents to two babies in the span of a year.

I didn't miss Owen's intake of breath on their words, nor did I miss Tate's hand tightening in mine after seeing it. But I quickly changed the subject to ease the tension, instead asking them about the charity they still run for the kids.

Tate spent the evening peppering me with kisses while Todd rolled his eyes before Owen suggested taking him into the gym for some workout. My brother jumped at the chance.

"Tate tells me he bought a cat?" Steph asked while filling up my lemonade.

I smirked into my drink while Tate mumbled about the cat being a fucking nightmare under his breath. "We did, it's from a rescue center. We got talking to one of the ambassadors there and he paired us with a cat he thought would suit us best."

Tate snorted, shaking his head.

Steph ignores his outburst. "That's so sweet. What did you call him?"

"He came with the name and Ava loved it so we're keeping it." Tate shrugged. "His name's Blinky."

Steph's hand rests over her chest lovingly. "Oh, that's adorable. I love it too."

"He's anything but fucking adorable. The thing pisses in my shoes, rips the goddamn curtains off the rail, and sleeps in the fucking fridge. I almost shit myself when he hissed at me for wanting my morning shake."

"You did jump." I nod.

Tate casts his eyes over toward mine. "Jump? I have claw marks, Ava." He held his hand up to show me the claw marks for the hundredth time.

He leaned back in his chair. "I think we should send the little fucker back. That prick, Reece, sent us a dud on purpose, I swear it." I roll my eyes at his accusation; it's not the first time Tate has mentioned being set up by Reece. He seemed like such a nice young guy, and I honestly don't think he's capable of being anything other than being helpful.

Steph gasped in horror. "Tate Kavanagh, we never sent you back and you were a nightmare too!"

Tate grimaced and dragged a hand over his head. "Yeah, fine. It can stay for now."

When I yawned, Tate insisted on us calling it an early night, and now, as I back into the room with Tate's hungry eyes eating me up, I can't say I'm disappointed by his insistence.

"This room holds so many memories for us, Ava."

"It does," I agree breathlessly.

"Lose the dress, baby, let me see those beautiful tits."

He kicks off his shoes and socks before popping open each of his shirt buttons. I slip my dress down, take my bra off, and delight as his eyes become hooded, desire oozing from them.

Watching in unadulterated lust as he slowly slips the belt from his pants, dropping it to the floor with a heavy clang.

Sitting on the edge of the bed, I lift my feet to open myself up to him, exposing my wet hole.

"No panties, baby?" he questions with a raised eyebrow.

"No." I shake my head. He drops his pants, taking his boxers with them. Then he fists his cock, faster and faster, my mouth waters with each stroke.

"Are you my little slut?" He steps between my legs.

"Yes," I breathe out on a whisper.

"Show me where you want my cum." His eyes flick from my face to my pussy and back again before he sucks in a sharp breath when I spread my pussy lips with both fingers.

"In here." I point toward my hole. His fist works faster, dripping precum over my inner thigh.

"Yeah?" his husky voice pants out.

"Mmm, I want you to fill me."

"Fuck yeah, you do."

The head of his cock runs over my fingers, around them, coating them in his juice.

He presses it roughly against my folds, over my clit, and down into where I'm begging to be filled.

"Is this cunt nice and tight for me?"

Our heavy pants fill the air. "Yes," I respond on a whimper.

Then he lines his cock up to my hole, and a hand wraps around my throat. "I'm going to fuck you so much I'm going to fuck a baby into you." I bite my lip to stifle the smile, knowing how much Tate gets turned on by the thought of getting me pregnant despite seeing our bump on the screen yesterday.

I play along. "I want your baby." He hisses through his teeth and pushes his cock to the hilt, slamming inside me so hard the wind is knocked from my lungs.

"Yeah, you do, little slut. You want my cum to fill you, fill you with my baby." He rears back, then thrusts forward with one hand around my throat and the other strumming my nipple. I continue playing with my pussy, circling my clit. "That's it, dirty slut, play with your clit for me. I want you to beg. I want this pussy to beg for my baby." His words send spasms of pleasure through me, and my head falls back against the mattress with Tate's hand still gripped firmly around it, and I realize he allowed me to fall.

He maneuvers me, lifting my legs over his shoulder so he can slam inside me at a different angle.

He tilts his head back and presses on my throat, my vision becomes hazy and when I feel the familiar flutter of my orgasm ebbing to the surface, he feels it too, "Come!" he demands on a roar.

Our orgasms collide, a tidal wave of pleasure surges through us, and Tate's footing stutters. "Shit," he grumbles, quickly moving to flip me over and letting him fall on the bed with me landing on top of him, his cock still seated deep inside me.

I chuckle at his swiftness, and he laughs too. The deep baritone sound of his voice rumbles in his chest as I lie on him in deep-seated satisfaction.

His fingers draw circles on my spine, and it feels euphoric that we're in the same place we were when we first met.

"What now?" I tease, lifting my head to face him.

"Marry me."

My mouth falls open.

"Say yes."

I nod.

He grins back at me like a Cheshire cat. "Say fucking yes, Ava. I need words, baby."

Tears brim my eyes. "Yes."

His lips meet mine, then he pulls back, holding my gaze.

"And now we fucking fly."

EPILOGUE

TATE

TWO WEEKS LATER...

I glance up the makeshift aisle on the jetty, taking a deep breath as I take in my friends and family gathered around us to help celebrate our day.

Of course, I wish Laya could be here today, but she FaceTimed me last week explaining she was moving home with her husband. Even her saying the word husband had me gritting my teeth in displeasure. I still haven't met the prick and already don't like him, simply for the fact he's made no effort with the people that mean so much to Laya.

"If everyone could please stand," the officiant declares, and a lump gathers in my throat knowing she's here.

"No Matter What" by Jamie Miller plays, and my legs almost buckle at how perfect the song is. My eyes sweep over my best friends, as they're the only ones to know the significance behind the song. They each nod, giving me their approval and loyalty, and I couldn't appreciate them more than I do in this moment.

My eyes latch onto hers, and my heart swells so wide I fear it will burst through my chest at any second. Todd is beside her, guiding her down the aisle where I wait at the end of the jetty by the lake.

Her bottom lip quivers and a tear slips down her face, and that's the final fucking straw. Before I know what I'm doing, I'm moving. "Fuck it." I march down the aisle, not prepared to wait any longer for my girl. Gasps of shock escape the small gathering as I scoop Ava into my arms and carry her back to the altar bridal style.

"You're insane." She beams up at me in jest.

"Only for you," I quip back with a wink.

"Hurry up and marry us, dude. I've waited too long for this day." My eyes don't leave Ava's.

The officiant's mouth opens and closes before he clears his throat and begins the ceremony while I hold her in my arms. Our eyes never disconnect as we utter the words he asks us to repeat, and when he tells me to kiss my bride, I do with every ounce of love I have inside me. Spilling it into her. Marking her as my wife.

When metal clinks behind me, I pull back and lift my head in time to witness the blue butterflies being set free above our heads.

I smile at the look of euphoria and admiration on Ava's face. "And now we fucking soar, baby."

THE END

MORE???

Would you like a sneak peek of Owen?

You can grab it HERE by signing up to my newsletter.

Or how about finding out what happened to Griffin's company Flawless? Office Infatuation is a short story based on the new owner.

MORE?

Would you like to learn more about **SHAW**? His story is available here: SHAW Book 1

Luca has his own story in Veiled In Hate. You can download here.

VEILED IN HATE

Finn O'Connell is part of the Secrets and Lies Series, available below.

Secrets and Lies Series

CAL Book 1

CON Book 2

FINN Book 3

BREN Book 4

OSCAR Book 5

CON'S WEDDING NOVELLA

ALSO BY BJ ALPHA

Born Series

Born Reckless

The Brutal Duet

Hidden In Brutal Devotion

Love In Brutal Devotion

STORM ENTERPRISES

SHAW Book 1

Secrets and Lies Series

CAL Book 1

CON Book 2

FINN Book 3

BREN Book 4

OSCAR Book 5

CON'S WEDDING NOVELLA

VEILED IN Series

VEILED IN HATE

ACKNOWLEDGMENTS

**Tee the lady that started it all for me.
Thank you, thank you, thank you!**

I must start with where it all began, TL Swan. When I started reading your books, I never realized I was in a place I needed pulling out of. Your stories brought me back to myself.

With your constant support and the network created as 'Cygnet Inkers' I was able to create something I never realized was possible, I genuinely thought I'd had my day. You made me realize tomorrow is just the beginning.

**To Kate, my crazy little smurfette.
Thank you for being YOU!**

To the admin and readers in the **Obsessive, Possessive Stalkers and OTT Jealous Alpha Group**, thank you for your continual support.

Special Mention
Jaclyn, Emma, Lilibet, Tash and Libs. Thank you for always being there when I call on you.

To My Readers
A special thank you to you all. I couldn't do it without you. Thank you for your constant support.

ARC Team
To my ARC readers you're incredible.
I have such an incredible team and I appreciate you all so much.

To my world.
My boys, continue growing into the amazing men I know you can be.
And remember you can be anything as long as you're happy.

To my hubby, the J in my BJ.
Love you trillions.

ABOUT THE AUTHOR

BJ Alpha lives in the UK with her hubby, two teenage sons and three fur babies.
She loves to write and read about hot, alpha males and feisty females.

Follow BJ on her social media pages:
Facebook: BJ Alpha
My readers group: BJ's Reckless Readers
Instagram: BJ Alpha

And don't forget to sign up to BJ's Newsletter for exclusive information and competitions. Newsletter sign up.

Printed in Dunstable, United Kingdom